Scar Tissue

Samantha Simard

ISBN-13: 978-1-7326392-4-9

Also by Samantha Simard:

Wolfe & Vaughn Mysteries
Stitches

For Mom and Dad, again. I couldn't do this without you.

And for everyone who picked up a copy of **Stitches**. *Thank you for welcoming my gang of misfits into your hearts.*

"From the day of a child's birth he is taught by every circumstance, by every law and rule and right, to protect his own life. He starts with that great instinct, and everything confirms it. And then he is a solider and he must learn to violate all of this— he must learn coldly to put himself in the way of losing his own life without going mad."

- John Steinbeck, *East of Eden*

"Mind is a battlefield
All hope is gone
Trouble to the right and left
Whose side you're on?

Thoughts like a minefield
I'm a ticking bomb
Maybe you should watch your step
Don't get lost"

- Foo Fighters, "The Sky Is a Neighborhood"

Chapter One

If Laine Parker slept, she always had the same dream.

If, not *when*, because sleep was not guaranteed. Sometimes she blacked out when her head hit the pillow, but more often the *thump-thump* of rotor blades and the screams of dying men rung in her ears. If she gritted her teeth against the noise and stayed in bed, that was when the dreams arrived.

The dreams started innocently, with the burn of the sun and grains of sand chafing her skin, but quickly morphed into one particular, nightmarish memory. She recalled all too clearly what it felt like to crawl on her belly up a rocky incline in the dead of the night, M4 strapped to her back and her uniform—including the field medic patch on her sleeve—coated in a layer of dust and sweat.

Laine's unit—12th Infantry, First Batt—was one of two backstopping a team of Rangers during an operation in a village about ten klicks outside Baghdad. One road in, one road out, curving up and around the left-hand side of a moderately elevated hill. The Rangers were looking for somebody the pointy-heads back home figured could give them intel, which meant the poor bastard needed to be taken alive; it also meant they had to make their way up the damn hill without any villagers raising the alarm.

The Rangers were ahead of Laine by fifty meters and on the plateau of the hill, crouched low to stay in the shadows of the fencing surrounding the village, the barely-visible green glow of their laser sights sweeping for threats. The road was to Laine's left, and she knew without turning her head that the other infantry unit was making the same slow on the other side of the road, ready to block the exit in the event something went FUBAR—*fucked up beyond all recognition*. If you were in the Army long enough, you got used to plans falling through.

In front of Laine, the lead Ranger signaled for everyone to stop by raising his closed fist. The Rangers had reached the curve in the road that turned into the village, and in the middle of the road was a motionless lump. The clouds in front of the moon moved along, providing some ambient light, but it was still tough to see without night vision goggles. Laine was top of her class during marksmanship training, and even she couldn't tell what the thing was, until a gentle breeze came along and ruffled its fur.

A dog. A goddamn dead dog in the road.

Something tickled at the back of Laine's brain, a remnant of a conversation she'd heard back on base—about dead dogs and what the hostiles had started using them for—but that tickle was drowned out by a flash of light up and slightly to Laine's right. The flash came from an open window in the top floor of a crooked little walkup, and it was something with which Laine was all too familiar.

The glint of a sniper's scope, trained directly on the Rangers who were in the middle of deciding how to get around the dead dog. In that moment Laine knew there was no informant, no intel, and there probably never had been. It was a trap, and they'd walked right into it.

"*Get down!*" she heard herself scream, right before the sniper fired and the improvised explosive device inside the dead dog's belly detonated.

The world went white, and Laine woke up.

~***~

A howl caught in Laine's throat, the noise smothered by the oppressive humidity that only late August in Boston could bring. Her red hair had worked free of its topknot, brushing against her sweat-soaked sleep tank when she rolled off her mattress (always too soft, no matter how many books she stacked underneath it). It took her a moment to orient herself, to realize she wasn't in some rattrap in the Middle East or one of the stark, prison-like rooms at Blakely Manor.

Laine rented a shitty one-bedroom apartment in Mattapan with her little brother, Aiden. Her window faced Blue Hill Avenue, across the street from a dilapidated strip of drycleaners, cell phone stores, and vacancies with garage doors pulled down over the storefronts. There was a small kitchenette and an even smaller bathroom, and Aiden slept on the futon in the living room, insisting that Laine take the bed. Her brother worked for a catering company and was in and out at all hours anyway, so it was no big deal.

She crossed the bedroom in three long-legged strides and stopped in front of the window, open to sparse two-in-the-morning traffic and the burn of a nearby trashcan fire. The scent of ashes drifted inside, a choking blight that reminded her of dead men, their charred bones crunching like glass under her boots.

Laine turned away from the window, leaning down to pull the long black plastic case out from under her bed. She flicked open the latches, pushing up the top to reveal the matte black pieces of her Steyr HS-50 M1. Not the same kind of rifle that had earned her sharpshooter patch, but it would get the job done.

A breeze pushed valiantly through the sludgy air, cooling Laine's overheated skin and making her scar tingle. It was bright pink and ran diagonally across her face, from the top left side of her forehead, through her pert nose, and into the right side of her jaw. The scar resembled a ropy trench, the furled tissue making her left eye lift with permanent intrigue and pulling the right half of her mouth into a permanent rictus grin.

There was only one thing that would make Laine grin for real. Considering the nature of the task, that grin would probably come right before she died.

~***~

Aiden Parker woke abruptly from a sound sleep. Not unusual—either a spring from the apartment's ratty couch was poking him in the ass, or Laine had yelled her way out of another nightmare. It was quiet for a handful of moments, and Aiden heard the latches on his sister's rifle case snap open, the sound echoing in the thin walls. That was his answer.

Maneuvering off the couch—Aiden was six-and-a-half feet tall and built like a brick shithouse—he headed for the bedroom. He didn't mind getting woken up in the middle of the night too much, since his job had him working events that took place on weekends. "Can't sleep?" It was a redundant question. Nearly every night since Laine left Blakely Manor was like this one, except now they had a plan to change things.

Laine made an affirmative noise. Her pale hands moved in the shadows, assembling the pieces of the rifle with practiced ease. "Is it bad that I'm excited?"

Aiden listened closely to understand what Laine said. They were whispering in an effort to not wake the neighbors, and the lisp caused by Laine's scar made her words drag at the ends.

"No, Lainey—I don't think it's bad at all," he said, coming further into the room and sitting on the edge of the mattress. It groaned under the combined weight of Aiden and the rifle case. "You got the hang of that thing?"

"More or less. Guy I bought it from took good care of it." Laine lifted the assembled rifle, biceps tightening as they hefted twenty-eight pounds of metal and plastic. The Steyr was intimidating enough in the daylight, but in the near-darkness of the bedroom it looked monstrous. "Glad I was able to find the five-shot model. Bolt-action blows if you miss."

"You don't miss often." Aiden reached out, put a hand over Laine's where it was curled around the Steyr's pistol grip. "Lainey…

we've only got to wait a couple more days. Just a couple more days, and we'll be able to send our message. Loud and clear."

Laine looked at Aiden with the same serious ice-blue eyes he'd known all his life, the shiny tautness of the scar across her face a stark reminder of what she'd endured. "You really think this is the right way to go? Knocking off a gubernatorial candidate seems like a drop in the bucket."

"It's big enough to draw attention, but it won't get us killed. We've been over this." Aiden was annoyed that Laine still had doubts; his sister might be a damn good shot, but she wasn't a brain trust. "Look, there's no reason this shouldn't work. As long as we stick to the plan, we'll be fine."

Laine blew out a breath and set about disassembling the Steyr. "Right. Stick to the plan." Her gaze lingered on the inside of the rifle case's lid, to which Aiden knew a picture of their intended victim was taped. "Stick to the plan, and we'll be fine."

She placed the pieces of the gun back in the case and slammed the lid shut, trapping the photograph of Christopher Sullivan against the weapon.

~***~

Chapter Two

Constantin Ionesco had watched his boss dish out a lot of bullshit over the years, but this party took the cake.

Tonight's dinner was a fundraiser for Christopher Sullivan's gubernatorial campaign, in its home stretch with Massachusetts's primary elections just two weeks away. The venue was Stela, a Romanian-American restaurant that occupied a glass-front building on Stuart Street in Boston's Theatre District. It was owned by Anton Codreanu, a wealthy restaurateur who was also a local magnate, a respected leader in the city's criminal underground, and Constantin's boss.

Every table in Stela was perfect down to the smallest detail, no placeholder askew and every napkin a bright blood red against draped white linen and gold-rimmed plates. The chandeliers toward the outer part of the floor were dimmed so the focus centered on Anton's table with Christopher and his family. The restaurant was maxed out at two-hundred and fifty attendees, each of whom had paid dearly to dine with the likely Republican nominee for governor.

Constantin stood in the shadows near the doors to the kitchen, his pinstriped Armani suit buttoned to conceal the Ruger SR45 in his shoulder holster. His stocky frame and closely-cropped black hair screamed *bodyguard*, but scarred knuckles and the way his eyes scanned the room said he was actually good at his job.

Beside Constantin, Sebastian Codreanu—Anton's son and the body Constantin guarded—made an amused noise. "You look like someone's attack dog, *cavalerul meu curajos*." Despite living in Boston's prestigious Back Bay neighborhood since the age of six, Sebastian's Romanian was flawless. "Swiveling your head like that must be painful."

My brave knight. Constantin almost cracked a smile at the term of endearment. It was from a game they'd played when Sebastian was a boy, wherein Sebastian was a prince in peril and Constantin was the courageous hero who saved the day. Constantin was often hard-pressed to reconcile the innocent child from his memories with the man Sebastian was forced to become, but he'd see that child in moments like this and feel a swell of platonic affection.

Not that he'd ever show it. "Your cufflink is crooked."

Sebastian swore under his breath, flicking a strand of jaw-length dark hair out of his eyes as he fiddled with the errant accessory. "This thing's been giving me shit all afternoon." His tone took on a bitter tinge. "But God knows what would happen if I did not show up to the party looking like Daddy's pretty little showpiece."

Pretty wasn't the word Constantin would've used, but even a straight man could acknowledge that Sebastian was attractive. The blue twill of his suit matched his eyes, points of color standing out in an otherwise gloomy corner. He'd shaved before the party, erasing his usual stubble and leaving the unfamiliar scent of Tom Ford Tobacco Vanille behind. Sebastian had previously worn Clive

8

Christian No. 1, until his one-night stand with Jake Wolfe and its aftermath; Constantin was the one who convinced the maid to throw the bottle away after she found the cologne in Sebastian's trash.

And just because Sebastian's comment about his father was accurate didn't mean Constantin had to like it. He glanced at his charge, a frown pulling his craggy face downward. *"Prințul meu—"*

His response to their game was cut off by the ring of a fork tapping the side of a champagne flute. Nearly in unison, the tables of attendees tore their attention away from alcohol and appetizers and focused on their host.

Anton Codreanu rose from his seat at the Sullivans' table, setting the flute down and smoothing down the front of bespoke suit. Not yet fifty-five, Anton had a plain face surrounded by a graying beard. His eyes were the same bottle-blue as his son's but colder in demeanor. His thin lips widened in a smile, genuine on the surface but hiding a rolling tide of contempt.

"Thank you all for being here, and for your incredibly generous donations to Mr. Sullivan's campaign," he said, raising his voice to be heard throughout the massive dining room. "He is going to speak momentarily, but I wanted to tell you that since endorsing Christopher's campaign, I have come to see him more clearly as both a politician and a man." The thin smile widened, and Constantin didn't like it a bit; that smile meant good things for Anton's personal ambitions and nothing good for the city of Boston. "And I like what

I see. Now, please join me in giving our next governor a warm welcome—Christopher Sullivan, everyone!"

The man of the hour stood up amid a clamor of applause, a grin on his face as he ran a hand through his head of curly brown hair. The hair appeared to be a familial trait, from what Constantin had seen of Christopher's siblings, as was his freckled nose and short stature. He was good-looking in the way that a father's ideal prom date for his daughter might be—cute, but not cute enough to lure her into the backseat of his car after the dance.

"Thank you, Anton, for that flattering introduction. Am I blushing? I hope I'm not blushing." As polite laughter filtered through the room, Constantin realized he was witnessing the so-called "awkward charm" the *Boston Herald* wrote about in their page-long endorsement of Christopher's campaign. "And thank you all for coming! I can't believe…"

He trailed off, and what followed happened in a matter of seconds—to Constantin, it felt like hours. Like most public speakers, Christopher had been coached to not focus on the crowd directly, but to look slightly above their heads. This practice reduced nerves for both speaker and audience, and put Christopher's gaze on the wall of windows at the front of Stela and the passing headlights on Stuart Street.

Christopher's sudden pause caused a confused murmur to spread through the attendees, but Constantin couldn't have cared less. He followed Christopher's stare and immediately figured out what caught his attention. A set of headlights attached to a van had slowed to a crawl, and the back door slid open.

Constantin saw the gleam of titanium and the six barrels of a minigun and felt the floor drop out from underneath his feet. *"Get down!"*

Stela's glass front collapsed in a cacophony of sound, NATO rounds twice the size of AA-batteries passing through the panes. The bass-deep *thud-thud-thud* of the minigun's rotational fire resonated through the building as the guests scattered in all directions, screaming and panicked if they weren't already injured and sprawled on the floor. Splinters of wood and shards of glass flew through the air, rocketing upward like fireworks with each bullet that hit.

Constantin's first priority was Sebastian. He tackled the younger man to the floor, sliding an arm under his head to save him a concussion. As soon as Sebastian was out of harm's way, Constantin hid behind an upturned table and aimed his Ruger toward the street, joined in the effort by several of his men. The shooters timed their attack perfectly, driving away in the scant seconds it took for Constantin and the other bodyguards to take cover and gather their wits. All that was left when Constantin lined up his sights was a faint smoke trail, a byproduct of the rubber the assailants burned on their way down the street.

Sebastian was at Constantin's side, kneeling on the floor, a hand clutching at the older man's jacket sleeve. "What the hell was that supposed to be, a goddamn execution?"

"I don't know," Constantin replied, hesitating only a moment before holstering his gun. "Are you all right?"

"I'm fine," Sebastian said, "but others are not."

"Constantin!" Despite their differing opinions on several subjects as of late, Constantin was relieved to hear Anton's voice. His boss was half-shouting due to temporary deafness and crouched next to Christopher Sullivan, who was lying prone on the floor. "Call for assistance—he's been shot!"

~***~

Detective Jeff Kamienski sighed as he unfolded his lanky frame from behind the wheel of his blue-and-white Boston Police cruiser. He was in his early thirties but felt his knees creak with the movement, making an attempt to smooth out the wrinkles in his brown business suit as he stood before leaving it to the humidity to sort out. Curly black hair hung down behind his ears and was greasy with sweat, the shitty air conditioning in the city-maintained cruiser doing nothing to fight the late summer swelter.

"Parked as close as I could get and we're still gonna have to walk a block," he grumbled to his partner, Detective "Silent Mark" Hale.

Silent Mark—an imposing black man who favored trench coats, fedoras, and moving like an apparition—predictably said nothing.

They were across and down the street from the crime scene at Stela, which was a mess of fire trucks and BPD cruisers. Up and down the block were metal barricades with *Property of Charles Playhouse* stamped along their top rails. They'd been dragged up the street for crowd control, in deference to the group of onlookers clustered at the front of the Revere Hotel. Several trucks from the local news channels were parked in a row down to the next street, and Kamienski could see an equal number of BPD uniforms and Anton Codreanu's black suit-clad bodyguards grouped together nearby.

Kamienski and Silent Mark had tangled with Codreanu—albeit indirectly—four months prior during the Mass Art Murderer case, during which they got suspended from the force because their captain was being blackmailed—again, indirectly—by Codreanu. They couldn't prove it, but Codreanu had paid the Mass Art Murderer to kill four college students and mutilate Jake Wolfe, all to forward his personal agenda.

Maneuvering around the gathering swarm of crime scene techs, Kamienski was relieved to see an officer he knew by name. "Sullivan! What's the situation?"

The youngest of the four Sullivan siblings, Frankie was the son of Chief Patrick Sullivan of the Somerville Police Department and in the fifth month of his tenure as a solo officer. He'd narrowly missed getting his ass handed to him for passing information along to Kamienski and Silent Mark while they were suspended. He stood near the entrance to Stela in his patrol uniform, hat clutched in a white-knuckled hand. The wild dark curls trademark to the Sullivan family were cut short and neat, but hazel eyes and strong eyebrows reminded Kamienski of Frankie's older sister, Caitlin, whom he'd had the pleasure of working with (unofficially) last April.

"Hey kid," Kamienski greeted as he and Silent Mark reached him, taking in the set of his jaw and his pallor. "You okay?"

Frankie swallowed hard and shook his head. "I just got here, but we've got seven gunshot wounds and dozens of others with minor injuries from glass and debris. One of the people that got shot was Dumbass for Governor, otherwise known as my fucking brother." He paused to mop the sweat from his brow with his shirtsleeve. "Sorry, sir. That was inappropriate."

"Christopher got hit?" Kamienski said. He glanced around at the throng of guests from Stela; some were being interviewed by officers while others were getting patched up by EMTs. "Did they take him in an ambulance?"

"They went to Tufts," Frankie replied. Meaning Tufts Medical Center, the closest hospital to the Theatre District and probably where most of the injured would be taken. "It's a shoulder hit, through-and-through—he lost some blood, but they said he'd be all right."

Silent Mark touched Frankie's shoulder, a quiet gesture of support, and moved off toward a gap in the crowd. Kamienski knew his partner front to back, which meant he knew Silent Mark had spotted someone of interest and went to catch them so Kamienski could speak with them when he was done talking to Frankie.

Turning his attention back to the junior officer, Kamienski said, "I want you to get over to Tufts right now, you understand? Your brother might be a dumbass, but you should still be with him. Get outta here."

Frankie left, and Kamienski followed the trail of Silent Mark's fedora to where he stood with Sebastian Codreanu. He was next to the Steinway grand piano near what was once Stela's front window, its black lacquer finish pockmarked by bullet holes. His head was bowed, and crooked yet elegant fingers brushed the faux-ivory keys, leaving idle smears of blood in their wake. He wore a white dress shirt stained red at the edges and pants that belonged to a blue twill suit; a tie or matching jacket were nowhere in sight.

"Hey, Sebastian?" When Kamienski got no response he stooped down, trying to see behind Sebastian's curtain of dark hair. "Kid, you okay?"

Bottle-blue eyes rose to meet Kamienski's, their gaze distant but still less glazed than half of the people in the restaurant. This wasn't Sebastian's first traumatic event. "I'm fine, *detectiv*. The blood isn't mine." He looked around, shadows from the broken chandeliers bouncing off the high planes of his cheekbones. "I tried to help Christopher… they took him away not long ago." Copper-coated fingers ran across the keys one last time. "I'm glad the pianist wasn't out here when this happened. She'd be dead."

Helping Christopher explained the blood, but Kamienski didn't like the sallow tinge to Sebastian's golden skin. "What about you? You're not hurt, right?"

Behind Kamienski, Constantin Ionesco cleared his throat. "*I* am fine, thank you so much for asking."

The bench that matched the piano was miraculously intact, and Kamienski gestured for Sebastian to take a seat, ignoring Constantin's smartass remark. "How about you take a load off and walk us through what happened? Mark and I just got here, and we could use all the help we can get. How was Christopher when you saw him last?"

"Christopher will be fine," Constantin said. The barrel-chested bodyguard, Kamienski noticed, wore his fair share of bloodstains and was picking pieces of glass out of his hands. He brushed past Kamienski and plunked his ass down on the piano bench next to his charge. "Sebastian's jacket staunched most of the blood flow. Luckily whoever is behind this was terrible at aiming their minigun."

Silent Mark raised an eyebrow at the word *minigun*. Not an easy weapon to acquire or to wield, so it was a potential clue.

"Your boss piss anyone off lately?" Kamienski asked. "I realize that's a pointless question, considering he pisses numerous people off on a daily basis, but I have to ask. Also, where the hell is he?"

"Addressing the media circus I am sure you saw on your way in here," Sebastian replied. He accepted the package of Wet Wipes that a passing crime scene technician offered and began cleaning the blood from his hands. "Appearances are everything, you know."

"We'll have to see if he can take some time out of his busy schedule to talk to us," Kamienski said with a touch of sarcasm. The same crime scene technician that gave Sebastian the Wet Wipes handed Kamienski a bagged and tagged cartridge from the gun that decimated Stela. He glanced at it briefly: a 7.62x52 NATO round. "You said minigun, Constantin? Any idea what kind?"

"Easiest one to get in the United States would probably be an M134." Constantin stroked at his beard thoughtfully. "The weapon with that designation is popular with the Army."

"Interesting," Kamienski said. "Problem is, a designation doesn't get you a manufacturer, which is what could eventually get us a buyer. Dillon Aero, Garwood Industries—a bunch of companies make variants on the basic design."

"You might have better luck tracking the bullets," a voice said, hard consonants and the *click-click* of hand-tooled loafers against the floor welcoming Anton Codreanu into the conversation. "But I suppose I do not need to tell two of Boston's finest how to do their jobs, do I?"

Deciding it would probably be better for everyone if Anton didn't know that he and Silent Mark already knew Constantin and Sebastian, Kamienski played it like they didn't. "I would hope not, Mr. Codreanu. I'm—"

Codreanu held up a hand. "I know who you are, Detective Kamienski, and obviously—" he gestured at the mess around them "—I know why you're here, so how about we get down to business? We'll all get back to work a lot faster that way."

Gee, never would've guessed this guy's a Communist, Kamienski thought. A glance at Silent Mark revealed he didn't look impressed, but then again, Silent Mark rarely did. "Okay, no problem. Are there cameras on the front of your building?"

"Yes, but I would imagine they were damaged or destroyed during the shooting," Codreanu said. "However, the Revere is directly across the street, and there are several high-end stores on this block. I would imagine you might be able to pull something useful from their cameras."

"Did anybody get a decent look at the vehicle?"

"It was definitely a van," Constantin said. "On the newer side. Not sure on make or model."

Sebastian cleared his throat. "Christopher saw it, too." When his father's icy gaze snapped toward him Sebastian didn't shrink away, which Kamienski imagined was due to years of practice. "He was in the middle of a speech, and I saw his eyes move toward the windows right before the shooting started."

"Thanks for the info," Kamienski said. "I'll get somebody asking for security camera footage, but we should get over to Tufts. I'd imagine they're seeing a lot of action tonight, but Christopher's probably in surgery by now."

Silent Mark nodded his agreement, and wordlessly handed Codreanu a business card printed with Kamienski's information.

"Call us if you think of anything else." *Or, you know, don't do that*, Kamienski added mentally, and they left.

~***~

Chapter Three

The next morning found Jim Wolfe—former Army Ranger turned one half of a private investigatory duo—struggling to hang a new sign on the door to his office and wondering how many people had accidentally driven a nail through some part of their body since the invention of the hammer.

The office of Wolfe & Vaughn Investigations was a one-room affair in an old brick building on Boston's famed Boylston Street, across the hall from an accountant and one floor up from a hairstylist who claimed that banana peel hair masks were rejuvenating. Wolfe cut his own hair with a pair of clippers, but even if he didn't, he was fairly certain he didn't want the discarded parts of somebody's snack pressed to his head for two hours.

From behind Wolfe and to his left—leaning against the accountant's doorjamb, no doubt—came the scratchy voice of his partner, Scarlett Vaughn: "A little to the left."

"That's not what you said when I had it more to the left," Wolfe said, the words slightly jumbled due to the nail clamped between his teeth. He glanced back at Scarlett, caught a glimpse of wavy honey-blonde hair and a smirking heart-shaped face. "Remind me why we didn't buy the fancy door with the fogged glass? You know, the one they could've just etched our names into?"

"Because you're a cheap bastard?" Scarlett suggested. She pushed off the doorjamb and came to stand at Wolfe's side, the top of her head a few inches short of Wolfe's shoulder; she was one of few people Wolfe had met who had never been intimidated by his six-foot-four frame, scars and all. "Either that or Trevor the Landlord didn't bring the form around because we're perpetually late with the rent."

"We're not *perpetually* late—I mailed the check early this month—and I'm not cheap!" Wolfe exclaimed, making a noise of triumph as he finally got the sign centered and took the nail out of his mouth to pound it into the door. "We even have an intern now, for Christ's sake. How can you call me cheap?"

Scarlett snorted. "Our intern is Sebastian, and we're not paying him—*and* he's not even here."

Wolfe stepped back to admire his work. "I texted him earlier but he hasn't answered. Doesn't necessarily mean anything—his old man thinks Sebastian's spying on us for him, and he needs to keep it that way."

After the events of the previous April, Sebastian and Constantin had both expressed the desire to see Anton pay for his crimes. Wolfe had a bone to pick with the elder Codreanu due to his role in the mutilation of Wolfe's younger brother, Jake, and Scarlett always backed Wolfe's plays, no matter how ill-advised they might be. They needed proof of wrongdoing, however, which was hard to come by—finding concrete evidence that Anton orchestrated the Mass Art

Murders was like looking for a particular needle in a disease-laced haystack of heinous but less important needles. Constantin and Sebastian were inside men, but they had limits on what they could do without being suspected by Anton's other employees or the man himself.

Beside Wolfe, Scarlett sniffed the air and nudged his arm. "Hey, do you smell coffee?"

"We really need to talk about your caffeine problem," Wolfe said. "I'm beginning to think you and Frogger should start a support group."

From the stairwell at the end of the hall, Caitlin Sullivan—Wolfe's ex-girlfriend from high school turned close friend—spoke up, a tray of cups from Dunkin' in one hand and a blue and white box from Kane's in the other. "I guess I'm an enabler now. I'm pretty sure that's like the opposite of what a nurse is supposed to be." She was shorter than Scarlett but curvy at her bust and hips, with a rounded chin and a smattering of freckles across her nose. The Sullivans' signature curly dark hair was cut just below Caitlin's shoulders, and she had her contacts in, blue-green eyes free to roam without her glasses.

"Hey, Caity," Wolfe said, surprised to see Caitlin there—especially when she was supposed to be at work at Massachusetts General Hospital. "What's wrong?"

Caitlin quirked an eyebrow, ducking into the office when Wolfe held the door for her and Scarlett. "I take it you haven't seen the news this morning? Or looked at Facebook?"

Scarlett and Wolfe exchanged a look, and then Scarlett said, "No, I picked Jimmy up from his apartment and we came straight here to hang the sign before we open. What did we miss?"

The office was a twelve-by-twelve box with gray walls and flooring, a set of double windows providing most of the light. Mounted on the walls were the duo's private investigator certifications and a watercolor painting of birds on a wire, along with some ceramic butterflies that Wolfe's mom made in an art class at the YMCA. The guest chair was falling apart but Caitlin sat in it anyway, setting down the coffees and donuts on the scratched-up top of the single desk Wolfe and Scarlett shared.

Caitlin waited for them to settle in their rolling chairs on the other side of the desk before she opened the Kane's box and fished out a Boston Cream. "Christopher had a fundraising dinner last night for his campaign," she began, taking a sip of her coffee. "At a fancy five-star restaurant in the Theatre District. You wanna guess which one?"

Wolfe had his own coffee cup halfway to his mouth and groaned. "Seriously? Why the hell did he have a fundraiser at Stela?"

"Because Anton Codreanu donated an insane amount of money to your idiot brother's campaign and now he's got him wrapped around his little finger?" Scarlett guessed, condescension dripping off the words.

Caitlin snapped her fingers and pointed at Scarlett. "You got it. I tried to tell him what he was getting into, but you know Christopher."

"Sometimes I wish I didn't," Wolfe muttered, eliciting a snort from Scarlett. "So what happened at the fundraiser?"

"A drive-by shooting," Caitlin said, face contorting grimly even as she licked custard off the back of her hand. "Bunch of people got hurt, but thankfully nobody died."

Scarlett looked at Wolfe and raised her eyebrows. "You think that's why we haven't heard from Sebastian?"

Wolfe's hand tensed around his coffee cup, worry tingling its way down from the back of his skull and crowding around his spine. "I don't know. Hopefully he and Constantin are just lying low until Anton's distracted."

"I don't think he was hurt—pretty sure that would've made the news," Caitlin said, snorting derisively. "My idiot brother getting shot sure did."

"With the amount of people Christopher's pissed off at your family reunions I'm surprised it didn't happen sooner." Wolfe reached for a Key Lime Pie donut, which Kane's only made during August. He had a stockpile of them at home in his freezer, but that didn't mean he couldn't have a fresh one. "He gonna be okay?"

"He's talking to the cops right now, so I think that's a yes," Caitlin said. "But I came here to see if you two could talk to him about hiring some security for the rest of his campaign."

Scarlett coughed up some donut crumbs in surprise. "He doesn't have any security? Is he nuts?"

Caitlin made a see-sawing motion with her hand. "Debatable, but would you believe me if I said up until last night he hasn't *needed* security besides what's provided at venues?" She twiddled her thumbs and looked at the wall beyond their heads. "*I* was hoping… you guys could be his security?"

"You've gotta be kidding, Caity," Wolfe said, slugging down the last of his coffee. "Christopher and I don't get along… at all. I'll probably be next in line to shoot him if I have to work for him."

"He's not my favorite person either, but I want you to consider something." Scarlett spread her arms to indicate how empty the office was. "Clients aren't exactly banging down our door, Jimmy— and besides, he's probably too damn stubborn to hire us anyway. What could a consultation hurt?"

Caitlin piled on, busting out the puppy dog eyes: "Come on, Jimmy! Christopher might be an ass, but if somebody kills him my mom's gonna cry. Do you want to see my mom cry?"

Wolfe sighed, running a hand through his short reddish-blond hair and making a face when he got it all sticky with sugar from his hands. "Ah, hell, okay. Where is he?"

"Well, he *did* get shot," Caitlin said, "so we figured the hospital was a good place."

~***~

A few blocks from Wolfe & Vaughn Investigations—across from where Boylston met Arlington Street and kitty-corner to the Public Garden—was a tailor's shop called Seams, which occupied a faux-vintage storefront and served as camouflage for one of Anton Codreanu's many "secret" offices scattered throughout the city. He owned it under an alias and collected the legitimate profits while avoiding most of the hard work that came with being a small business owner.

David Wolfe—back-from-the-dead ex-Army Ranger and current CIA spook—and his partner, Diana Johnson, sat in a rented sapphire-blue Toyota Camry a few cars down from the intersection next to the Arlington Street Church, its Black Lives Matter banner blowing gently in the humid breeze. The Camry was arguably one of the most nondescript cars in the United States, and while David appreciated that, he hated that it had the approximate legroom of a Tinker Toy.

"I have a question for you," Diana said, Serbian accent barely touching the words, even to David's trained ears. "Did you pick up worms while we were on that job in Spain?"

It took a second for her words to percolate through David's brain—maybe the dye he'd used to color his hair from its natural blond to brown killed off some brain cells. "What? No, I don't have worms!"

"Then how do you explain all the squirming you are doing?" Diana gestured at him with silver rings that distracted from gun calluses, long black hair slipping over her shoulders like slick oil. "You haven't been still for longer than thirty seconds in the past four hours and it's driving me insane."

"Sorry," David said, and he meant it, because he was shifting around again. People who were six-foot-two were *not* meant to drive mid-sized sedans, let alone a six-foot-two person teetering the line between *capable field agent* and *old man who should be golfing*. "There's zero leg room behind the wheel of this thing and I can't feel my ass." He paused. "I blame Otis. Why did he have to go missing?"

"I don't know, but I just hope Anton didn't have anything to do with it." Diana frowned, glancing down at her watch. David gave that to her for her eighteenth birthday; he was surprised it still kept time, and that she still wore it. "It's almost ten o'clock—Seams is supposed to open at nine, and we haven't seen anyone go inside."

"Well, we already know there's no delivery door," David mused, "so maybe we should take a walk over and see what's what?"

His partner rolled her hazel eyes as she reached for her door handle. "Your detailed, nuanced planning style is why I keep you around."

They hustled through the crosswalk right as the light changed—much to the dismay and honking horns of every driver at the intersection—and when they got closer to Seams, it became apparent that something was off. The shades were drawn down over the windows, and the security cameras positioned at the building's corners had been coated with black spray paint, obscuring their lenses.

David's eyebrows drew down as he tried the door. Locked. "Somebody covered the cameras but they didn't break in?"

"*Sranje*," Diana cursed. She glanced around covertly, looking for Anton's goons but seeing none. "This isn't good news for Otis."

David automatically maneuvered his large frame between Diana and the street when she pulled out her lock picks—the worst thing an outsider would see was a guy loitering in front of a tailor shop. "You think Anton knows what we're up to?"

Diana shook her head as she felt out the lock with a torsion wrench and a pick. "If he did, I'd already be dead." Someone in Anton's inner circle—adopted daughter or not—wouldn't last long if he discovered they were a spy. "Perhaps he suspects Otis was going to talk to the police?"

"The idea that the only guy you trusted inside Anton's operation vanished right when we were going to ask him to testify against his boss doesn't fill me with the warm fuzzies," David said. He held the door for Diana when she got it open and slipped inside, running up her back when she stopped short of the front counter. She smelled like orange blossoms and gun oil. "Sorry."

She waved away the apology—a privilege, since Diana didn't like people in her personal space—and together they silently examined the scene. Enough daylight filtered in through the slats in the blinds for them to see without turning on the overhead fluorescents. The business part of Seams was fairly small, with a couple of chairs for people who wanted to wait for their alterations, a tall freestanding magazine rack, and bead board paneling crawling up the walls. David knew from Diana that the door behind the counter went to a hallway, which led to the tailoring space and Anton's office.

Diana hopped the counter with ease, boot heels clacking against the linoleum. She shuffled some work orders around and rifled through the drawers under the countertop. Each time she moved something she always put things back exactly the way she found them, like only a careful spy—or in Diana's case, child assassin turned spy—would know to do.

Something crunched under David's foot when he took a step forward, and when he looked down he saw the glint of broken glass on the floor; it was swept to the side like someone was in a hurry, and he followed the trail of shards to the magazine rack. Sticking out from under the rack was the corner of a picture frame, and David bent to pick it up.

"D?" he said. "Otis is married, right?"

"Yes, but his wife is ill," Diana replied, coming around the counter to look at the picture in David's hands. It was faded with age and showed a pretty young woman with short dark hair and a button nose, standing in front of a remnant of the Berlin Wall. "I wondered where this was—it's been on the counter every time I've come here."

"If there was a struggle, the picture was the only casualty." Carefully, David pried the picture from the wrecked frame and slid it into the inner pocket of his denim jacket. He looked a little odd wearing a coat in the summer swelter, but it was the only thing that concealed the gun in his waistband. "How sick is his wife?"

"Last I heard Anton paid for some new high-tech treatment for her cancer, but it didn't work," Diana said. "She's in hospice care in Lynn, and I'm fairly certain Anton's paying for that too." She paused, head tilting in a way that always reminded David of a bird of prey considering its next meal. "Perhaps we should drive up there and see if Otis has been by to see his wife."

"Exactly what I was thinking," David replied. The picture of the curly-haired woman felt uncomfortable in his pocket, almost like an omen. "Lead the way."

~***~

"Explain this to me again," Scarlett said. "Real slow this time, to make sure I understand."

Wolfe huffed out a laugh and spun the wheel of Scarlett's 1969 Chevrolet Corvette, falling in behind an ambulance as it turned down Stuart Street. "I don't know what's so hard to understand. I've had four accidents in the past year, and my insurance agent told me if I reported another one he'd drop me like a hot potato, even though I'm ridiculously sexy. That's a direct quote, by the way."

The last of those accidents had occurred in the driveway of Wolfe's mother's house about four months prior. A lot of things changed that night in April, all of them more important than Wolfe losing his Mustang to the wrath of Frankie Sullivan's police cruiser. Within the span of a few hours, Wolfe had found out his dream girl was engaged to another man, his brother Jake was almost tortured to death by a serial killer, and his… friend Sebastian had almost died after being poisoned with an experimental drug by his own father.

"You're not using your car for work anymore—I get that part." They were approaching Tufts Medical Center, and Scarlett took the opportunity to pull her long blonde hair into a ponytail. With a hairband clamped between her teeth she continued, "What I don't get is how that equates to *you* driving *my* car."

"… I have control issues?" Wolfe guessed, banging a U-turn so he could park on Stuart before it became Kneeland Street. They'd have to walk a little ways, but it was better than trying (and failing) to park in the garage. "Plus you hate parallel parking."

Scarlett snorted. "Bitch, I'm from New York. Parallel parking is an Olympic sport."

Tufts Medical Center was a sprawling network of buildings that resembled a protractor when viewed from the air, the middle of the complex arching over Washington Street like the arm of a compass. This center branch connected the parking garage and the Floating Hospital for Children to the rest of the facility; Scarlett and Wolfe went in through the main doors, and once the receptionist called up to Christopher's room to double-check, they were directed to an elevator that would take them to correct floor.

It was the little things about hospitals, Wolfe thought as they stepped out at MedSurge, that made him want to run back the way he'd come. The clashing aromas of chemicals and sickness were mixed with TV chatter, beeping machinery, and the moaning of people in pain. Nurses and other medical personnel shuffled between rooms, the sallow lighting making everyone look half-dead. Before he knew it, the spider-web of scar tissue that spanned Wolfe's side was aching, and the space behind his eyes throbbed in time with his pulse. Everything seemed more vivid, and the tang of copper stung the back of his throat even though the blood wasn't there anymore, even though they told him they'd gotten rid of it all—

Scarlett's hand on Wolfe's arm snapped him back to reality. The way his scarred skin felt under her fingers had never bothered her. "You okay, big guy?"

Wolfe blew out a breath and rolled his bad shoulder; his muscles felt like stone, they were so tense. "Sorry. Last time I was in a hospital was…"

"With Jake. I remember." Scarlett's pale green eyes knew Wolfe too well as they gazed into his face. "But you weren't a traumatized big brother just now. You were a solider."

Wolfe mustered up a smile, just for her. "I'm always a big brother… and I never stopped being a soldier, Scar."

She squeezed his arm in a gesture of support, and knocked on the door to Christopher's room once before entering.

The gubernatorial candidate was asleep in his bed, tubes and wires trailing from his chest and arms to an IV stand and some monitors. He was in a private room that looked like it belonged in a hotel, outfitted with couches, a television, and its own coffee maker. Melissa Sullivan was curled up in a recliner in the corner, a conservatively-cut pencil dress taut around her drawn-up knees. Her Jimmy Choo heels lay discarded nearby, red toenail polish visible through her pantyhose. Frankie Sullivan sat in an armchair at the opposite end of the room, murmuring quietly into his cell phone and pinching the bridge of his nose.

Melissa jumped up from her chair. "Jimmy! Oh, thank God!" She threw her arms around Wolfe's neck, her platinum blonde hair throwing off notes of Guerlain perfume and sheetrock dust from Stela. Despite her height—she reached Wolfe's chin without her heels, a rare thing—Melissa's rounded face and wide-set eyes gave her an almost childlike in appearance. At that moment, she looked less like Massachusetts's next first lady and more like a worried wife. "I'm so glad you're here—Caitlin asked you, didn't she? You just missed a couple of detectives from the police department." She made a face. "One of them had a funny name and the other one didn't talk."

"Yes, Caitlin asked us to come," Wolfe said, easing Melissa back into her chair before he and Scarlett took seats on a nearby couch. He had a feeling the detectives were Kamienski and Silent Mark from that description, so he cut to the chase: "How is Christopher?"

"They have him on pain meds, and the surgery to remove the bullet went well." Melissa said. She bit her lip, cutting into lipstick that probably cost as much as an oil change. "We haven't put the TV on because we didn't want to wake him up. Was anyone…?"

Killed was not a word she used often, Wolfe thought, which explained why she had a hard time saying it. Melissa grew up in Cambridge and was the only daughter of Reuben Quinn, a founding partner at Quinn, Goldstein and Wickersham, the Boston-based law firm that made its money from representing only the scuzziest criminals the state had to offer—providing they could afford a hefty price tag.

"Thankfully, no. It looks like the most serious injury was Christopher's," Scarlett said. She leaned forward, arms braced on her knees and her hands clasped. "Look, Mel, we know this is a shitty time to be asking questions—"

"But if they're gonna protect this idiot when I have to go back to work, then they need to know stuff," Frankie interjected, coming over to join the powwow. "Mom and Dad are on their way, and Kevin says he'll stay with the kids as long as you need, Mel."

"Okay, okay—Christ, I almost forgot about the kids." Melissa dropped her face into her hands and took a deep, shuddering breath before she looked up again. "I'm sorry. How can I help you guys?"

"You don't need to apologize." Wolfe grabbed a box of tissues off a nearby table and offered them to Melissa; tears had been streaming silently down her cheeks since they got there. "Why were you guys at Stela last night?"

"It was a campaign fundraiser," Melissa said, dabbing carefully at her mascara-ringed eyes. "The cover charge bought dinner and an open bar for two. Mr. Codreanu was gracious enough to host us."

"Did he donate to Christopher's campaign?"

"Of course. Why do you ask?"

"Anton Codreanu has a lot of legitimate business interests, but he also keeps some interesting company," Scarlett said. "Danh Sang, for example."

Melissa sniffled, blinked in confusion. "Who's that?"

"The leader of the Red Dynasty. They're the big Vietnamese outfit that runs Dorchester," Wolfe said. "We suspect—but can't prove—that Anton Codreanu hired the Mass Art Murderer to help him achieve certain goals. Getting Sang out of prison was one."

"Seriously?" Melissa looked at Frankie. "Did you know about this?"

"Yep." Frankie shrugged his shoulders. "Tried to tell Chris that Codreanu was bad news, and Caitlin did too. But you know brother dearest."

"Once he gets an idea in his head, he's as stubborn as a fucking donkey," Melissa said. "And the million dollars Anton donated to the campaign would have only made him more pigheaded." She rubbed her forehead. "I realize I don't sound like the most sympathetic spouse right now, but sometimes that man drives me *insane*."

"He wouldn't be your husband if he didn't." Scarlett patted Melissa's knee. "It's more likely the real target of the shooting was Codreanu and the campaign fundraiser was as good of a bullseye as any."

"I hate to ask this," Wolfe began. He scratched at the scruff growing along his jaw. It was too short to be called a beard, but he rarely bothered shaving down to the skin. "Does Christopher have any enemies? Anybody who dislikes him enough to try something like this?"

Melissa snorted out a laugh. "Chris is a politician. He makes enemies everywhere he goes." She sobered quickly. "But no, I can't think of anyone. That's what I told the police."

A groan came from the hospital bed, startling all four of them. "Jesus Christ on a pogo stick," Christopher rasped, "what does a guy have to do to get some sleep in this hospital?"

"Chris! Oh, I'm so glad you're okay," Melissa exclaimed. She rushed over to pour him a cup of water from the pitcher on the bedside table. "How do you feel?"

"A lot like I got shot, hon." Despite the somewhat snarky answer to her question, Christopher grabbed Melissa's hand and held on as he took in the rest of the faces in the room. "Wolfe? Vaughn? What are you doing here?"

"Your sister stopped by our office," Scarlett said. She'd never liked Christopher for a few reasons, not the least of which was his less than amicable relationship with her partner. "She bribed us with coffee and donuts—and we all know Jimmy here is a sucker for anything from Kane's."

Wolfe snorted. "Yes, and the rest of those donuts *definitely* won't meander back to your condo." He leaned forward. "Caitlin's worried about you, man, and so are a lot of other people after what happened last night. I can't tell you what to do, but it's probably in your best interest—and the best interest of your family and the people working on you campaign—if you retained us as bodyguards, at least until the primary is over. We already know your family, and I bet our rate is significantly cheaper than most protection firms out there."

Christopher pulled a face. "Look, I appreciate you guys stopping by and all, but—"

"No buts," Melissa cut in, squeezing her husband's hand a little too tightly. "We'll take the protection, Jimmy. Thank you."

"Of course you will," Frankie said, shooting his older brother a look that suggested he shouldn't argue. "Jimmy and Scarlett are good at their jobs, Chris—they'll keep you safe and you can focus on the campaign."

Christopher's face twisted into a sneer. "Oh, you mean like they kept those kids safe back in April?"

Everything stopped. Wolfe bristled like an angered cat, shoulders tensing as he squared his jaw, and Scarlett went pale and red in the face in quick succession.

"Chris!" Melissa admonished. "Jesus, did you *have* to say that?"

Frankie shook his head. "Dick move, bro."

"Well it's true," Christopher argued, sounding a lot like the politician he was, determined to argue a point even when the majority was against him. "Matt O'Donovan's dead, Jake Wolfe looks like hell, Captain Bach lost her sister—"

Wolfe stood up from the couch, anger coiling in his gut. "I need to have a word with Christopher. Alone."

"Gladly, partner," Scarlett said, a little too cheerfully. "We'll go down to the cafeteria and get some coffee."

She gave Wolfe a pat on the shoulder and left the room with Caitlin, Frankie, and Melissa.

Once they were gone, Wolfe dragged Frankie's vacated chair over so it was next to Christopher's bed. "You've got a lot of balls, saying that. About two more than I thought you did."

"I'm sorry, okay? I had to get everybody else to leave so we could talk, and I knew that would piss you off enough to want to tell me what a prick I am in private," Christopher said, pitching his voice low. "I know you tried your hardest to catch that bastard, and so did those detectives."

"Yeah, and none of it was good enough," Wolfe replied. He almost couldn't believe Christopher was clever enough to clear the room in the way he had. "Now what did you want to talk to me about?"

"Nobody's gonna let this protection thing go, are they?" When Wolfe shook his head, Christopher continued, "Fine, but my brother is the only person from BPD I trust."

Wolfe raised an eyebrow. "Why?"

"The police union hates me because I'm on the Republican ticket against Big Mike," Christopher said. Michael "Big Mike" Draymond was the former chief of the Boston Police Department, and while Wolfe had never met the man, he'd heard you either loved him or wanted to punch him in the face. "And with that information leak they had during the Mass Art Murders—"

"From what Kamienski told me they think the leak was somebody associated with the department, not actually in it." Wolfe knew the department's IT faction had been trying to figure out where the leaks to the media had come from for months, and they'd managed to trace some cyber evidence back to the medical examiner's office. "Do you think Draymond had something to do with the shooting at Stela?"

"I don't know, but I wouldn't be surprised," Christopher said. "He's been hounding me like a dog with a bone—says I'm not conservative enough, that I've 'been corrupted by the liberal media'."

Wolfe huffed out a laugh. "Is that code for 'I'm afraid of the internet'?"

Christopher tensed weirdly, like he wanted to shrug but stopped himself because of his shoulder. "Could be. Draymond is pretty old-school."

"Okay, but what about Anton Codreanu?"

"What about him?"

"You're sure he didn't plant the idea of police corruption in your head?"

"Anton and I barely know one another," Christopher said, annoyance bleeding into his tone. "And any conversations we've had have strictly been about the issues. Melissa probably told you he's been a generous donor to the campaign."

Speak of the devil and he shall appear. Before Wolfe could respond, the door to the room opened and Anton Codreanu walked through it. He was trailed by two bodyguards sporting near-identical buzz cuts and harsh Eastern European facial features. They wore crisp black-on-black suits that offset their boss's Sunday-golf-casual look, jackets cut to conceal the handguns they undoubtedly had holstered under their beefy arms.

"Of course I've been generous, Christopher! You are the best candidate for governor Massachusetts has seen since I arrived in this country," Anton said. His Romanian accent had been sanded down over the years, and he spoke with no true affectation despite his grand words. Eyes that matched Sebastian's in color but were blank like a snake's landed squarely on Wolfe. "My, my, if it is not Boston's finest!" He extended a hand. "I do not believe we have met."

Wolfe thought: *You had my brother tortured. You make your son do terrible things. You want to kill my father.*

Wolfe said: "We haven't." He forced himself to stand and shake Anton's hand. He wanted to crush the other man's fingers, to whip his arm into a spiral fracture and throw him on the floor, stomp his head beneath his boot. He did none of those things. "I'm Jim Wolfe."

"Ah, the illustrious *detectiv*." Wolfe didn't know it was possible for a human being to sound so sardonic in the space of four words, but Anton managed it. "My son speaks highly of you—nothing but praise for the lovely private investigator who did not report an unfortunate car accident."

It wasn't an accident, Wolfe wanted to say. *You ordered him to rear-end me on purpose, wanted him to get under my skin when Diana couldn't.* Sebastian had admitted as much back in April, but Wolfe had that part of Anton Codreanu's crazy scheme figured out before his confession.

However, Wolfe knew that while Anton may not have been expecting to see him in Christopher's hospital room, he was now trying to figure out how to twist this situation to his advantage. The easiest way to play into Anton's hand would be to reveal exactly how much Wolfe knew about his theory that his eldest son Vladimir's murderer—Wolfe's father, David—was alive, despite being declared dead by the Army over two decades ago. Since David was in fact alive and Wolfe had gotten the majority of his information about Anton's lust for revenge from Sebastian, it was safer for everyone for Wolfe to play dumb.

That didn't mean he had to like it. "My driving record isn't spotless, and your son made an honest mistake." *And I have a crush on him that's approximately the size of Alaska so I kind of want to kill you.*

Anton looked at him with a critical, calculating eye, but he appeared to buy the dumbass act Wolfe was trying to sell. He turned his attention back to Christopher: "Mr. Sullivan, you have my deepest apologies for what transpired at Stela last night. I would like to offer as many of my men as you require for personal protection until the primary election."

Christopher opened his mouth to reply, but Wolfe didn't trust him to not fuck it up.

"That's a generous offer, Mr. Codreanu," Wolfe said, "but we have it handled. We'll be providing Mr. Sullivan with security and doing some investigating of our own until BPD knows more about what happened."

"Well, I'm sure the department will be working on it night and day," Anton said. He clasped his hands behind his back, the picture of false humility. "Tell me, how is Captain Bach? It must have been so painful to lose her sister in such a gruesome manner." A cruel imitation of sympathy twisted his expression. "And speaking of which—how is your brother, Mr. Wolfe? Is Jake all right?"

"Hanging in there," Wolfe replied. If he gritted his teeth any harder he'd crack a molar. "We're taking it one day at a time."

"And I wish him nothing but the best." Anton was such an adept liar that he had no tells, something that Wolfe had only seen in true crime films about psychopaths and sociopaths. "Mr. Sullivan, if you need anything, you have my number." He made to leave, his two bodyguards following along like overdressed gorillas. "Best of luck with your investigation, *detectiv.*"

"About that," Wolfe said, causing Anton to pause in the doorway. "*You* wouldn't have any idea of who'd want to shoot up your restaurant, would you?"

Anton smiled, and it was reminiscent of the way a shark might grin if it sensed blood in the water. "None at all. Have a pleasant day."

~***~

Chapter Four

Down on Brookline Avenue, Laine and Aiden Parker strolled past Fenway Park, greasy slices of pepperoni pizza from Sal's in hand. They were dressed like the tourists milling up and down the block, in shorts and tank tops and brand new Red Sox hats. Laine's distinctive red hair was tucked up underneath her cap and large tortoiseshell sunglasses mostly obscured the scar across her face.

Aiden took a bite of his pizza and raised his phone, snapping pictures like any young man would—he even took a few of his sister when she stopped to pose in front of a restaurant. "People probably think you're an Instagram model."

Laine snorted even as she flashed him a cheesy grin. "Only from a distance."

They passed the intersection with David Ortiz Drive and Jersey Street, Laine pausing again to pose in front of the baseball-shaped sign for the Kenmore parking lot. She took a good, long look at the building directly next to the lot, inspecting it from top to bottom from behind her shades.

"I've got one security guard," she murmured, smile still plastered on her face as Aiden snapped away. "He's by the entrance closest to the street, but I doubt he'll still be here at game time."

"You prepared to do something about him if he is?" Aiden asked, and there was an undercurrent of malice in his voice that made Laine tense. "I won't be around to help you if he's a problem."

"He won't be," she replied, hoping she sounded surer than she felt. "I have no interest in hurting anyone besides the target, Aiden, and neither should you. We're not like those idiots that shot up Stela last night—we have a message to send."

They kept walking, past the building and the security guard, and Aiden licked pizza grease off his fingers. He gave his sister a harsh once-over out of the corner of his eye and said, "Don't forget that part, Lainey. The message comes before anything—and any*one*— else."

Laine swallowed the last bite of her pizza, the doughy treat suddenly a hard ball in her stomach. "I know, Aiden. I'll do what I have to."

~***~

Christopher Sullivan's campaign office was in his hometown of Somerville on the stretch of Broadway west of I-93, crammed between an optician and a bank in a small strip mall. The windows were papered with large photographs of Christopher's face, bordered by a red and white stars-and-strips motif that was probably meant to be patriotic but looked tacky to Wolfe's jaded eyes. There were conflicting odors from a taco place at one end of the street and an Ethiopian restaurant at the other, and some local kids rolled on their skateboards near the corner Gulf station, soaking up the last dregs of summer before they were forced back to school.

Constantin and Sebastian were loitering outside the campaign office, both of them leaning against the optician's brick wall, albeit in vastly different stances. Constantin stood at attention in his usual black-on-black suit despite the heat of the sun, hair slicked back and a perpetual frown on his craggy face; Sebastian slouched next to him in designer skinny jeans and a blue t-shirt, booted feet crossed at the ankles and a lit Camel dangling from crooked fingers. There were a couple of trucks from the local news channels camped out across the street, but the reporters and their cameramen seemed too preoccupied with setting up the perfect backdrop for their shot to be interested in anything actually happening at the office.

The Corvette purred to a stop behind Constantin's black Mercedes sedan. Sebastian elbowed his bodyguard to get his attention, taking one last drag from his cigarette before grinding it underfoot. Constantin shrugged his shoulders with disinterest, because evidently now that he knew Scarlett and Wolfe weren't a threat to his charge, he'd rather continue daydreaming.

Scarlett hopped out of the passenger's seat of the 'Vette and got to them first, wrapping her arms around Sebastian in a hug. "Hey, dude—you okay? Last night sounds like it was pretty fucked up."

Sebastian looked pleasantly surprised but returned the embrace. "I'm fine. I heard on the news that the others who were injured are all going to be okay. How is Christopher?"

Scarlett snorted. "A pain in the ass, but he'll live… at least if we have anything to say about it."

"Which we will since we're getting paid, but also because Caitlin will literally force me to watch her mother cry if he gets murdered," Wolfe added, stepping up in Scarlett's place and going for a hug of his own. He came from a family of huggers—Scarlett had learned it from them—so he figured it wouldn't be weird if he hugged Sebastian too. Friends hugged all the time, toxic masculinity surrounding the idea of men showing affection be damned.

What Wolfe wasn't expecting was how *nice* it would be.

Sebastian was just under six feet tall, so he could hook his chin over Wolfe's shoulder and not get his face smushed somewhere by his armpit (which was something that Wolfe liked to avoid). His dark hair tickled the side of Wolfe's face where it curled behind his ear, and his smaller frame was solid with muscle even though he was thin enough that Wolfe could feel his ribs through the back of his shirt. He'd sucked in a sharp breath initially but let it out a second later, hands coming up to grip Wolfe's back as he returned the hug.

"I met your father today," Wolfe said as he pulled back, clenching his hands into loose fists to stave off the urge to brush that one errant piece of hair off Sebastian's forehead. "He was shorter than I expected."

Sebastian's eyes went wide. "You met Anton? How?"

"He probably went to see Christopher in hospital," Constantin guessed, and when Wolfe nodded he let out a snort. "That is Anton, always pretending to possess the capacity for feelings. Like guilt."

"He offered Christopher some men for protection, but thankfully Jimmy managed to dissuade him," Scarlett said. She'd gotten the whole story on the ride from Tufts to the campaign office. "Hopefully he gets the hint and backs off."

Constantin snorted again. "Not likely. It's Anton."

In an effort to fade the worry lines from Sebastian's face, Wolfe changed the subject: "So how's your mom? She need anything else fixed?"

Stela Goodyear née Codreanu remarried to a kindhearted and well-off accountant, but Nathan was one of those people who insisted on trying to be a handyman while knowing nothing about home improvement. Therefore he failed, sometimes spectacularly, to get anything done. His most recent folly involved setting some painting rags on fire when he left them by a well-lit garage window to dry and they promptly caught on fire. It wasn't a surprise that once Stela met Wolfe and realized *he* was handy, she would call or text occasionally to have Wolfe fix Nathan's mistakes while he was at work.

Sebastian smiled, bringing out the dimples in his cheeks and the light in his bottle-blue eyes. "Actually, she asked me to ask you to come by when you get a chance. From what I understand, Nathan managed to coat the entirety of the cabinet under the kitchen sink in silicone but he didn't fix what was wrong with the sink in the first place."

Constantin grunted, shaking his head. "That man is a menace. Is that not the exact situation in which most people would call a plumber?"

"Why bother when you know a guy who's got a master's degree in engineering that he never uses and will work for plum dumplings?" Wolfe opened the door and held it for the others, stepping into the air conditioned space last and breathing in the scent of copy paper and old coffee. "Wow, this is... not what I was expecting."

The office was all one room, with cream walls and dark green carpeting that was meant to hide dirt. Large gray filing cabinets lined one wall, and the rest of the space was taken up by several post-form desks that looked like they had been assembled by a drunk blind man and plastic folding chairs that were either from a rental company or somebody's backyard. One sad-looking houseplant sat atop the water bubbler, directly below yet another poster with Christopher's face on it.

"Disappointing, isn't it?" a female voice said, emerging from one of two doors along the back wall. "I told Christopher we needed to spice up the décor, but his sense of style is about as exciting as a piece of white bread." The woman was around Scarlett's height, with brown wavy hair cut in a short layered style and eyes like polished pieces of onyx. She wore a pale lilac jumpsuit that looked light and flowy, but shoulder pads and black pumps gave her a *don't fuck with me* edge even as she stuck out her hand. "Nikki Shaw, campaign manager for the next governor of Massachusetts—you know, providing he doesn't die."

Wolfe shook her hand and introduced her around. The lack of people other than Nikki in the office was surprising, so his first question was: "Where is everyone?"

"Told them to stay home," Nikki replied with a shrug. "Everyone's a volunteer except for me, and the last thing we need right now is someone blabbing to the media." Crossing her arms over her chest, she looked Wolfe up and down. "From the way your military record describes you I expected you to be a spit-shined asshole."

Wolfe raised an eyebrow. "How the hell did you get your hands on my file?"

Nikki smiled, red lips glossy under the fluorescent lights. "Got a guy at the Pentagon who owes me about twenty favors. Even he could only get a heavily-redacted version, of course, but it told me enough. Three tours of every shithole the Middle East has to offer with a Silver Star and a Purple Heart to show for it, honorable discharge at Sergeant thanks to grievous injury. You know what that tells me about you?"

Scarlett looked like she was debating between being impressed and strangling Christopher's campaign manager. "Please, enlighten us."

"It tells me you're loyal, brave, and maybe a little bit crazy," Nikki said, not unkindly. "What it *doesn't* tell me is how well you choose your friends." She looked at Sebastian. "I advised Christopher to stay the hell away from your father, but Anton provided us with a donation at an important time."

"My father has the ability to make himself invaluable to whomever he's trying to manipulate," Sebastian said. Glancing at Wolfe and Scarlett, he added hastily, "I can assure you I am not here to act as his spy. That is what I *told* him I was doing, but I'm actually their intern."

Nikki took that in, nodded to herself, and turned to Constantin. "What about you?"

Constantin jutted his chin in Sebastian's direction. "I go where he does. No exceptions."

Scarlett pulled a face. "That makes it sound like you stand over him while he takes a shit, which, ew." Her expression went flat when she met Nikki's dark gaze. "What about me, huh? You're not gonna psychoanalyze me based on my record?"

"You're a former NYPD detective that got scapegoated by the force as part of a cover-up, and your father runs one of the most well-known and wide-ranging private security firms on the planet," Nikki said, chuckling a bit. "I was actually going to call Vaughn Securities to get a quote, and then I got the word that the boss hired you two. Seemed almost poetic."

The door Nikki had come out of opened again, and this time Detective Jeff Kamienski stuck his head out. "Ma'am, are you coming back to the interview, or—ah, hell."

Wolfe perked up. "If it isn't our favorite detective!" He elbowed Scarlett in an attempt to sell his cheer. He and Kamienski were friendlier post-Mass Art Murders—nothing brings people together faster than a serial killer—but that tenuous thread could fray with one wrong word. "What are the chances we'd wind up on the same case twice?"

"Slim to none," Constantin commented, the sarcasm going over his Eastern European head. "Is Silent Mark with you?"

Kamienski pinched the bridge of his nose, opening the door further to reveal the trench coated form of his partner leaning against a wall in the conference room behind him. "I feel like I'm in a bad crime novel—you know, the kind they sell online for a couple bucks? Or maybe the oncoming migraine is making me delusional."

Scarlett patted him on the arm as she shouldered her way into the conference room. "Take it easy with the Excedrin or you'll wind up with liver failure at a critical moment in the plot." She nodded a greeting at Silent Mark and sat down in one of the chairs arranged around the large conference table. "So what is this, the two-for-one special?"

Nikki nodded, taking her own seat. "Something like that. I figured since all of you would like to know the same things, I could kill two birds with one stone."

"That's not usually how this works," Kamienski said, "but I'm getting the feeling that you don't give a damn, Ms. Shaw."

"I got a similar impression," Wolfe agreed, stretching out his legs and immediately coming boot-to-loafer with Constantin, who glared at him with only slightly less malice than he would've a few months ago. "I guess the first question to ask would be the obvious one—what have you told the press?"

"As little as I can get away with, but that comes with its own problems." Nikki leaned over and opened a mini-fridge that sat in the corner. She passed bottled water around, taking a long sip from hers before she continued. "The other candidates are sympathetic on the outside, but they're also the ones spreading the rumors."

"Rumors?" Sebastian asked.

Nikki rolled her eyes. "Christopher slept with a mobster's wife and got caught, he's secretly addicted to cocaine and the cartel is after him—oh, and apparently aliens use miniguns now."

Wolfe winced. "Sounds like a real clusterfuck."

"Is it possible that one of the other candidates could've had something to do with the shooting?" Kamienski asked. "Because as usual, Mr. Codreanu—not this one, his father—conveniently had no idea why someone would want to trash his restaurant and injure a bunch of people."

The campaign manager hummed thoughtfully, drumming a manicured nail against the cap of her bottled water. "Well,

Christopher *did* get into a little spat with Governor Halliday at a community service event a while back..." Roy Halliday was the Democrat all the Republican candidates were frothing at the mouth to unseat, and it wasn't *too* surprising that the extremely liberal governor and a conservative candidate had argued publicly. "You all spoke with Christopher earlier, correct? Did he name a suspect?"

Kamienski and Silent Mark shook their heads, but Wolfe said: "He mentioned something about not trusting the police because he and Mike Draymond don't get along."

Scarlett huffed out a laugh. "I don't think anybody gets along with Big Mike Draymond except the thick necked weirdos that follow him around."

Kamienski glanced at Silent Mark, who gave him a thumbs-down. "Draymond's an acquired taste—a drive-by wouldn't be out of the realm of possibility for him. Problem is we can't go at him directly. Nobody really *likes* Big Mike, but they all respect him. If we bring him in for questioning and it's *not* him, I might as well invest in charcoal briquettes, because Captain Bach will burn my ass. That suspension a few months ago did *not* make her any more sympathetic to bullshit."

Constantin made a face. "That metaphor was lackluster, but you got your point across." He looked at Sebastian. "What if we were to speak with this Big Mike? We have no association with the department."

Silent Mark's thumbs-down turned into a thumbs-up, and Kamienski said, "I don't like it, but if it's the best idea we've got then I guess we go forward. You do that, and Silent Mark and I will speak with the governor."

"Don't be surprised if you get voicemail," Nikki said, before she turned her attention to Wolfe and Scarlett. "Meanwhile, you two should get ready for your big televised debut alongside Christopher and Melissa."

"Whoa, whoa, *televised*?" Scarlett repeated, eyebrows arching into her hairline. "What the hell are we doing?"

Nikki reclined her chair, her expression indicating she was glad it was them and not her that would be enduring a night out with her client. "Baseball game, Red Sox and Yankees at Fenway, tonight. As quintessentially American as hot dogs and apple pie. Oh, and you both need to bring a date—Mel's mom and the kids were going originally, but given the circumstances I nixed that idea."

Wolfe turned to Sebastian. When their eyes met, he suddenly found himself flustered, and brought a hand up to rub the back of his neck. "You could, uh, come with me? We could go together?"

Ignoring the way Scarlett snorted at Wolfe's less-than-smooth delivery, Sebastian chewed his lower lip in thought. "Like a… date?"

"No! I mean, not if you don't want it to be," Wolfe reassured, even as something seemed to deflate in his chest. "Work date. A date at work."

"I like it," Nikki said, nodding as she no doubt visualized how progressive it would seem for a Republican candidate to have a male friend who was dating another man. "The media will eat that up."

"Good Christ," Scarlett muttered, shaking her head before saying in a louder voice, "What about me? Who am I supposed to bring?"

Nikki tapped her chin in thought. "Hmm… what about Kevin? He's close in age, and that way we don't have to bring in an outsider and expect them to keep their cool if the bullets start flying."

Kamienski groaned. "No flying bullets, please—I don't want to be the one to scrape Wolfe's corpse up off home plate."

Scarlett, meanwhile, looked as shocked as a person could look without passing out. "*Kevin*? Kevin *Sullivan*? You want me to go to a ball game slash potential life-or-death scenario with a *librarian*?"

"And me," Wolfe piped up. "I'll be there. So will Sebastian." He looked at Constantin. "You know you can't go, right? You're way too conspicuous."

Constantin nodded. "I figured that out. I also figured you are smart enough to understand that if anything happens to Sebastian while he's with you I will cut your nuts off and hang them off my menorah during Hanukkah."

Sebastian rubbed his forehead and muttered "*Constantin*," in a way that suggested this was not the first time someone had been threatened with genital mutilation by his bodyguard.

"Well!" Nikki exclaimed, clapping her hands together and rising to her feet. "I think that's a good place to adjourn this meeting. I'm off to run damage control."

The rest of them got up as well, heading for the door and back out into the rippling waves of humidity on the sidewalk. Nikki locked up the office and gave them a little wave as she got behind the wheel of a brand-new white BMW and roared off toward Boston. Constantin and Sebastian left next, intent on tracking down Mike Draymond before lunchtime.

Kamienski grabbed Wolfe's elbow before he could get into the Corvette. "Hey, can I ask you a question?"

Wolfe looked at him over the tops of his aviators. "You just did, technically."

Silent Mark hid a smile at Kamienski's growl of frustration.

"Okay, smartass, *let* me ask you a question," Kamienski said. "We both got invitations to Caitlin's wedding in the mail a while back—are those legit?"

Wolfe leaned against the car, only wincing a little as hot metal practically sizzled against his back. "Why wouldn't they be?"

"I don't know anybody who's in the business of sending out counterfeit wedding invitations," Scarlett added, from behind her pair of the same gold-rimmed, brown-lensed aviators Wolfe wore—two-for-one sales at Sunglass Hut were no joke. "And since I don't see Ashton Kutcher anywhere, I'm pretty sure you're not on *Punk'd.*"

Kamienski took a surprised step back. "Seriously? Why the fuck would a nice girl like Caitlin Sullivan want two cops she met once at her wedding?"

Wolfe shrugged. "Why not? You helped save my brother—that counts for a lot in my book, so I'm sure it does in Caity's." He clapped Kamienski on the shoulder. "Stay in touch, man. Hopefully we can keep her brother alive for the big *I do.*"

~***~

Angel Wings Hospice was a three-story prewar brick building on the west side of Lynn, separated from Boston Street by a wrought-iron fence and a sweeping lawn. A parking lot and the equipment necessary to take care of people in the last stage of their lives had been added during a massive retrofitting at the turn of the century. According to their website Angel Wings boasted one of the highest online ratings for a private pay hospice facility in Eastern Massachusetts.

Diana had pulled up the site on her phone while she and David sat across the street from Angel's Wings in their rented Camry. They drank large iced coffees from a nearby Dunkin' and debated how to talk their way into the facility. Being convincing was usually as simple as pretending to belong somewhere, but a hospice facility—

which was less porous than a hospital and would be very concerned with patient privacy—required more tact.

"They've probably been given information about Martha's family," Diana said, digging around in the cardboard box propped on the center console for a donut hole. "Better to pretend to be related to Otis, I think. I could be his niece?"

David nodded. "I'd buy that. Who am I?"

Diana smirked mischievously. "You could be my father again."

David choked on a sip of coffee. "Nope—I told you that wouldn't work last time, and it didn't!"

"Not even with this?" Diana questioned, reaching out to tug at a stray section of his dyed hair—which, in fairness, was currently a lot closer in color to hers than the hair of his actual children. "The eyes don't sell it, though. Why'd you pick gray?"

Because it reminds me of Angela without me getting up the balls to see her, David thought, blinking against the contact lenses covering his irises. "Covers the green pretty well."

Diana snorted. "You're a shit liar."

David smiled, jostling her shoulder as he popped his car door. "Only to you, kid. Let's do this."

Diana took David's hand in hers as they crossed the street, as naturally as if they were a real couple. When they weren't pretending to be father and daughter, they were husband and wife; the juxtaposition made David severely uncomfortable and Diana liked to tease him about it. Just because Diana didn't *look* fifteen years old anymore didn't mean David didn't think of her as the cynical teenager the CIA had paired him with after the death of his previous partner. She thought he was ridiculous and told him as much, with a little smile on her lips that never failed to make something old and fond twist in David's chest.

They were hit by a blast of frigid air as they walked through the hospice's automated doors, immediately faced with a reception desk and a smiling woman in a dress shirt and cardigan. Large glasses took up most of her face and her gray hair was cut in the shape of a slightly-wilted flower. She looked like someone's grandma, which David thought was apt since lots of grandmas wound up in places like this.

"Hi there!" she said, cheery but not forced. "Welcome to Angel Wings Hospice—are you here for a tour, or a visit?"

"A visit," Diana said, any trace of a Serbian accent gone from her voice, replaced by something vaguely Beacon Hill. "We just got back from vacation and wanted to see my aunt. Her name is Martha Webber."

The receptionist tapped at the keyboard in front of her for a moment, the good-natured smile slowly fading from her face. Adjusting her glasses, she got up out of her chair and came around the desk, worrying the edge of her cardigan between her fingers. "I'm afraid I have some bad news, Miss…?"

"Mrs. Johnson," Diana corrected, the hand that wasn't clutching David's rising to her mouth. "Diane, and this is my husband, Daniel. Are you telling me… is she…?"

The receptionist nodded, sucking in her cheeks and looking at the floor. "I'm afraid your aunt passed away over a week ago." She glanced up again, eyes narrowing as she thought of something. "I'm surprised your uncle didn't tell you."

Bringing Diana into his shoulder as she pretended to sob, David explained: "We were on a cruise off the coast of Alaska. Spotty cell service—Otis's messages must not have come through." He rubbed Diana's back and knitted his brows together. "Do you think we could at least see her room? Unless someone else is in it, of course."

The receptionist's expression softened back into sympathy, her suspicion overridden by Diana's convincing display of grief. "Yes, that's fine. Martha's belongings haven't been collected yet, so we've kept the room closed."

Diana sniffled as she pulled away from David. "We can take her things—I'm sure Uncle Otis is just busy planning the funeral." She reached out to squeeze the receptionist's hand in both of hers, forcing a smile. "Thank you so much."

The receptionist patted Diana's arm and ushered them through a pair of doors behind the desk that she unlocked with the electronic badge hanging around her neck. A generic-looking linoleum hallway led to a small private room equipped with a hospital bed, a dresser with a few knickknacks on top, and a couple of chairs for visitors. A door near the back of the room led to a bathroom, and some cardboard boxes were stacked in the corner, overflowing with clothes that must've belonged to Martha Webber.

"Just let me know when you're done—take as long as you need." With that, the receptionist left, shutting the door quietly behind her.

"Good job back there," David said, deliberately keeping his voice down; their conversation didn't need to be overheard by a patient or staff member. He glanced around, studying the corners of the room without looking like it. "I don't see any cameras, do you?"

"No." Diana moved toward the dresser. "This place is high-end, though. Anton must've chipped in to put Otis's wife here, don't you think?"

"Probably," David replied. He unstacked the boxes and began sorting through the clothes, looking for anything that might give them a clue as to where Otis could be.

Diana was quiet for a moment, and then she asked, "Have you spoken with Jake?"

David was used to Diana's frequent non sequiturs, but the new topic threw him for a loop. "Uh… no? I've never even met the kid."

"Sebastian mentioned to me in passing the other day that nobody's talked to Jake much since he moved out of Caitlin and Ryan's place last month," Diana continued, rummaging in the empty dresser drawers like David hadn't spoken. "Perhaps you should try getting to know him a little."

Jake was another man's son with the love of David's life, but David wasn't going to hold his and Angela's issues against him. He wasn't opposed to the idea of introducing himself and hanging out with Jake, but David wondered why Diana was interested. "What brought this on?"

Diana shrugged, a deceptively casual gesture. "I know what it's like to get fucked over by Anton—and from what Sebastian tells me it sounds like our father was very much behind the mess with the Mass Art Murderer. That, and he *is* Wolfe's brother—maybe you could earn some brownie points with your son."

"I'll think about it," David conceded. He'd found nothing interesting in the clothes and restacked the boxes, the clothes inside folded much neater than they were before. "We've got to find Otis first."

Diana had picked up a jewelry box off the dresser to make sure nothing was underneath it, and when something caught her eye, she grinned. Setting the box down, she picked up a business card embossed with the shiny golden logo of Quinn, Goldstein and Wickersham, also known as Boston's ritziest law firm. "This should help with that."

~***~

"How'd things go with Big Mike?" Wolfe asked, taking a sip of his chocolate frappe—which would be called a milkshake anywhere but New England—from a red-vinyl booth in Ryan's Diner. He and

Scarlett managed to secure their table an hour before the lunch rush, which meant they were the only customers.

A fifteen-table establishment in a run-down storefront on Washington Street in Boston's South End, Ryan's Diner was kitty-corner to the Burying Ground and overlooked by tourists unless they accidentally walked in the door. The menu above the counter featured typical greasy spoon fare ranging from pancakes to club sandwiches and everything in between; Wolfe had been eating there since he was a little kid and he knew from personal experience that everything was delicious.

Sebastian made a face at the question, sliding into the booth across from Scarlett and Wolfe. "Not so good. I might not be associated with the police department, but he knew who I was right away."

"Word of Anton's generosity to Christopher's campaign seems to have spread," Constantin said, plonking down next to Sebastian in the booth and resting his beefy forearms on the table. "We were escorted out of Draymond's campaign office, which was probably good in retrospect."

Scarlett munched the strawberry that came with her frappe of the same flavor. "Oh yeah? Why's that?"

Sebastian gave Constantin the side-eye and answered, "Because Big Mike did not hesitate to let us know how he feels about my father, and about... people like me."

Wolfe's fingers tightened around the bottom of his glass. "What do you mean?"

"He called him a faggot." Constantin's voice was hard, his craggy face harder. "Among other things. Sebastian made me leave before I could break his jaw."

"That's definitely worth breaking a jaw," a new voice interjected, echoing Wolfe's thoughts. It belonged to Ryan Murphy, namesake and owner of Ryan's Diner after inheriting it from his father when he retired to Florida. Like Wolfe and most of his friends, Ryan was in his early thirties, a mop of black hair swept to one side and a perfectly-placed set of dimples giving him boyish charm that was at odds with his gym-honed body and hard jaw. He also happened to be getting married to Wolfe's ex-girlfriend Caitlin in about a week's time, and while Wolfe had a range of feelings on that topic, he liked Ryan (and his food) too much to let it be awkward. "Do we need to round up a posse and curb stomp someone?"

Scarlett looked at Ryan like she was seeing him for the first time. "You know how to do a curb stomp?"

Ryan laughed and shook his head, gesturing back toward the kitchen. "Nah, Kevin does. We were talking about different ways my relatives might start a fight once they get drunk at the wedding."

Wolfe craned his neck and spotted Kevin Sullivan's perpetually messy brown curls from where he was putting together a salad behind the counter. "How the hell do you know what a curb stomp is? You're a librarian!" He paused. "Also, since when do you work here?"

"I don't," Kevin replied around a mouthful of avocado, bringing his salad—some kind of all green kale thing that looked too healthy—and loped over to the table, glancing at Constantin before deciding sitting next to Scarlett was the safer bet. He pushed his wire-rimmed glasses up his hooked nose and mercifully finished chewing before he tried to speak again. "Work here, I mean. I come here for lunch on my days off. I *do*, however, know how to perform a curb stomp. Theoretically."

After a poke to the ribs from Wolfe, Scarlett cleared her throat and asked, "Are you also theoretically free tonight? Because I could use your help with something."

"*We* could," Wolfe confirmed, before explaining where they were going and why, pausing while Ryan took their lunch orders. "And yes, before you say it, I'm aware that your brother is a dimwit of the highest degree."

"*Dimwit* was not the word I was going to use," Kevin sighed. "But yeah, I'll come with you guys." He nibbled on a piece of broccoli and rubbed his brow. "I can only imagine what he's going to be like at the wedding. You heard Christopher's standing up for Ryan too, right?"

Wolfe choked on his frappe. "Who the fuck thought *that* was a good idea?"

"I cannot believe I'm saying this, but I agree with Wolfe." Constantin looked up as Ryan returned with more drinks; black coffee for Constantin, and a Shirley Temple for Sebastian, who was evidently intent on rotting all his teeth before he hit forty. "You told us there were, what, three hundred people coming to your wedding? And Wolfe is already your best man—why in the name of God did you include *him*?"

" Because the guys standing up for you write speeches," Ryan replied calmly, "and since Christopher is inevitably going to give a speech whether I want him to or not, at least this way I get to read it first."

As Ryan went back to the kitchen, Sebastian's eyes widened as the bell above the door to the diner jangled. He paused, cherry from the Shirley Temple halfway to his mouth, and asked icily, "What the fuck are *you* doing here?"

Old vinyl creaked as Wolfe, Scarlett, and Kevin all turned in their seats only to come face-to-face with Danh Sang, head of *các triều đỏ*—or the Red Dynasty, Boston's largest Vietnamese gang— and his right-hand man, Thanh Ngo. Both men were middle-aged and dark-eyed, but that was where their similarities ended; where Sang was tall and svelte with collar-length hair and a designer linen jacket folded over his arm, Ngo was short and chubby, his black hair cropped close to his head and his face sweaty from the heat outside.

Two unremarkable men in white suits filed in after Ngo and Sang and stood in front of the door, flipping the diner's OPEN sign to CLOSED and blocking the most obvious exit with their bodies.

Sang flashed a crooked yellowed smile, the one thing about his appearance that wasn't prim and proper. "Now Sebastian, is that how you greet all your old friends?"

"You are not his friend," Constantin spat, rising from his seat. The bodyguards jolted forward to intervene but a raised hand from Sang stopped them. "You are a pig, and so are your men. I can't imagine how you get anything done when you are so busy wagging your dicks everywhere."

"Careful, Mr. Ionesco," Sang chided. "Those are words that could get Anton's restaurant shot up in a drive-by... again."

Ryan was coming to the table with their tray of food and froze upon seeing Sang and his men, but Scarlett beckoned him forward, eyes never leaving the mob boss's face. "What do you know about that? And how did you know we were here?"

"The second question is easier to answer than the first." Taking a seat at the counter, Sang folded his jacket across his lap. "I have eyes everywhere, Ms. Vaughn, and most of them look less like me and more like you—white as snow and altogether unremarkable." He examined his nails. "As for what I know about the shooting at Stela, I can tell you no one in my organization had anything to do with it."

Wolfe folded his arms on the tabletop, the club sandwich he'd ordered all but forgotten. "And why should we believe that?"

Sang's angular face took on an amused bent. "Because it would be awfully hard for me to steal the Rapture formula from Anton if he accidentally took a bullet, seeing as he's the only one who knows where the drug is being made."

Sebastian made a disgusted sound. "Why am I not surprised? You've been in business together for all of three months, and already you intend to stab him in the back."

"Your father does not make friends well," Sang responded mildly, "and he does an even worse job keeping them. He is a cunning businessman, but he has no idea how to deal with people."

It was Kevin who piped up next: "Did you come in here just to gloat, or do you have useful information?"

One of Sang's guards choked on a laugh and earned a scathing look from Thanh Ngo.

Sang tilted his head, studying Kevin with dark, reptilian eyes. "Quite ballsy for a librarian, aren't you?" His gaze moved to Wolfe and became no less unfriendly. "I suggest looking a bit closer to home for your culprit—and I don't mean your father."

A winter-cold chill of dread shot up Wolfe's back. "How do you know about my father?"

Sang snorted. "Please. He gallivants around my city with Anton's adopted daughter on his arm and you think I don't know about it? Don't worry, I'm not going to tell. If Anton tried to go after David Wolfe he'd wind up dead for his trouble, and then I'd never get what I want. I was referring to your uncle." He paused. "You know, the one who took over the Winter Hill Gang."

~***~

Jake Wolfe liked routines… ah, fuck it, that wasn't true. He hated routines, loathed schedules, and detested anything binding. However, all of the above were necessary to keep what was left of his sanity from fraying, and his new roommate's consistently horrible quiches and the PTSD-fueled nightmares didn't cut it.

Cut it…

Jake shut his green eyes, forehead creasing with the effort of keeping That Voice at bay. He smacked a fingerless-gloved hand against the steering wheel of his 1985 Chevy Camaro in frustration. "Come on, Wolfe, get it together. You're better than this." A moment passed with blood and a curved knife teasing the edges of his mind, and he snorted. "Well, so much for that positive self-talk crap."

Instead of lying to himself, Jake shut his eyes again, though not as tightly as the first time, and took in a deep breath through his nose. He calmed down as he slowly flexed his fingers and wiggled his toes. If he could move any which way he wanted, then he was free, and alive, and not trapped in a basement with a psychopath.

These episodes—not quite panic attacks, but close—were happening more frequently since Jake peaced out of Caitlin and Ryan's place. His rational for leaving was threefold: he was all healed up (physically, at least) from his tangle with the Mass Art Murderer, Ryan and Caitlin were getting married and didn't need a fourth wheel (Kevin lived with them too), and Misha (also known as the roommate with horrible quiche) had desperately needed someone to split the mortgage on his house. Together they were barely making the payment, but Jake's only other option would be to move back in with his mom, and he'd eat his shoe before he'd live in his childhood bedroom and endure Angela's pity.

Sighing out his resignation, Jake emerged from the car into the heat of the parking lot at Caruso's Grocery. A behemoth single-story eyesore, Caruso's occupied almost a block of Broadway in Cambridge, right off Route 2A and less than ten minutes from Harvard and the Massachusetts Institute of Technology. The building had no windows and was striped with garish yellow-and-black paint, revolving doors like you'd see at a hotel serving as the entrance for customers. Recently, the owner replaced the piece of sheet metal above the doors that once served as signage with a billboard that displayed the store's name and hours.

Jake took a step toward the familiar building and froze, the thought of actually going inside enough to curdle his stomach. Every time he'd been out until today, he'd had someone with him—now it felt like he was the only man on an island, far away from everything he'd ever known. Sweat broke out on his brow and at the small of his back, insulated by the long coat and jeans he wore despite the weather. The itch under what was left of his skin started at his chest and moved outward, and suddenly he knew there was no way in hell he was going inside Caruso's to be gawked at like a circus monkey. Not alone.

A streak of burgundy light flared near the corner of his eye, offering a momentary distraction from Jake's mounting panic.

The light was a sign across the street from Caruso's, on a storefront that was minuscule by comparison. It read *Voici Spiritueux* in cursive tube-lighting, which Jake translated through what he remembered of high school French to *Here Is Liquor*. This was a store owned by runway model turned businesswoman Joanne Lavinge, who according to Sebastian had played an indirect role in the execution of the Mass Art Murders. She'd needed more retail zoning for her stores, and Sebastian's father Anton—who wanted sell some kind of new party drug using bottles of wine as a disguise—was more than happy to oblige.

Jake shifted from foot to foot as he examined the store, noting the crush of cars parked out front and the shadows of people moving around behind the half-frosted windows. He could see clusters of wooden shelves holding row after row of seemingly identical wine bottles, including what looked to be a special section behind the cash register.

It's a fancy liquor store, he thought. *One your best friend died for. You don't need to go over there and torture yourself.*

The jangle of Jake's car keys in his still-trembling hands, however, made him mull it over. If nothing else, he could sate whatever curiosity he had about Lavinge's operation... and maybe pick up something to take the edge off his nerves?

Going over there was a terrible idea. A colossal mistake.

A break from routine.

"Ah, screw it," Jake said aloud, and jogged across the street.

The air conditioning inside the liquor store was like a slap in the face, and Jake felt the tension ebb out of his shoulders as he slunk between the racks. Though the predominate inventory did seem to be wine—most of it with names Jake couldn't pronounce and high price tags—there was the occasional stack of Scotch bottles or sale on goblets to keep things exciting. The other customers were scattered through the place and kept to themselves, not appearing to be interested in the only survivor of the Mass Art Murderer's torment.

There was no sign that said *Hey Kid, Wanna Buy Some Drugs?* so Jake presumed you had to ask for the special wine. He eyed the middle-aged guy slouched behind the register, who looked like an overly-cliché, not-skunk version of Pepe Le Pew, complete with a popped collar on his Ralph Laruen polo shirt and too much cologne. Was there a code word you had to know to get the Rapture? Was it like a speakeasy, where you had to memorize a phrase?

Or was it ridiculously simple?

Pepe Le Pew noticed Jake watching him and didn't look impressed, sniffing haughtily as Jake approached him even though it was doubtful he could smell anything beyond his own cloying stench. "Can I help you find something, sir?"

Jake was startled to hear a South Shore accent come out of some dude who resembled a low-rent mime, but he took it in stride. "I sure hope so. You got any Communion wine?"

Evidently being a recovering Catholic had its perks, because Pepe scowled like he hated his mother but reached under the counter, producing an unremarkable bottle of pinot noir with something solid floating in its black depths. Whatever it was clinked against the glass as Pepe set the bottle down on the counter and reached for a paper bag. "A hundred dollars. Cash only."

Jake fished the grocery money out of his wallet with only a hint of guilt, a glance out the window at Caruso's enough to make his hand shake slightly as he took the wrapped bottle from the fake Frenchie. He thanked him and headed out the door without a backward glance.

~***~

Chapter Five

David and Diana were exiting the offices of Quinn, Goldstein and Wickersham when David's phone buzzed with an incoming call from his son. They were in the Financial District and fresh off a multi-story elevator plunge to get down from the law firm's top-floor offices in a black-glassed skyscraper on Congress Street. As soon as they hit the corner and turned on to State Street they were assaulted by the smell of exhaust and a crush of sweaty tourists heading for the Old State House, heedless of the DON'T WALK signals flaring at the crosswalk.

Diana shook her head in amazement. "I will never understand how those people do not get flattened with the way we drive in this town." She glanced at David, who had stopped walking to look at his phone, now ringing in his hand instead of his pocket. "Are you going to answer that?"

David snapped out of his reverie—it baffled him to think that after all these years of running, his family was only a phone call away—and moved aside for a guy pushing a cart of Boston-related hats. "Yeah. Sorry." He slid his thumb over the green button on the screen. "Hey, Jimmy. What's up?"

"Hi Dad." Wolfe's voice was deep but not abrasive, and David heard him clearly despite the clamor of traffic on both ends of the call. "You see the news?"

"If you mean did I hear about Christopher Sullivan getting shot, then yes," David said. He followed Diana's lead down State Street toward the garage where they'd left the rental car. They hadn't learned anything new about Otis—according to the lawyers he'd never made it to the office—but at least their parking got validated. "Please tell me it's you and Scarlett protecting him and not some two-bit security firm."

"We are, and that's what I'm calling about." Wolfe swore and honked his horn. "I just dropped Scarlett off at Christopher and Mel's place—Frankie was there earlier, but he's got patrol, and I'm trying to get to Uncle Bobby's favorite bar."

David stopped walking again, much to Diana's chagrin. "Bobby? What the hell does he have to do with the shooting at Codreanu's place?"

"Apparently he might be the one who ordered it."

"Who'd you hear that from?"

Wolfe's response was wry: "Danh Sang."

"Not exactly a trustworthy source of information, Jimmy," David pointed out, but as much as he'd hate to admit it, it was possible the Red Dynasty leader had a point when it came to his brother. "Where's Bobby hanging out these days?"

"When he's not busting heads, you mean? He's usually at Dirty Dan's. It's a shithole barroom."

"And where's Dirty Dan's? I'll meet you there and we can have a chat with Bobby."

Wolfe sighed. "Where else would it be? Winter Hill."

~***~

Four hours ahead of the baseball game's 7:15 start time, Laine Parker was dropped off several blocks away from her destination by her brother Aiden, the Steyr rifle broken down in pieces inside a rucksack she'd picked up at the Kenmore Army/Navy store. Despite the time to go until the first pitch, the crowd of people in the area around Fenway Park had grown since earlier in the afternoon, outdoor tables at nearby restaurants full to bursting and traffic moving at a crawl on Lansdowne and Van Ness Streets.

Laine waited until she almost pulled level with the office building they'd scouted earlier on Brookline Street before cutting a sharp left down the neighboring alleyway. She kept her head down to avoid cameras, red hair once again tucked away under her ball cap. When she reached the back corner of the building she threw the rucksack up on to the fire escape first before she bent at the knees, springing upward with as much force as she could muster and grabbing the railing to haul herself up. She crept up the metal stairs, aware of noise potential despite all the nearby activity—the last thing she needed was a curious tourist wondering if they could catch a glimpse of a real-live city rat.

Soon she was on the roof, the hot sun making its slow rotation westward. Laine made a note of where the fire escape was in relation to the roof access for the building, and then she headed to the northeast corner. Dropping the rucksack, she took shelter from the sun's rays on the shadowy side of a large air conditioning unit, which was working overtime in the scorch and dripping condensation that sizzled away almost immediately.

Laine checked her watch. Three and a half hours to go.

She settled in to wait.

~***~

Wolfe was leaning against the hood of Scarlett's double-parked Corvette when his dad showed up, looking like the fucking Hunchback of Notre Dame behind the steering wheel of a Toyota Camry. *Secret agent, my ass*, Wolfe thought with a snort.

They were on Broadway in Somerville's famed Winter Hill neighborhood, the old stomping grounds of Whitey Bulger given way to college students and Brazilian cuisine as warehouses got rehabbed and storefronts changed hands. Unsurprisingly, parking was a bitch, and that was why Wolfe had taken two parallel spaces and hoped if a cop came along it was somebody he went to high school with; luckily that didn't happen, and he was able to move the Vette to make room for his father's rental.

"Nice ride," Wolfe said, after David flopped out of the sedan with all the grace of a dying trout. "Don't you think you could've gone smaller, though? For the environment?"

"Funny," David replied with the same level of snark, but his eyes softened at the corners. "It's good to see you, Jimmy. Keeping busy?"

"Living the dream." Wolfe accepted his dad's back-slapping man-hug—things were weird enough when your dad pretended to be dead for most of your life, he didn't need to start a debate about traditional masculinity—before gesturing toward Dirty Dan's. The bar was situated across the street in a run-down building with a Post Office and a pizza shop. "Bobby's car's outside. You ready to see your brother?"

David took in a breath and exhaled slowly, studying the bar's dirty windows and flickering neon sign. The first D in Dirty Dan's wore a cowboy hat, and the S was a rattlesnake. "It's been a long time. Before I left on that last tour I asked him to watch out for Angela, and for you and Josh."

Wolfe winced. "Yeah, he maybe didn't do a great job at that." He thought of Angela's abusive ex-husband Keith, and the way Josh had changed after David's "death". His brother had become more distant—still friendly, but detached from Angela and Jake in a way that Wolfe had never dreamed of being. "How do you think he'll take finding out you're alive?"

"Knowing Bobby, he'll probably hit me," David remarked, thumbing the crosswalk button as they waited for the stream of cars on Broadway to subside. "That's how he solves most of his problems."

Wolfe nodded his agreement, hands shoved in the front pockets of his jeans. He felt sweat beading on the back of his neck and he'd only been out of the Corvette for a few minutes. "Hey, when are you gonna tell Ma you're back?"

David seemed caught off-balance by the question. "I… don't know, Jimmy."

"Well, you better figure it out," Wolfe said, not unkindly, but in a way that suggested his patience with David's spook bullshit was wearing thin. "It's going to be pretty damn awkward if you show up at Caitlin and Ryan's wedding and Ma still thinks you're dead." The light turned, and he sighed, giving his dad an olive branch: "When Bobby heard I was going to enlist and Ma couldn't talk me out of it, he made me an offer."

David shot him a curious glance as they crossed the street. "Oh yeah? What'd he put on the table?"

A grin pulled at Wolfe's mouth as he held the door for his dad. "A laundromat. All mine as long as I started cracking heads for the boys on Winter Hill."

"Jesus Christ," David said, taking two steps inside Dirty Dan's and making a face when the soles of his boots stuck to the floor. "I can see the name of this place is literal."

Dirty Dan's was, as David surmised, fucking dirty. A rickety-looking bar ran along the back wall of the one-room establishment, which was wider than it was long, its cheap Western-themed décor aged at least thirty years by the weird yellowed glass lamps hung from the water-damaged ceiling. What must've been one of the first flat screen televisions hung above a dusty rack of bottles, airing a rerun of a Patriots-Dolphins game in which Tom Brady's ass looked, as usual, fantastic.

From the jukebox, Jim Morrison howled about breaking through to the other side. *Been there, done that*, Wolfe thought. You died on an operating table a couple times and you got less fascinated with what comes next.

Robert "Knee-Bustin' Bobby" Wolfe was the only person in Dirty Dan's besides the bartender, who was a mullet-sporting forty-something twig who looked like he'd rather be snorting coke off a toilet seat. The oldest of David's five siblings (Catholic family), Bobby's considerable height wasn't enough to draw attention away from the paunch at his waistline or the crags in a face that had seen too much sunlight and cigar smoke. Grayed-out hair under a brown flat cap and heavy eyebrows over dull, sunken eyes completed Bobby's visage, one large liver-spotted hand clenched around the handle of a glass beer mug full of Sam Adams.

Those sunken eyes moved to the mirror behind the bar to size up the newcomers, and Bobby's face registered surprise when he saw Wolfe and outright stupefaction at the sight of his dead brother.

"What, no Guinness?" David spread his arms. "I feel like you're missing out on a branding opportunity, Bobby."

Bobby spun on the barstool. "Holy fucking *shit*—Davey, is that really you?"

"You bet your ass it is." The brothers hugged (not a lame back-slapper, Wolfe noted, but a real embrace), and sure enough, as David pulled away Bobby punched him square on the jaw. The hit wasn't as hard as it could've been, but it was enough to stagger David back a step. "Christ, Bobby! You haven't seen me in twenty-five years so you slug me?!"

"I haven't seen you in twenty-five years because *you were dead*!" Bobby shouted, his cheeks going red. He sat back down hard on his stool and looked at Wolfe. "Did you know about this? Is this some of that fuckin' stupid military man bullshit?"

Wolfe bit his tongue against reminding Bobby he dodged the draft during Vietnam (bone spurs) and said, "I only found out a while ago, and he didn't want me to tell anyone. Not even Ma."

"I still don't," David ground out, accepting the makeshift icepack the cokehead bartender handed him with a grunt of gratitude. "It's too dangerous for this to get out everywhere, but when Jimmy told me you might be involved with the shooting at Stela I knew I had to talk to you myself."

Hearing the name of Anton Codreanu's restaurant caused Bobby to stiffen and then sag in resignation. "Ah, fuck me. You want a drink?"

Wolfe crossed his arms. "I'm on the clock. So it was the Winter Hill boys behind the shooting?"

"Yeah, yeah, it was us," Bobby replied, draining half of his beer in one go. "But it's not what you're thinking. I could give a shit less about whether or not your girlfriend's brother gets elected governor."

"Ex-girlfriend." Wolfe leaned against the wooden cactus that served as the bar's coatrack. "What about Codreanu's new business venture?"

Bobby's thin lips turned downward. "You mean Rapture? Nasty stuff. Gotta admire the man's business acumen, though—teaming up with Joanne Lavinge was a slick move." He looked down at the scratched bar top and heaved out a sigh before meeting Wolfe's stare. "We did it for your brother. To send a message."

Wolfe took a moment to digest that, bringing one hand up to rub at his brow. Several responses flitted through his mind, ranging from *what the fuck* to *you could've killed someone*, but he settled on, "Did you honestly think blasting holes in a dinner party would make Jake feel better?" When Bobby hung his head, Wolfe scoffed, turning to scowl at a framed vintage advertisement for Miller Lite so he didn't break that beer mug over his uncle's thick skull. "Of course you didn't. You wanted to make *yourself* feel better."

"Everybody knows Codreanu was behind what happened to Jake!" Bobby exclaimed, rising from his seat. He flapped his arms a little, like an old rooster trying to take flight. "What else were we supposed to do, Jimmy? Sit back and ignore an attack on one of our own?"

Wolfe turned on his heel and took two quick steps toward Bobby, so he was right in his face and his uncle had to look up at him. "Let's get something straight right now: Jake is *not* yours," he said, the lowness of his voice and deliberate cadence of his words betraying his anger. "I told you years ago you weren't gonna drag him into this stupid mob shit, and I'm not going to let you use him being tortured and almost killed to further some fucking agenda Winter Hill has against Codreanu."

David put a hand on Wolfe's shoulder, tugging him backward gently. "Easy, Jimmy."

Wolfe exhaled harshly and moved away, walking backward toward the door. Suddenly Dirty Dan's seemed to be shrinking around him, the lukewarm breeze coming from the window air conditioner not enough to stop red from creeping in at the edges of his vision. He pointed at Bobby, who looked a little scared in his posture and around the whites of his eyes. Wolfe didn't blame him; his size and the occasional thousand-yard stare meant he could be scary as hell when he wanted to be. "You stay the hell away from Codrenau, and you keep Jake out of your shit."

Bobby brought his hands up to the level of his shoulders, palms out, in the universal gesture for *I get it, don't hit me.* "Alright, alright, Jesus! I was just trying to help, that's all."

David shook his head, following Wolfe's path to the exit. He paused before he left, hand gripping the edge of the open door, waves of humidity battling it out with the air conditioning. "Watch your ass, Bobby. Codreanu's not somebody you wanna fuck with."

"Cross my heart and all that shit," Bobby said, waving him off. "Don't worry about me."

He watched through the window until his brother and nephew were out of sight, and then he picked up his cell phone off the bar top to make a call. Danh Sang wasn't going to like this, but the bastard would only pay the Winter Hill boys if they kept rattling the Rom's cage. If Bobby was going to bring home the bacon, he'd have to find a way to circumnavigate David and his son… which gave him an idea.

~***~

Around the time Wolfe and David had their conversation with Bobby, Sebastian Codreanu played the piano in a dive bar called The Hole. Four was a little early for most drinkers, but Sebastian provided musical entertainment for both the college kids and chronic alcoholics on a regular basis at no charge. After hearing about his near-death experience a few months back, the owner gave Sebastian a key to the bar and said he could come in whenever he wanted.

The Hole was located in the basement of a brick walk-up at the intersection of Massachusetts and Columbus Avenues. It was a popular spot for the kids from Northeastern University due to its cheap beer prices and the way the bouncer overlooked fake driver's license or baggie of weed. A simple red door served as the entryway and neon paint splattered the cement walls inside; a battered bar ran the length of one wall and faced a dozen booths and some scattered tables and chairs, with an elevated stage occupying the back wall.

Despite its reputation and general lack of cleanliness, The Hole served as a kind of sanctuary for Sebastian. Constantin was the only bodyguard he would allow to join him on his visits to the bar. The older man often found himself the victim of leaning against a sticky tabletop and engaging in conversation with a drunk while Sebastian plunked out bits and pieces of music with his mangled fingers.

It was at a Steinway grand piano just like the one on The Hole's stage that Sebastian had lost so much at sixteen years old. His hopes to go to music school, the ability to play without pain, and any trust in his father were all destroyed the instant one of Anton's cronies slammed the fallboard down on Sebastian's unsuspecting fingers while he attempted to flee death inside Stela. Ironically, Stela was named for Sebastian's mother, who had been a famed concert pianist at the *Sala Patatului* in Bucharest before she married Anton. He'd learned everything he knew about music from his mama, and they were still close.

Though he eventually regained the use of his hands, the severity of his injuries meant Sebastian lacked the flexibility necessary to play the piano at a professional level. Each note brought him pain, but he pushed the discomfort aside for a chance to feel normal again. The idea of going on a date with Wolfe, however—even if it was cover for a job—was so far from Sebastian's sense of *normal* that he missed several notes while picking his way through the first movement of Beethoven's *Moonlight Sonata* (his hands were too bad to attempt the second, let alone the third).

Constantin noticed, glancing up from the *Boston Globe*'s crossword puzzle. "You seem distracted."

Sebastian licked his lips, counted beats in his head and rolled into "Impossible Year" by Panic! At the Disco. "What makes you say that?"

The bodyguard tapped his pen against his chin in mock-contemplation. "Oh, I don't know, maybe the fact that your little outing tonight is likely to give your father an aneurysm?" He looked back at the crossword. "I still do not approve, by the way. What is a ten-letter word for anxiety?"

"'Foreboding'," Sebastian said, then frowned, his hands stilling against the ivory. "You don't approve of what, exactly? Me going to the game without you? Anton still thinks I'm spying on Jim and Scarlett—he'll understand me bringing you along in this scenario would make them suspicious."

Constantin snorted. "It might be hard to believe, but sometimes I have more pressing concerns than your father's megalomania. I *meant* I do not approve of you going on a date with the son of the man that your father wants to know is alive so he can kill him himself. Especially since we both know David Wolfe is not dead."

"It's not a date." Sebastian was quick to correct him—too quick, if Constantin's withering stare was any indication. "Not a real one, anyway."

"That does not mean you do not wish it was," Constantin pointed out.

Sebastian regarded his crooked fingers, golden-tan against the same white and black keys that had wronged him. "Wishing has never gotten me anything," he murmured, the ghost of expensive vodka against his lips paired with the phantom burn of cocaine in his nostrils. Wishing for things to be different, it seemed to Sebastian, did more harm than good. "What is your next crossword question?"

The set of Constantin's face suggested they'd continue the conversation at a later date, but he was willing to let it slide for now. "Ten letters, the title of Brooke's sonnet."

"'The Soldier'," Jim Wolfe said, and oh, Sebastian had it *bad* if the sound of the man's voice alone made his palms sweat. He'd slipped through the door of The Hole without calling attention to himself; Wolfe moved soundlessly when he wanted to, despite his size. The bar's shitty lights made the blond strands in his red hair stand out, and he ran a compulsive hand through it when his eyes found Sebastian's. "Hey, Bash. You ready to go?"

Sebastian nodded stupidly, belatedly remembering that standing was a good idea. He slid off the piano bench with as much grace as he could muster, catching the tan bomber jacket Constantin tossed to him without looking. No doubt it was still muggy outside now, but the evening would cool the city. "*Da*—yes, I'm ready."

Wolfe smiled at him, reaching back for the door handle and saluting Constantin at the same time. "I'll have him back by midnight."

Constantin grunted, arms folded across his barrel chest. "I'm holding you to that, *detectiv*. No funny business."

I wouldn't mind some funny business, Sebastian thought, not for the first time. But he kept it to himself, even with Wolfe's hand resting lightly between his shoulder blades as they stepped into the waning sun.

~***~

"What do you think of Jimmy's new ride?" Scarlett asked Sebastian when the gang met up on Jersey Street after paying an arm and a leg to park in the Kenmore lot. "If I didn't know better I'd say he was compensating for something."

Sebastian took a glance back at the lot, where a brand-new black Ford Mustang GT Fastback sat like a proud panther, similar to and yet so different from the cherry-red Mustang Wolfe had driven before Frankie totaled it. "It's… very fast." He faced Scarlett again and furrowed his brow. Licking the side of his thumb, he set about fixing the large "B" for Boston someone had painted on her cheek in burgundy lipstick. "How do you know what Jim's dick looks like?"

Scarlett arched an eyebrow. "Um, we're partners? Have been for years? With the amount of times he's been puked on by clients it would be weird if I *hadn't* seen him naked."

Wolfe made the mistake of walking away for five minutes to buy Christopher a ball cap so he'd be less recognizable on the street, and he sighed as he caught the last part of the conversation. "Can we please stop talking about my dick?"

"Oh no, go on," Melissa said, pulling her hair into a ponytail. She was doing a better job of pretending to be casual than her husband, wearing a Red Sox shirt and some old jean shorts. She winked in Wolfe's direction. "I was invested."

Christopher made a face, the tops of his cheeks coloring the same pink as his Ralph Lauren polo shirt. His injured shoulder was supported by a sling, which he flapped around indignantly. "I hardly think that's appropriate, Mel." He craned his neck. "Can we go in yet?"

"Only if you get your ass moving," Kevin grumbled. He'd been taking pictures of Fenway and the sunset for his Instagram, but now he offered his arm to Scarlett as the crowd of people on Jersey began to shuffle toward the gates into Fenway. "Shall we?"

"We shall," Scarlett confirmed, taking his elbow. "Let's get inside before your brother gets shot again."

~***~

Up on the rooftop about a thousand yards away, Laine Parker leaned away from the scope on the newly-assembled Steyr, unsure yet again if her frayed mind was playing tricks on her. She thought, for a split second, that Sergeant Wolfe had crossed through her Plex sight… but what were the odds of that?

Why would the only man she'd been able to save on her last trip to the Sandbox just *happen* to be going to a baseball game on the same night she was supposed to kill Christopher Sullivan? She knew Wolfe was a private investigator because he'd been on the news a few times over the summer after what happened to his brother. Mostly she'd just gotten glimpses of him shoving cameras out of his face on his way in and out of hospitals… so maybe she was confusing one thing for another, superimposing someone in a situation from another memory.

They'd told her the human brain was capable of that much and more at Blakely Manor, in between the electrical shocks.

The scar on Laine's face tightened like her hand around the rifle's grip, and she went from prone behind the gun to curl up in a fetal position on the roof, warm despite the settling darkness. Her brain felt like it was curling in on itself too, like one of those plants that closes up at night; she had a hard time believing that was Wolfe, but how many other men did she know that appeared in a flash of red-blond hair and scars? And if that *was* Wolfe down there, when push came to shove, could she still pull the trigger?

Of course you can, Aiden's voice said in Laine's head. *What's that guy ever done for* you*? The objective hasn't changed.*

Was that right? Was *anything* Laine thought right? Had she really saved Wolfe? Had all those men actually died? Sometimes she didn't know, but she *did* know that men like Christopher Sullivan were the reason she'd wound up this way, and she wasn't going to sit back and do nothing while another generation of boys and girls got sent to terrible places to die.

And if a bullet needed to blow off Sullivan's head in front of Sergeant Wolfe to make that happen, then so be it.

~***~

Chapter Six

The last time Wolfe was at a baseball game he was five or six years old, and the only things he remembered clearly was that his seat smelled like vomit and that his dad was pissed because the Red Sox lost (not an uncommon occurrence before 2004). Other details—the tightness of a new hat on his head and the way Josh had talked him into forking over the foul ball Wolfe caught—were blurry, running together like beads of sweat on the back of a player's neck.

Nothing about tonight was blurry. They'd already been on camera at least once that they were aware of, Christopher nodding in modest acknowledgement before putting his good arm around his wife, ignoring the equal amount of cheers and boos his presence received. Wolfe was surprised someone hadn't either tossed nachos at them or asked Christopher to kiss their baby.

On the outside, Wolfe looked like any other guy out with his friends, sitting in the primo seats behind the Sox's dugout, nursing a singular overpriced cup of Bud Light with an arm draped over his "date's" seat. Inside, however, his situational awareness was cranked up to maximum, eyes constantly moving as he watched the stands across the field, the field itself, and took the occasional inconspicuous glance backward at the rows of fans behind them. At the other end of their little grouping, he knew without checking that Scarlett was doing the same thing while laughing at Kevin's lame jokes and destroying a hot dog with onions.

Beside him, Sebastian shifted in his seat, a vertebrae in his back cracking audibly. "How the fuck do people sit in these chairs for so long?" he whispered. "I can barely feel my legs."

Wolfe looked at him sidelong and smiled, saying in a conspiratorial tone, "Most people buy more than one beer and they're so hammered they can't feel their legs anyway." He flicked his gaze toward the Green Monster to check the score. "And it's the top of the ninth—three more outs and I'll pry you out of that seat."

Sebastian snorted. "That may not be an exaggeration." He shifted again, knee brushing against Wolfe's, warm and firm even through two layers of denim. He pulled away quickly, like he'd been burned—or like he figured Wolfe would read more into it than he should. "Sorry."

Wolfe swallowed the last of his beer and squeezed the hard plastic of the chair back, squashing the urge to do something catastrophically stupid, like lean in and brush his lips across Sebastian's razor-sharp cheekbone. "Don't worry about it."

He felt Scarlett's eyes on him, telling him without saying a word that he was an idiot.

The Yankees bats went down in order and the Red Sox won, much to the jubilation of the fans, who leapt up to scream and clap as soon as the final out was called. "Dirty Water" by The Standells blared from the speakers around Fenway, and everyone began the tedious shuffle out of their seats and up the concrete stairs to the exits. This was the stretch of time that concerned Scarlett and Wolfe the most; if nothing happened on the way *in*, it was entirely possible somebody would make a run at Christopher and Melissa while they were leaving the ballpark. And of course when they walked outside, they were immediately greeted by a group of thirtyish people who wanted to talk to the Republican candidate.

"Christopher, maybe you shouldn't—" Scarlett began.

He waved her off with his working arm, moving in to shake the proffered hand of his nearest supporter.

Wolfe took a panning look around the area, and in that single instant, something moved in his peripheral vision, a visceral flashback to the worst day of his life. Most people didn't realize it, but bullets travel faster than the speed of sound, meaning that by the time a shot "rings out" like it does in the movies, someone is usually bleeding or dead. Then again, most people weren't trained to see light reflecting off the scope on a high-powered sniper rifle right before the shooter pulled the trigger.

"*Get down!*" Wolfe shouted, pushing those closest to him— Sebastian on one side, Kevin on the other—to the relative safety sidewalk.

Adrenaline licked through his chest like fire, and he saw Scarlett tackle Christopher to the pavement as the hood of the car parked on the street next to where he'd been standing crumpled under the velocity of a bullet. The sound of the shot reached their ears in the next instant, and the screaming started as panic rolled through the crush of people exiting Fenway. Nearby BPD officers were mobilizing but not fast enough to catch the shooter, and they were about to have their hands full with frantic tourists and locals alike.

Wolfe grabbed Scarlett's shoulder, pushing aside a cascade of blonde hair. "You okay?"

"Yeah, I'm fine!" She had to shout to be heard over the commotion. "Did you see where it came from?"

Wolfe nodded, glancing back to check on the others before refocusing on the rooftop where he'd seen the glint. "Stay with them!" he said to Scarlett, and took off running.

~***~

The instant after she squeezed the trigger, Laine knew she'd missed the shot.

Her aim had faltered when Christopher Sullivan emerged from the ballpark with his wife and siblings—she recognized them from the research materials Aiden had complied on Sullivan—to a crowd of admirers. The same short blonde and model-type guy who were with them earlier came next, and bringing up the rear was the tall redhead. She got a good, long look at him, and he was most definitely Sergeant James Wolfe.

Her whole body had jerked like she'd been poked with a live wire, and in the same second her index finger had applied the pressure necessary to fire the Steyr. The fifty-cal round ripped through the night air, missing its intended target by less than a foot and embedding itself in the hood of parked car. Laine didn't see where the bullet went because she was already hefting the Steyr under her arm, hooking the rucksack over the opposite shoulder and rushing for the fire escape.

~***~

Wolfe followed the shooter's southwest path down Brookline Avenue, dodging around the people on the sidewalk they shoved out of their way and ignoring the occasional scream from someone who noticed their giant sniper rifle. He kept his eyes trained on that gun and forced his legs to move faster, knowing that even if he'd been allowed to bring his Glock 22 into Fenway it wouldn't make a damn bit of difference now; the after-game flow of people was thick, and it would've been too easy to catch a bystander in the crossfire.

That and Wolfe liked to think he wasn't the type to shoot someone in the back.

After it passed Fenway Park, Brookline continued for a few blocks before hitting a busy four-way intersection, the right-to-left one-way of Park Drive meeting with the end of Boylston Street in a star shape. Even at ten o'clock at night, the stoplights had to work to contain the cars, and both the shooter and Wolfe had to slow down to try and navigate between the piles of pedestrians waiting to cross.

The shooter glanced back at Wolfe over their shoulder, the movement loosening the ball cap on their head and causing a bright red ponytail to slip out. She—and it was almost certainly a she, between the hair and the feminine jawline—didn't like what she saw and picked up her pace, even going as far as to use the butt of the rifle to push people out of the way. As they reached end of the sidewalk Wolfe made a lunge for her arm and missed, but caught a better glimpse of her face before she stepped out into the intersection against traffic.

A woman with red hair and a ghoulish scar that sliced her face in half.

Wolfe felt the ice of recognition freeze his spine, and thought, *no, it can't be her* as the people around him gasped and shouted as the oncoming traffic threatened to run her down.

A silver sedan tore down Park Drive and screeched to a brief halt less than a foot from the shooter, who had never stopped moving even though in Wolfe's mind, time had. In fact, he mused dully as she folded herself into the getaway vehicle and it raced off to the west with the snarl of burned rubber, it was almost like time had rewound, wrenching him back to a place and a person he'd thought he'd never seen again.

Wolfe was positive the woman who had almost killed Christopher was also the woman who'd saved his life in Iraq.

~***~

By the time Wolfe jogged back down Brookline, the area around Fenway was cordoned off by BPD officers and campus cruisers from neighboring Boston University. He probably wouldn't have had a hope in hell of reaching Scarlett and the others—everything was a cacophony of lights, sirens, and the murmurs of latent fear—except that right as he arrived, two familiar figures emerged from a BPD cruiser.

Kamienski took one look at Wolfe and started rubbing his forehead. "Oh, Jesus Christ—what the fuck are you doing out here? Aren't you supposed to be protecting Sullivan?"

Wolfe nodded, slightly winded from the chase. He worked out every morning, but now that the adrenaline was fading, every scar on his body (and there were a lot) felt taut like a bowstring. "Scar and Bash are with him. I need to use your dash computer."

Kamienski and Silent Mark exchanged a look, and then Kamienski gesticulated toward the crime scene, saying, "Uh, we're a little busy? Active shooter?"

"She's gone." Wolfe gave the detectives a quick rundown of what had happened during and after the shooting before clasping his hands in front of him imploringly. "Seriously, Jeff, I wouldn't ask to use your goddamn police property unless it was important. I think I know who the shooter is, but I have to look something up to be sure."

Kamienski sighed, his whole gangly body shifting with it. "Fine, fine—Mark, open your door."

Silent Mark obliged, and Wolfe slid halfway into the passenger's seat of the unmarked car, legs sticking out onto the sidewalk so they could all see the monitor and he could reach the computer's keyboard without folding himself up like a pretzel. He clicked around for a minute until he found the database he wanted and typed LAINE PARKER into the search box. It wasn't a common name, and the right result came back immediately.

A former corporal in the United States Army, specialization in field medicine and proud owner of a marksman patch, Laine received almost as many medals as Wolfe had for what happened in Iraq. She'd been honorably discharged about three months earlier than him because her injuries were less severe. She had a brother named Aiden who lived in Mattapan, and her last known address was someplace called Blakely Manor; other than that, current information about Laine Parker was scarce.

Kamienski whistled. "That's an impressive service record. You know this lady?"

"You could say that." Wolfe licked his dry lips, suddenly aware that he was almost painfully thirsty. For the bottle of water he'd left in the Mustang, sure—but with the memories boiling under the surface of his consciousness, a bottle of whiskey wouldn't hurt either. "She's the only reason I'm here talking to you. Corporal Parker kept me breathing until we were rescued."

Silent Mark's eyebrows furrowed, and Kamienski voiced the question the three of them were all thinking: "Why would she do this?"

Wolfe pushed the dashboard computer away and wiped the sweat from his face with his forearm. "I have no idea."

"We'll look into her, keep you guys updated," Kamienski said. "Good job running after her like that. I mean, you're fucking crazy, but good job."

Wolfe shrugged, a modest smile gracing his features. "Been accused of worse." He got out of the cruiser in time to see a flash of Scarlett's blonde hair by the area cordoned off closer to Fenway; he waved, and she came trotting over with Sebastian after a quick word to the cops who were standing guard near Christopher, Melissa, and Kevin. "Hey. You guys okay?"

Scarlett punched Wolfe in his good shoulder—she was considerate like that. "We're fine, dumbass."

"Ow! What was that for?"

"For taking off after a goddamn sniper without backup!"

Sebastian cut in, calmer than Scarlett but no less agitated: "We were worried, Jim."

"I get that, but what was I supposed to do? Somebody needed to watch out for Christopher and Mel, and I didn't figure Kevin and a bunch of ballpark cops were going to cut it." Wolfe did not rub the spot where Scarlett hit him, even though it burned like a bastard. "Besides, I was just telling our favorite detectives I think I know who our shooter is."

He told them about Laine, and in the midst of the conversation Kamienski interjected to say that he had a couple of cruisers he could spare to shadow Christopher and the others home. Scarlett reminded Wolfe she had to be at Caitlin's last dress fitting for the wedding the following morning, so she volunteered to take the overnight shift at the Sullivan home and Wolfe would spell her in the morning.

They parted ways, with Wolfe and Sebastian walking back to the Mustang amongst the continuous white-blue flashing of cruiser lights and the ever-growing glare from news reporters setting up their lights for live shots. Police helicopters circled the neighborhood, and even though the noise from their propellers was different from the choppers in the Sandbox, Wolfe felt the muscles in his arms twitch as they tried to reach for an M4 that wasn't on his back anymore. Even getting behind the wheel of the Mustang brought back flashes of Humvee dashboards and trying to drive and shoot at the same time.

Careful fingers touched a ridge of scar tissue on his wrist. "Jim? Are you sure you're all right?"

Wolfe glanced at Sebastian's face, his features earnest in their concern. "I'm…" he trailed off, the lie caught on his tongue. "Actually, no, I'm not fine. The shooting alone I could've dealt with, but seeing Laine again… it threw me a little."

"She saved your life the last time you saw her, and this time she tried to kill our client," Sebastian said, raising his voice to be heard over the roar of the Mustang's engine starting up; Wolfe pretended he didn't feel a warmth in his chest when Sebastian called

Christopher *their* client. "It is understandable that you would be upset."

"I guess." Wolfe swung the car out on to Brookline Avenue, passing through the police barricade and over the David Ortiz Bridge, I-93 a trail of lights in either direction underneath them. "But it also bothered me because her sniping us like that was a lot like what happened… over there." *A lot like what made me like this*, he added mentally, trusting that Sebastian would understood what he meant.

Sebastian opened his mouth to respond but closed it again, lips pressed into a hard line as he peered into the rearview mirror. "Jim, I think we have a problem. We appear to have picked up a friend."

Wolfe looked in the mirror too, and didn't like what he saw. A large black SUV—Cadillac, he noted as they passed under a streetlight—had fallen in behind them when they made the right turn on to Commonwealth Avenue, and it was gaining on them with alarming speed. The traffic at this time of night was thinner than during the day, so it was easy to tell when two more identical SUVs flanked the first, clearly preparing to try and cut off the Mustang.

"Hang on, let me see if I can lose them." Something occurred to Wolfe. "Those aren't from your old man, right?"

Sebastian shook his head. "No, he only uses German cars. Don't ask me why."

"Something to do with slovenly Americans, I'm sure."

Wolfe hit the gas, and the Cadillacs followed, once again much closer than he would've preferred. Instead of taking the first left on to Beacon Street—the way he would go to take Sebastian home—Wolfe continued down Comm Ave, wishing for once in his life that a BPD cruiser would appear out of nowhere to pull him over. No luck. "They're gonna cut us off at the Charlesgate bridge," he guessed. "I can probably outrun them, but it'll be messy."

Sebastian shrugged, retrieving Wolfe's Glock 22 from where he'd left it in the glove compartment before the game, racking the slide to check the load in the chamber. He flashed him a grin that, despite the situation, was so damn pretty it made Wolfe's heart skip a beat. "I can handle messy. Go for it."

Wolfe punched the gas, and they made it under Charlesgate first, if just barely. He heard the grind of fiberglass on concrete and saw sparks in his rearview as one of the SUVs clipped a concrete pylon but kept coming. Ahead, Comm Ave eastbound narrowed from four lanes to two as it intersected Massachusetts Avenue. Sebastian buzzed his window down and leaned outside, firing off three rounds from the Glock in quick succession. The same SUV that had lost some paint back at Charlesgate got a blown tire and skidded off the road into a tree.

Movement flickered in Wolfe's side mirror, and his brain instinctively recognized the shape emerging from the window of one of the two remaining vehicles as the muzzle of an assault rifle. "Nice shooting, but I don't think they liked that—*duck*!"

He jerked the wheel as hard as he dared while going eighty miles an hour in a sports car, trying to avoid the incoming spray of bullets. Thankfully either the goon with the M16 wasn't used to firing while moving or he was just a bad shot, because Wolfe didn't hear the telltale thump of a bullet punching through the Mustang, nor did any of the windows shatter. The intersection with Mass Ave wasn't clear as they approached, and Wolfe made a fishtailed right turn into the traffic, garnering a lot of angry honks but also losing another of the SUVs to a broadside crash with a pickup truck.

The last SUV was swerving in and out of the flow of cars trying to get to them, and over the hammer of his own frantic pulse and Sebastian's breathing, Wolfe could hear the distant wail of police sirens. He doubted BPD had many units to spare given what went down at Fenway, but at least it might dissuade whoever was in those crashed Cadillacs from following them on foot. The more immediate problem was approaching much faster than Wolfe liked: the Mass Ave intersection with Westland Avenue and Falmouth Street by Symphony Hall. The unmistakable molar-shaking hum of a semi truck's engine to his left signaled incoming from Falmouth, and with it came opportunity.

He had one chance to get this right. "Hang on!"

The Mustang rocketed into the intersection at full speed, missing the nose of the giant truck by less than a foot and going temporarily deaf from the blare of the driver's horn. Wolfe was close enough that he saw the whites of his own eyes in the reflection of the chrome grille, right before he cranked the wheel again and jammed on his brakes, rotating the Mustang a complete three-hundred and sixty degrees so they could face their pursuers head on.

The semi-truck continued to Saint Stephen Street, and by the time the trailer was out of the way, the last SUV that chased them was gone.

~***~

Chapter Seven

Unforgiving Friday morning sunlight pierced through the thin skin of Jake Wolfe's eyelids, and he groaned as his retinas attempted to char themselves into briquettes. It took his brain a moment to equate the sudden brightness with the *whooshing* sound of the curtains in the living room being thrown wide open, but when he did he squinted in his roommate's direction. "Misha, what the fuck?"

Mikhail "Misha" Aleksandrov stood by the front window, arms crossed over his chest. About the same height as Jake but a couple of years older, Misha had a mouse-brown tumbleweed on his head that he called hair, equally brown eyes, and a cleft in his chin that would've made Johnny Bravo jealous. He was dressed for work as an intern in a local law office, and somehow his plaid blazer only served to make him look more annoyed. "Pretty sure *I* should be asking *you* that question, Jakey, since I'm not the one who passed out on the couch for fourteen hours after a binge-drinking episode."

Jake was confused until he noticed the empty pinot noir bottle on the coffee table. The vial that had contained the Rapture was nowhere to be seen; at least he'd had enough forethought to throw away the evidence of his crime. To Misha, it must've seemed like Jake came home and guzzled down the entire bottle, when in fact that was the furthest thing from the truth. But with interning during the day and classes at Harvard at night, Misha wasn't likely to notice much these days unless it was shoved right under his nose.

When Jake didn't respond, Misha sighed and rubbed a hand over his five o'clock shadow. "Please tell me you at least made it to the store and got some food."

"Uh," Jake said intelligently. The high from the Rapture—more pleasant than the pain pills from the hospital and more euphoric than weed—had mostly worn off, but he still felt a pleasant buzz in his fingers and toes, blood thrumming underneath his numerous scars for what felt like the first time. "Not exactly?" Reluctantly, Jake told him what went down in the Caruso's parking lot, emphasizing his near-breakdown and glossing over the details of his trip into *Voici Spiritueux*. He mentioned buying the wine, of course, but not the vial of Rapture that had been hidden inside of it.

"So what you're telling me," Misha began, enunciating each syllable of every word at a glacial pace, "is that you blew our grocery money on *one* bottle of wine? You don't even *like* wine!"

"I'm sorry," Jake said, and he meant it. Whether he was sorry because he wasted the money or sorry because he got caught was up for grabs; a lot had changed since the Mass Art Murderer's rampage, not the least of which was the stability of Jake's moral compass. "Look, I know I fucked up, okay? I'll go back to Caruso's tomorrow and put the groceries on my credit card."

Misha stared out the window he'd uncovered a moment ago, no doubt watching the cars pass in front of their red Colonial-style house, which sat on the corner of Pearl and Granite Streets in Cambridgeport. Misha's ultra-rich hippie-dippy parents had put a down payment on the house as a gift to their son for getting into Harvard; problem was, they'd stuck him with the mortgage before they left to hike the Andes for a year. Enter Jake, desperately in need of someplace to stay so he could from home as a call center jockey. It wasn't a perfect relationship—there was the awkwardness that came with Misha having dated Jake's best friend, who was a Mass Art Murder victim—but it was a symbiotic one, at least until today.

"Promise me you'll go to the store," Misha said, tone resigned. He glanced at his watch. "And do it fast—I'm gonna be late."

Jake raised three fingers. "Scout's honor." No need for Misha to know he'd never been a Boy Scout—that was Jimmy, and he got kicked out for kissing another boy. "Now get out of here."

~***~

Otis and Martha Webber owned a brick-front Greek revival on Hutchings Street in Boston's Roxbury neighborhood, a few blocks from the Franklin Park Zoo. Diana had never visited their house before today, but she presumed that before Martha got sick she had been a gardener, judging from the breadth and scale of the flowerbeds that stretched from the front door to the sidewalk. The gardens were overgrown with weeds and looked as if they hadn't been tended in years, but Diana was less interested in plants and more invested in the battered blue Kia sedan sitting in the Webbers' driveway.

"Curtains are all shut," David observed from the driver's seat of the Camry, which they'd parked a few houses down from the

Webbers' abode, the front end partially concealed by an overgrown hydrangea. "That's Otis's car, right?"

Diana glanced at the Kia and nodded. "Yes. Should we go knock?"

David sighed and popped his door. "Don't see any point in putting it off." He waited for Diana to get out of the car before heading toward Otis's house, the morning air slightly cooler than the day before but no less humid. "Oh, I forgot to tell you I saw Bobby yesterday."

Diana tilted her head to the side, considering. "Your son and the only sibling you're on speaking terms with know you're alive, but you *still* haven't told your wife? There is a pun there somewhere, I think."

"Jimmy asked me when I was gonna tell Angela when I saw him yesterday, and I... didn't have an answer for him," David said, his halting tone telling Diana this was hard for him to discuss. "I don't know what to do, but he's right in that I have to do something before the wedding."

"What are you so afraid of?"

"I don't know," David repeated. (*Liar*, Diana thought but didn't say.) "Maybe it's because she remarried?"

Diana snorted. "Yeah, to a prick." At David's surprised glance, she raised her eyebrows. "Wolfe didn't tell you about Keith?" She gave him the short version—which she'd heard through Wolfe during the ill-fated six-months when she'd pretended to date him—beginning with Keith's drinking and verbal abuse and ending with Wolfe putting Keith's head through a wall when he came home from basic training. "As far as I know, Jake's father is in prison and nowhere near his life, and that is most likely for the best."

David's expression was a mixture of shock and horror, but in true spook fashion he covered it well as they approached Otis's house. "Why the fuck didn't Jimmy tell me about that?"

"There is one thing your son values above all else: honesty." Diana climbed the porch steps ahead of her partner and rang the doorbell, trying without success to get a glimpse of the interior through the sheer curtains blocking the window. "You were not honest with him for the majority of his life, so is it really surprising that he isn't telling you shit?"

David scrubbed at his dyed hair in frustration. "I guess not." They waited a beat or two, and when nobody came to the door, he nudged Diana's arm. "Go ahead and pick the lock, I'll keep a lookout."

Much like at Seams, Diana whipped out her lock picks and got them through the Kwikset deadbolt in under a minute. She was of the mind that *Quick-Pick* would be better branding, since the cheapest lock you could buy also happened to be the simplest, but that was a debate for another day. Walking inside revealed no immediate dead body stench, which was good, and they drew their Glocks and made quick work of clearing the house. Nobody home, and from the state of the dirty dishes and the trash, it looked like no one had been around since Martha passed away.

"Place seems abandoned," Diana noted, returning her gun to the holster at the small of her back, concealed by the length of her flower-print shell top. "Do you think we should—?"

The back door to the house banged open and Otis Webber himself came barreling inside like his ass was on fire. A huge man at well over six-five and two-fifty, Otis was far more intimidating when he wasn't partially concealed behind the counter at Seams. His t-shirt and jeans were ripped and dirty, eyes bulging in their sockets with mania and his entire body soaked in sweat. Without preamble, he let out an angered shout and ran at them, covering the distance from the kitchen to the living room in seconds.

David and Diana dove to opposite corners like they were avoiding a charging bull, and Diana raised her hands in placation as Otis whirled on her. "Otis—it's me, Diana! Please, what's the matter?"

He came for her with his arms outstretched and a snarl on his face. Diana turned quickly at the waist and brought her leg up, planting her foot on the coffee table and using it as leverage to spring upward. She grabbed Otis's shoulders and spun around him, hooking her legs around his neck and using her momentum to throw him to the ground; she flew through the air and landed on all fours, skidding on the hardwood floor in David's direction.

"What the hell is his problem?" David wondered aloud, as Otis got his feet under him, seemingly unaffected by a headscissors takedown.

Diana shook her hair out of her face. "I have no idea, but I do not see us reasoning with him in this state."

David was ready for it when Otis tried going after him, using the slick polish of the wooden floors to his advantage and sliding out of the way. He hopped up on the larger man's back and got his arm around Otis's neck, trying valiantly for a chokehold. Unfortunately, Otis was wise to this and turned around, slamming both his back and David into the nearest wall.

"Uh, D?" he said, voice strained due to his ribs being crushed between a giant and unforgiving sheetrock. "A little help?"

"Only since you asked so politely." Straightening out of her half-crouch, Diana picked up the nearest solid object—in this case, a ceramic table lamp—and slammed it into the side of Otis's skull. It shattered on impact, chunks of painted pottery and metal bits from the lamp's innards hitting the floor at their feet.

The big man went down like a sack of potatoes, falling to his knees and allowing David to stumble away from the wall and catch his breath. Otis didn't lose consciousness, but he did curl up in the fetal position on the floor, moaning and grabbing at his head. David pulled a zip-tie from his pocket and handed it to Diana, who rolled Otis on his belly and secured his hands together behind his back. She noticed what looked like a small cut of some kind on the back of

Otis's neck near the base of his skull, but wrote it off as a result of the fight.

"Dijana?" Otis groaned, peering at her from the corner of his eye. "How... why are you here?"

"We've been looking for you, Otis," Diana said. She didn't bother correcting him on the usage of her true name, since David was the only witness; it didn't matter that hearing *Dijana* brought back a slew of memories every time, not the least of which were a cold orphanage and the feeling of a gun in her small hands. "You have been missing for over a week."

Otis thunked his forehead against wood. "Has it been that long? That long since... Martha died?"

"I'm afraid so," David confirmed, a note of apology in his voice that made Diana's heart do something funny in her chest. "Otis, where have you been?"

Otis looked up at him, eyes going wide. "*Mein Gott*, you're David Wolfe! Anton wants to kill you! What on Earth are you doing here?"

"That's not important," Diana interjected, even though it *really* fucking was—just not to Otis. "Answer the question, please. We've been looking for you, but not for Anton. I was hoping you would be willing to testify against him."

"The problem was not you, Dijana," Otis said, hands clenching and relaxing involuntarily. "Anton has done so much for Martha and

I over the years. He brought her to all the best doctors, funded experimental treatments, even paid for her hospice care… but once she died, I think he realized he could no longer buy my loyalty because he had no more leverage against me. Perhaps he was fearful of exactly what you wanted to ask me." The big man took in a shaky breath. "They came for me in the night. Injected me with some kind of drug and wrapped me in a—oh, *verdammen*, what is it called—?" He made a motion with his arms like he was hugging himself too tightly.

David's eyebrows shot up. "A straightjacket?"

"That's it! They put me in one of those awful things and took me away in some kind of ambulance." Otis squinted at them, his head tilting slightly to one side. "I do not remember much else, but they brought me to a place, a terrible place called Blakely Manor."

Diana opened her mouth to ask what was so bad about Blakely Manor, but in that same instant Otis collapsed back to the floor and began convulsing violently. David bent down to try and help him, but Diana yanked him backwards, away from the sparks skipping across Otis's skin from the back of his neck, as if he were hooked up to a car battery.

Otis convulsed for a moment more, made one final haunting sound, and died.

"Don't! You'll get… shocked…" Diana trailed off, exhaling harshly when she caught sight of the smoke coming from the same area as the sparks. "What the hell is that?"

David was leaning against her chest, both of them sprawled on the hardwood, and when he noticed this he jerked away. He cleared his throat loudly and said, "No idea. Think he's safe to touch now?"

"Probably, but do it quickly," Diana advised, pushing herself up to peek out the front windows. Her throat tightened with emotion but it never made it to the surface, and she studiously ignored the burning behind her eyes. "This place is either bugged or someone's watching it. There is no other explanation for why Otis was fine one minute and dead the next."

David rolled Otis's corpse over with a grunt, and after some squishy-sounding searching he tapped Diana's shoulder. She stood and examined the small, bloody device David held in his palm. "What is that? Some kind of microchip?"

"Not exactly," David replied. "See this part on the back? That's a transmitter, but it's been modified to receive a bigger electrical signal than your typical tracking device. Someone killed Otis, and you were right—they did it because he talked to us."

~***~

If there were something Scarlett Vaughn despised more than strapless tops and Junior Mints, it was shopping malls. And in her opinion, the Burlington Mall was one of the worst. There was nothing *wrong* with it—in fact it was full of bustling stores and extremely clean—but it was also kitty-corner to I-95 and Lahey Hospital, making it primo real estate for lost tourists and a breeding ground for all kinds of crazy germs. Between that and the design of the parking lots, driving by the place was enough to set Scarlett's teeth on edge; being *in* it was a completely different animal.

Yet she sat in the too-white bridal section at Nordstrom on an overstuffed bench upholstered to look like a shaggy dog. She held her phone in one hand and a flute of champagne in the other, the latter which she hadn't touched since she was technically on the clock with Melissa seated two chairs away. They were waiting for Caitlin to emerge in her newly-tailored wedding gown before Scarlett and Frogger—expert hacker, certified genius and a good friend of Wolfe's—tried on their bridesmaids' dresses.

Across from Scarlett sat Angela Wolfe and Maureen Sullivan, best friends for twenty-something years and the mothers of Scarlett's partner and the bride-to-be. They were both in their fifties and at the low end of five feet tall, but that was where the similarities ended. Where Maureen was heavy Angela was light, and Angela's flaming-red hair hung straight as a pin to her shoulders, while Maureen kept her dark curly hair—which all four of her children had inherited—in a stylish bob. Angela liked to wear ripped jeans and t-shirts, while Maureen was usually sporting some kind of New England Patriots merchandise and a colorful bag designed by Vera Bradley.

Scarlett opened her conversation thread with Wolfe (he was currently in her contacts as "Big Tuna" for no particular reason) and shot him a text: *Pretty sure your mom and Mrs. S are taking bets on how long we'll be here.*

Wolfe's response came almost instantly: **Can't see how waiting for Caitlin to try on her dress for the 8th time could be worse than following Christopher around while he knocks on doors.**

Scarlett snorted. *You sure he's a gubernatorial candidate and not a vacuum cleaner salesman?*

Francine "Frogger" Sampson came back from her quest for a champagne flute and sat down next to Scarlett on the bench. Younger than the rest of the wedding party by a few years—she graduated MIT at the ripe old age of eighteen—Frogger had a beautifully structured face with a prominent nose, bowed lips, and rich dark brown skin. Her tightly-curled black hair hung loose down her back, and she wore a pair of overalls with a yellow t-shirt and beat up Converse sneakers. "You talking to Sarge?"

Scarlett wasn't sure why Frogger chose to call Wolfe by his rank more often than not, but knowing Frogger, there wasn't a reason; she probably just liked how it sounded. "Yep. We're debating who's suffering more so we can argue about who deserves extra dim sum the next time we order out."

"Nice." Pushing her oversized, clear-framed glasses up her nose, Frogger lowered her voice to ask, "On a scale of one to George Kirk blowing up the *Kelvin* five minutes into the *Trek* reboot, how much of a clusterfuck is this wedding gonna be?"

Wolfe had sent a thumbs-down emoji after Scarlett's crack about vacuum cleaners, so she changed topics: **did you and Bash get up**

to anything adrenaline-fueled and/or naughty after your adventure last night??

In response to Frogger's inquiry, she said, "Not sure yet. I mean, it's always a little crazy when you get more than five Sullivans in one room, so I'm having a hard time imagining what a hundred of them plus Ryan's family is going to be like."

Frogger leaned her forehead on Scarlett's shoulder and groaned in despair. "That's *so many* people already, plus all the other guests! You'll be lucky if I don't pass out cold with that many eyeballs staring at me."

Scarlett patted her leg reassuringly. "Don't worry—with any luck, they'll all be staring at Caitlin and *she'll* pass out cold."

Her phone buzzed with another text from Wolfe: *no! just talked to the cops, then i dropped him off with Constantin*

Caitlin emerged from the dressing room and suddenly there was a lot of hand-flapping and crying as all the other women jumped up and surrounded the bride-to-be. She glanced up from her phone and saw a lot of white lace and chunks of Cinderella amidst an outpouring of estrogen. She sent back a quick **doesn't mean you didn't want to! ;)** to Wolfe before stowing her phone and going over to get a better look.

Caitlin was flushed a light pink from all the attention, and once the others backed off she grabbed Scarlett's arm and said, "Be honest with me—what do you think?"

Scarlett eyebrow shot up. "Of your dress?" She glanced down at her faded Metallica t-shirt and cutoff shorts. "I'm not exactly a fashion expert."

"Neither am I!" Caitlin said, pulling her over to the three-way mirror. "Is it too much, though? I was going for Disney princess, but… now I'm having second thoughts."

"Better to have second thoughts about the dress than the man," Scarlett remarked, smiling when that drew a snort of laughter. She put her hands on her hips and studied Caitlin's reflection. The dress was pure white, capped-sleeved and full-length, lace flowers of varying sizes making up a pattern broken by a satin belt at the waist. It was tailored to accent Caitlin's natural curves and fell in a bell-shaped cascade to the floor. "Seriously, what do you expect me to say? You look incredible, babe."

Caitlin beamed at her, a shot of pure sunshine that made even Scarlett's little black heart feel warm. They hugged, and Scarlett was selfishly grateful—not for the first time—that things hadn't worked out in a romantic sense between Wolfe and Caitlin. If the high school sweethearts had gone on to get married, the chain of events that led to Scarlett basking in her friend's joy wouldn't exist. And damn it all, just thinking about that made Scarlett feel as sad and alone as she had as a rookie beat cop in New York.

The Nordstrom lady came along and shooed Frogger and Scarlett into the fitting room, where their bridesmaids' dresses waited on hangers. Caitlin graciously allowed them to choose what they wore, so long as they didn't clash with the groom's sky-blue tie and pocket square. It had taken a lot of texting back and forth (the private investigator lifestyle didn't lend itself well to in-person socialization) to settle on something flattering for both of them: knee-length emerald green satin dresses with sweetheart necklines and lacy three-quarter sleeves.

Scarlett was in the middle of changing when she heard her phone ring from inside her purse. It was a leather satchel precisely big enough to hold her cell, her wallet, and her weapon of choice, a Colt M1911 pistol. "Goddammit, if that's another telemarketer—"

"Remember when the Do Not Call list was a thing and everybody thought it was going to work?" Frogger's tone was wistful as she tried and failed to untangle her bra strap. "Ah, to be young and naïve."

Scarlett shimmied into the dress and zipped herself up before traipsing over to inspect her phone. She froze when she saw the caller ID: one missed call from her father. No voicemail.

"Hey, you okay?" Frogger asked. "You just did that thing Wolfe does when he sees something he doesn't like—your shoulders went up around your ears."

Part of Scarlett wanted to confide in a friend like a normal person, tell Frogger it was her dad who called and explain the myriad number of reasons why that was a bad thing. The words stuck in her throat, barricaded inside by years of repression and not wanting to unleash the ugly, in-your-face anger that came from talking about Peter Vaughn. Today was supposed to be about Caitlin, and if Scarlett started spilling secrets now, she probably wouldn't stop.

"I'm fine," Scarlett replied, tossing the phone back in her bag before turning around to flash Frogger a smile that looked real but didn't feel it. "I just get pissed off when people call to sell me a warranty on something I don't even own."

A sliver of doubt creased Frogger's forehead but it disappeared as quickly as it came. "Ain't that the truth, girl. You ready?"

Scarlett offered her arm, and this time her smile was genuine when Frogger took her elbow. "Hell yeah."

They went back into the store and were greeted in much the same way Caitlin was, complete with hooting and hollering from the bride-to-be herself. The atmosphere was so happy and insular that none of them noticed Laine Parker dressed as a mall custodian, watching them through the storefront window.

~***~

Chapter Eight

At around eight o'clock that evening Wolfe found himself in the same Nordstrom store that Scarlett and the ladies were at earlier in the day. He was in the men's section watching Christopher examine himself in a three-way mirror—not Wolfe's ideal Friday night, but at least he was getting paid. The gubernatorial candidate needed a tuxedo for a charity gala the following night at the Four Seasons; since Sebastian was easily the most fashionable person any of them knew, it'd been a no-brainer for Christopher to ask him to come along on the shopping trip. Sebastian was currently over by the mirrors with Christopher, humming contemplatively and tugging at various parts of the tux like they offended him.

Sitting beside Wolfe on a bench was Constantin, who looked just as bored as Wolfe felt. "You know," the bodyguard said, "I've been on countless trips like this with Sebastian, and they never get more interesting."

"I can believe that," Wolfe replied. He stretched his scarred arm out along the back of the bench, hiding a wince when the movement popped an adhesion. Luckily it was a small one and didn't burn too badly, but to distract himself, he allowed his eyes to wander Sebastian's lean, graceful frame. "I take it you haven't developed an interest in fashion?"

Constantin frowned. "I know some things—for example, Christopher's ass looks terrible in those pants."

"Hey, don't drag me into this!" Christopher exclaimed. Contrary to that statement, he turned to study his body from the side before looking at Sebastian in concern. "My ass looks terrible, doesn't it?"

"If people at a charity gala are paying that much attention to your ass, you've got bigger problems," Wolfe said. "What charity is this thing for, anyway?"

"The Delaney Veterans Center," Christopher said, fiddling with his cuffs. "They do a lot of great work. I cut them a check and they were gracious enough to invite Melissa and me to the event. There's going to be finger food, obviously, but also a silent auction and some other stuff. They didn't even mind when I told them I'd need to bring along security."

"You'll need a tuxedo too," Sebastian said to Wolfe. The look in his eyes was simultaneously wry and fond. "I don't suppose you own one?"

Before Wolfe could respond, Christopher snapped his fingers and pointed at him. "Better idea! Can you wear your uniform? The press will eat that up."

Wolfe's mind flashed to his closet at his apartment, where his Army dress uniform hung perfectly pressed under the protective cover of a suit bag, the shoes polished and in their box below it. He knew every ribbon and medal on the jacket in the order they appeared, and his initial reaction to the question was a hearty, visceral *no fucking way*. The last time he'd worn that uniform was to visit the graves of the Rangers—*his* Rangers—who died in the ambush that nearly destroyed half his body. The idea of putting on that monkey suit for something as vapid as a gala with finger food and a silent auction felt about as good as taking a bath in battery acid. But Wolfe forced himself to remember that the gala was being held to benefit other vets who were a hell of a lot less fortunate than him, and he knew from firsthand experience that the Delaney Center did in fact do good work in the community.

For those reasons, even though he knew Christopher would find a way to twist this into a political stunt, he found himself saying, "Sure, okay. I can do that."

They wrapped up at Nordstrom a few minutes later, with Christopher arranging to have his manager, Nikki, pick up the suit the following afternoon once it was tailored. It would be a rush job, but Wolfe supposed these things were easy to get done when an election was seen as a formality. The four of them piled into Constantin's Mercedes and headed back to Christopher and Melissa's house, a sprawling six-bedroom, beautifully restored Tudor-style manor on Benton Road in Somerville's Spring Hill neighborhood.

They ran into the Sullivans' housekeeper on her way home for the day as they entered the house. She informed Christopher that Melissa had retired to the master bedroom and the children were in bed. He thanked her, but it was Constantin who walked to her to her car and held the door while she got inside; Sebastian waited for his bodyguard on the front porch, lighting up a cigarette at the railing.

"You guys stay up as long as you want," Christopher said, keeping his voice low so as not to disturb his kids. He yawned as he turned and headed for the sweeping front staircase. "Beer's in the fridge, help yourself. I'm going to bed."

Wolfe said goodnight and toed off his Wolverines before padding into the marble-floored kitchen to see about those beers. He grabbed one for himself and Constantin, thought for a moment, and swiped one of Melissa's sparkling wine coolers for Sebastian. When he came back into the living room, he noticed the housekeeper had left him a fresh pillow and blanket on the couch, neatly folded, and made a mental note to thank her in the morning.

Constantin came inside first, following Wolfe's lead and taking off his shoes. Sebastian joined them a few seconds later, kicking off his combat-style boots, smelling like Camels and the new cologne he'd started wearing after the Mass Art fiasco. They both sat down on the loveseat opposite Wolfe's couch and thanked him quietly for the drinks, Sebastian folding his legs underneath himself instead of sprawling them like he would to distract and/or seduce. Constantin was a giant among doll furniture, everything around him seemingly too delicate for this man who was not large in stature but big in intimidation.

They chatted in soft tones about the job and the gala tomorrow until Constantin glanced at his watch, setting down his empty beer bottle on the glass coffee table. "Sebastian, we should get going. It is late, and if I have to deal with that *prost* Christopher again tomorrow I need a full eight hours of sleep."

127

Wolfe huffed a laugh. He was trying to learn Romanian in his spare time, and like most languages, the easiest thing to pick up on was swearing. "He may be a dumbass, but he's also our client."

"Which means not shooting him, no matter how sleep-deprived you are," Sebastian chided, poking Constantin in the ribs and grinning when the bodyguard grumbled and swatted at him. He looked at Wolfe, sharp features softening at the edges in a way that few people got to see. "Are you going to be all right, Jim?"

Wolfe smiled and raised his own beer in salute. "I'll be fine. Drive safe."

For a moment, Sebastian looked like he was going to say something that had nothing to do with work, or being friendly. But that must've been Wolfe's imagination, because as he headed for the door with Constantin all he said was, "We will. See you tomorrow."

Not long after that, Wolfe walked the perimeter of the house to make sure everything was locked up tight. He double-checked that the security alarm was armed and then he took advantage of the blanket and pillow, falling asleep on the couch.

~***~

When Jim Wolfe slept, he didn't always have the same dream.

Sometimes he dreamt of his childhood, vague snippets of memories too strong to be bleached away by the white-hot air of the desert. He dreamt of being little Jimmy Wolfe again, small enough to swing between his parents' hands over puddles and cracks in the sidewalk. He played hide-and-seek with his older brother and only cried a little when Josh scared him into losing his balance and skinning his knee. Jimmy held his baby brother for the first time, a red-faced, screaming creature named Jake that he would swear to always protect and fail miserably.

And other times, Wolfe had one particular dream.

It was the one he dreaded the most but couldn't escape, with him and his guys from the 3rd Batt on the curving road to that village about ten klicks outside Baghdad. He dreamt of the quiet murmur of his men moments before disaster, the young faces of the infantrymen backstopping them, and the dead dog used to disguise an improvised explosive device set off with a single sniper shot.

Wolfe was thrown fifty feet through the air and landed hard on his back, the breath punched out of his lungs like air escaping a popped balloon. Half deaf and temporarily blinded, he spat out a stream of blood from biting his tongue and wrestled his rifle strap away from his throat. His broken earpiece whined and screeched until he yanked it out, leaving the busted tech discarded in the sand.

There was another explosion as Wolfe got to his knees, and agony shocked through his left side and rattled into his brain. He looked down, and where camouflaged fabric should've been was blood and flayed muscle and bone. Deeper, pulsing things that Wolfe knew intellectually were his organs made him recoil into himself, his gorge rising. The skin around the mess was peeled back like wrapping paper on the most gruesome present, blackened from the heat with shards of metal and Kevlar embedded in the gaping wound.

Wolfe collapsed backward in a heap, hands clenched around the mess that had once been his torso. The desert around him was silent, save for the crackle of the burning Humvees and the wet sound of his own breathing. With the remainder of his strength he turned his head, noticed a body that was shredded and burned almost beyond recognition. Other corpses were scattered around the area, the overwhelming stench of cooked meat and burning mingled with low-hanging black smoke.

The world around Wolfe grew darker. Before it faded away completely, he saw two things: a medic's arm patch, and a curtain of blood red hair.

Franklin "Frankie" Sullivan let himself in to his brother's house around five in the morning using the spare key on his keyring. It hung in between the fob for his cruiser and one of those little plastic picture frames that contained a shot of the entire Sullivan family on the flume ride at Canobie Lake Park, all screaming their heads off in delight as they plunged down the falls. He entered the house as quietly as possible, thumbing in the code for the security system before toeing off his shoes. He was just coming off a ten-hour shift, and wanted to catch a few hours of sleep before he watched Christopher's back for free on his day off. Ah, the glamourous life of a rookie police officer.

A noise from the living room caught Frankie's attention, and it took his brain a moment to figure out what it was: a muffled sob. Tiptoeing in, he wasn't surprised to find Jim Wolfe's large frame sprawled out on the couch, but he was disturbed when he realized his friend was caught in the throes of a nasty nightmare. Sweat glistened on Wolfe's forehead, and he'd thrashed around enough in his sleep to knock his blanket and pillow on to the floor; one leg dangled off the cushions, twitching occasionally like he was trying to run away from something.

"Jimmy?" Frankie whispered, worry creasing his brow. "C'mon, man, wake up."

No response except an awful whimper, Wolfe's eyes ticking back and forth furiously under closed lids. Not knowing what else to do and fearful that if the dream got much worse Wolfe might hurt himself, Frankie reached out and touched his trembling shoulder.

That was not Frankie's best idea.

Wolfe's gray-green eyes snapped open and his hand shot up, wrapping around Frankie's throat like a python's jaws for one, two, three seconds of crushing airless pain. Frankie made a garbled noise and immediately started clawing at Wolfe's scarred forearm, which was enough to bring him back to reality. He released Frankie as quickly as he'd grabbed him, but the damage was done.

Frankie doubled over, wheezing for breath and wondering idly why it was always him on the rough end of somebody else's problems. "Nice... to see you... too."

"Jesus Christ, Frankie!" Wolfe exclaimed, lowering his voice when Frankie pointed upward to remind him of the people sleeping over their heads. "Are you okay? I didn't—I woke up and I didn't know—"

Cautiously, Frankie straightened up and felt at his own windpipe. Although everything in the area burned and was already swelling, it all seemed to be in working order. "It's okay," he said, and winced at the sound of his own voice; it was like a brick rattling around in a dryer. "Are *you* all right? Looked like one hell of a nightmare."

Wolfe sat up on the couch and scrubbed his hands over his face. "Not really. I think seeing Laine last night—" a glance at his watch, worn with the face turned inward toward his body to prevent reflections "—or the night before last, I guess, fucked me up." He rested his elbows on his knees and looked up at Frankie, eyes ringed red with fatigue. "She's the one who saved me, Frankie. Without her I wouldn't have made it out of Iraq."

Frankie blew out a breath. "Damn, Jimmy. That's rough." He took a seat on the coffee table, wriggling the tactical belt off his uniform and tossing it in a chair, gun and all. "You think we need to bring someone else in on this thing? I'm starting to think the five of us aren't enough."

Wolfe didn't look thrilled at the idea—he liked to keep his circle small and trustworthy, and Frankie respected that—but he didn't shoot it down either. "I'll think about it, maybe talk to Scarlett tomorrow." He clapped Frankie on the knee. "Let's try to get some sleep, yeah? Big day once the sun's up."

~***~

A few hours later at the apartment on Blue Hill Avenue in Mattapan, Aiden Parker awoke to his sister bolting from the bedroom to the bathroom. The hollow echo of vomit hitting the toilet bowl brought him fully out of sleep, and he reached under the couch cushions for the repurposed acetaminophen bottle he kept there before trudging in to join her.

He stood in the doorway, wincing in disgust as Laine heaved some more, and distracted himself by pouring a single capsule about half the length of his pinkie finger into his palm. The capsule was clear and contained a swirling silver liquid that Laine thought was medicine to help her PTSD. It was actually the capsule version of Rapture, the highly-addictive and dangerous party drug pioneered by Anton Codreanu—but in Laine's case, the Rapture's reality-altering properties were being used to reinforce the subliminal messages planted in her brain during her time at Blakely Manor.

If this was the only way to get his hardheaded sister to listen to him, Aiden would gladly take it. "Here, swallow this. And for God's sake, rinse your mouth out."

Laine did as she was told and flushed the toilet, leaning back against the vanity cabinet and shutting her eyes while she waited for the "pill" to take effect. "I'm sorry about yesterday. It won't happen again."

"It better not," Aiden said, half threat and half statement of fact. If Laine fucked up again like she had last night with Wolfe, it wouldn't be long before she'd be back in the basement at Blakely Manor—and this time, Aiden thought with a shudder, he would be joining her. Codreanu was just as vindictive and conniving as the Parker siblings; they'd had a less than friendly text exchange after the mess at Fenway that contained specific instructions on their next assignment. "Our best shot to stir things up is that big charity gala happening at the Four Seasons tonight. We can't go after Sullivan directly, not after last night, but maybe there's another way to destroy him."

Laine's body was relaxing in increments, the knot of scars across her face smoothing out. "How?"

"Findlay Catering is doing the food, so I already have an in. They always need extra sets of hands for shit like this, and who's going to say no to a vet volunteering to help out at an event *for* veterans? That gets you into the gala too." Aiden laid out his plan with sweeping gestures that were a little too grand for their dingy bathroom. "You're a knockout except for that damn scar, so you find that Mike Draymond asshole and start chatting him up, buy him drinks. You slip something in one, he takes a tumble—maybe he kicks the bucket, maybe not—and meanwhile I'll find some evidence to plant that points to Sullivan."

Laine nodded along, wiping the sweat from her brow with the back of her hand. "That… makes sense."

"Good," Aiden said. "Because we don't have a lot of choices now that you fucked up."

He left the bathroom, the details of the operation spinning themselves out in his mind like twisted cotton candy.

~***~

Like a scene out of his own fucked up *Groundhog Day*, Jake found himself sitting in the Camaro in the parking lot at Caruso's Grocery, the inside of the car already sweltering in heat that just wouldn't break. Sweat sliding down his temple, Jake stared across Broadway at the front of *Voici Spiritueux*. It didn't look as busy as it had when he was there the last time, and he warred with himself, wanting to go back and get another hit of Rapture. He knew if he did that Misha would be apoplectic enough to do something damaging— like tell Jimmy about Jake's new hobby.

Then again, if anyone would understand Jake's need to escape himself for a while, it would be Jimmy. His brother was good at hiding his PTSD most of the time, but when he'd first come back from the Middle East, Jimmy was like one of those creepy jointed puppets getting rattled around by an unseen master. He wasn't himself and never would be again; he recovered bits and pieces of that person, but his time in the desert changed him irrevocably.

Jake's time in the Mass Art Murderer's basement had changed him too. Not in the same ways, maybe, but in the ways that mattered. His naturally optimistic nature about people was crushed like a bug, as had any dreams of being an artist for a living. Between the debilitating injuries to his hands that cost him dexterity with a paintbrush and the nightmares that plagued him even when he was awake, Jake hadn't been able to paint one single stroke since he got out of the hospital. Not one.

And all of that was bad enough without considering the worst part of the whole ordeal. Not the pain, not the scars, not even the friends he'd lost (to death and social stigma alike) or the constant hounding from the media. No, the worst part was the secret, the answer to the riddle countless pundits and cops and online theorizers had been trying to solve for almost four months.

Jake knew the identity of the Mass Art Murderer.

It would be so simple to tell someone. Jimmy, their mom, even Frankie or Detective Kamienski—those last two weren't his biggest fans, but he knew they'd believe him. But every time the words bubbled up into his throat he swallowed them back like tar, because the Mass Art Murderer's final threat (his *oldest brother's* final threat) was frighteningly clear. If Jake told anyone who'd committed the torturous murder spree in Boston, when Josh came back the next time he would start with their mother and Jimmy, making Jake watch while they died slow, miserable deaths.

"Fuck it," Jake muttered, unbuckling his seatbelt and stalking across Broadway, sweat breaking out on every part of his body thanks to his long sleeves and pants. If he had to live with this shit he was going to do it on his own terms. He yanked on the door to *Voici Spiritueux* and frowned when it didn't budge. "What the hell?"

"They're closed," a voice said, behind him and to his right. "Sign says it's for cleaning, but I don't see anybody inside, do you?"

Jake spun around, heart hammering. He'd never been a fan of surprises before, but now the slightest unexpected sound had him jumping for the ceiling. A derogatory comeback was on the tip of his tongue but he swallowed it back when he saw a woman around his age with short, choppy hair dyed bright orange and skin as fair and likely to burn as Jake's own. She stood with her arms crossed over a green tube top and linen shorts, a pair of Ray-Bans masking her face from the nose up.

Even with the sunglasses, Jake recognized her from the news stories that had aired around the same time as his—this was Lacey Stahl, rock n' roll heiress and fellow kidnapping victim.

"Well if they're not cleaning, then why are they closed?" Jake asked.

Lacey pulled down her sunglasses and regarded him with bloodshot eyes. "Why do you want to know?"

Sensing this was some kind of test, Jake replied, "Because I wanted to buy a bottle of Communion wine."

Lacey's mouth twitched into a smile, but it wasn't particularly happy. "Me too. My boss is just dying to try some." She stared hard at the darkened interior of the wine shop for a moment before turning on the heel of her sandal. "I have an idea about how we can get all the Communion wine we want, but I'm not talking about it here. Too many eyes and ears—you want a fix, come back to my place."

Jake's gut told him this was a colossal mistake, worse than coming home without groceries or trying Rapture in the first place. Jimmy and Scarlett had told him about how they'd found Lacey Stahl with Sebastian in a motel room, both on the brink of death thanks to Danh Sang. He was ninety-nine percent sure the boss to which she was referring was Sang, but his feet moved on their own and he followed Lacey down the road.

Chapter Nine

Due to the less than natural circumstances of Otis's death and not knowing whether their voices were heard by whoever had killed him remotely, David and Diana decided the best thing to do was lie low for a while. Neither of them went home, choosing instead to buy some cheap suitcases and clothes at the Primark in Downtown Crossing before renting a queen suite at the Courtyard Marriott across Tremont Street from Tufts Medical Center. It was a nice room with luxury finishes and a view of the Chinatown skyline, and the complimentary breakfast meant they only had to venture out for two meals a day.

David let himself back into the room while balancing a drink tray and paper bag from the McDonald's across from Boston Common. He was greeted by the sight of Diana tapping away at her laptop at the desk in the corner of the room, black hair like a cascade of ink over one shoulder. She wore a ruby-red tank top and a pair of high-waist denim shorts, bare feet hooked over the bottom rung of her chair, eyes narrowed at her computer screen. She was the single most beautiful thing David had ever seen, and just thinking that made him feel like a dirty old man.

Diana didn't look up as he entered the room, which showed how well they knew each other; if he were anyone else, she would've been out of her seat with a gun in her hand before the door had opened. "Did they have the hot sauce?"

"Yep." David swallowed down his feelings in favor of tossing a couple of sauce packets in her direction, which she caught effortlessly, gaze never leaving the laptop. "Find anything good on Blakely Manor?"

"They have a nice website," Diana replied dryly, opening her box of chicken nuggets and nodding toward the laptop. "Pretty pictures of the outside, a bit of property history, but nothing much on its current purposes."

David leaned down to read, inadvertently breathing in the scent of Diana's shampoo, some heinously expensive thing from Sephora that smelled springy and fresh. He eyed a black-and-white picture near the top of the webpage. "Who's the guy dressed like Colonel Sanders?"

"Doctor Donald Blakely. His family bought the manor after the Vietnam War and converted it into a nonprofit asylum for veterans with post-traumatic stress disorder—not that they were calling it that then." Diana scrolled down to some photos of the manor, which was a vast, sprawling thing made of stone and high arches; to David's untrained eye, it looked like a cold place to put someone with mental health issues. "It stayed that way until Dr. Blakely died a few years ago—he had no known relatives, and as far as I can tell the place is kept alive through charitable donors."

David sipped his Diet Coke contemplatively. "Where is it?"

"In the middle of fucking nowhere," Diana said. "They don't list an exact location on the website, so I had to run a reverse image search." She clicked on another tab open to Google Maps. "The closest town to the property is Petersham, and that is the biggest thing northwest of the Quabbin Reservoir." She showed David a satellite image of the town, which contained maybe two intersections, a few houses, and not much else. "The back of Blakely Manor shares a border with the Petersham State Forest, and the main attractions there are a gun club and a priory."

"I don't suppose that phone number they list at the bottom of the site works?"

"It rang when I called, but no one answered."

"That means someone pays the bill—any idea who?"

"The property is held in a trust, and the executor is a place called Morningstar Holdings, which is almost certainly a shell corporation."

"Morningstar?" David repeated. He hadn't set foot in a church in decades, but he wasn't likely to forget Sister Margaret from Sunday school or her ruler against his knuckles. "Like the Bible? Because that's another name for Lucifer."

One of Diana's eyebrows twitched upward. "Well, that is about as subtle as a flying brick." She nibbled at a French fry, eyes narrowing. "What are the chances it's a coincidence Anton releases a drug with a name like Rapture and is also indirectly connected to Blakely Manor, which is owned by a shell corporation that is named after an actual devil?"

"Pretty damn slim," David answered. "How do you want to play this?"

Diana shrugged. "We could bring in Byrne, see if she can find more information in the cyber world."

Tara Byrne was a world-renown hacker and part of a group of misfit agents David and Diana had recruited to the CIA for an ongoing op called Project Renegade. While Byrne's skills could be useful in finding out more about the shell company, David shook his head. "You know if we bring in Byrne, the rest will follow. I lost both eyebrows the last time we worked with Devereux and Walker and I'm not eager for a round two."

"Wuss," Diana accused, but there was a barely-detectable fondness behind the word that made David feel warm. "Fine, we don't call them in—what's our next move?" Before David could reply, Diana's phone vibrated with an incoming call where it sat on the desk. She checked the display and frowned. "It's Anton. What should I do?"

"Answer it." David took a seat on the end of the bed and unwrapped his cheeseburger. "I'll do my best impression of a church mouse."

"Just don't start nibbling at the walls." Diana waited a few rings before she accepted the call, turning up the in-call volume so David would be able to hear Anton's end of the conversation too. "*Da?*"

"Dijana." Anton had a habit of calling Diana by her given name even though he knew she disliked it; David suspected it made him feel like he had more power over her than he actually did. "I need a favor from you, my dear."

Diana and David exchanged twin looks of surprise. They had both expected him to open with outrage regarding what happened to Otis and the fact that Diana was working with David. Maybe he didn't know about the circumstances surrounding his former employee's death, but then who had killed Otis?

"And what would that be?" Diana asked.

"I wondered if you would be able to speak with Sebastian. I suspect, although I cannot prove, that someone is attempting to copy the Rapture formula. I would like to make sure that information is not being leaked from him, but I fear that if I attempt to have that conversation with your brother things will turn... unnecessarily contentious."

"Do you not trust Sebastian, then?"

"It is not a matter of trust, Dijana. With the work he is doing, spying on Wolfe... it is easy to become complacent. Get back to me with his response."

Anton hung up, and Diana stared at her phone screen for a second before she did the same. "What the fuck was that about? The Rapture's selling out of Lavinge's shops, and nobody's tried to copy it."

"Evidently Anton's paranoid," David said, resisting the urge to brush an unruly lock of Diana's hair out of her face. "So Agent Johnson, what's our next move?"

"I will gather some supplies for a trip to Blakely Manor and talk to my brother," Diana replied. She threw a French fry at him for the *agent* quip and rolled her eyes when David caught it out of the air and winked at her. "Why don't you take a drive by the shell corporation? I'll get you the address."

~***~

Scarlett Vaughn was the proud owner of a two-bedroom, one-bath condominium in a cluster of buildings located off Warren Street in Boston's Dudley Square neighborhood, which was all winding tree-lined streets that featured an eclectic combination of churches, mosques, and funeral homes. Normally on a Saturday morning Scarlett would be up and jogging the block, stretching while she waited at crosswalks with music blaring in her headphones. But this particular Saturday she'd elected to catch a few extra hours of sleep in order to be fresh for the veterans' gala that evening.

She'd slept like a rock all night, so an alarm bell started ringing in the back of her mind when her eyes snapped open to stare at the ceiling. Her bedroom was the bigger of the two, with a picture window covered by teal curtains and an off-white country-style bedroom set she'd bought from a second-hand store; the wall-mounted air conditioner hummed away, filling the space with cool breezes. Scarlett glanced at her alarm clock—almost eleven in the morning, damn—and wondered what woke her.

A faint but unwelcome sound reached her ears: a shoe scraping against the tile entryway.

Scarlett rolled off her mattress, grabbing her M1911 off the nightstand and landing in a silent crouch on the floor. She racked the slide to check the load and was thankful that she didn't sleep naked, even if all she wore was a too-big Army t-shirt she'd stolen from Wolfe. Nearly everyone in the former sergeant's life had appropriated at least one for their own purposes. Despite being a gigantic overfunded war machine, the Army manufactured some of the comfiest shirts around.

She slipped out of her bedroom, walking on the balls of her feet down the short hallway that led to the kitchen and living space. Stepping out with her gun raised, she was ready to confront just about anything—except her father. "*Dad*?"

Peter Vaughn was in his early fifties but could've easily passed for ten years younger, with a thick head of brown hair and a neatly-trimmed beard that made him look like a business-casual version of Wolverine. The only thing that alluded to his past work as a soldier and later a military contractor were his hands—broad and scarred, they reminded Scarlett a lot of Wolfe's, but with less of a naturally gentle temperament. He wore a dark blue sport coat over a white dress shirt and a pair of chino pants, a copy of the morning's *Boston*

Herald folded under one arm; he set a drink tray from Starbucks on the kitchen island and turned to face her.

"I could've *shot* you," Scarlett griped, lowering her weapon. "What the hell are you doing in my condo, anyway? I thought you got the hint yesterday when I didn't answer your call."

"We need to talk," Peter replied, calm as anything. He sipped from one of the Starbucks cups and held out the other one toward Scarlett. "You still take it black, right?"

Scarlett put the gun on the counter and took the cup. The coffee was so hot it was burning her fingers through the cup and the little cardboard sleeve, and she recalled something Wolfe said once about the only thing Dunkin' and Starbucks having in common was that they heated their coffee using nuclear fission. She wasn't sure about that, but she did know whatever her father wanted, it would be annoying. "You get five minutes. Talk."

Peter leaned against the counter. "How's Wolfe?"

That was not the opener Scarlett had expected. "Since when you do you give a shit about the man you once described as, and I quote, 'an overdeveloped, underqualified nematode who lost his last two brain cells in an explosion'?"

"I care about Wolfe because he's the one you've decided should watch your back. I don't agree with that choice, but I figured you both might be feeling some strain from your latest job."

"He's fine, we're fine—now what do you *really* want?"

Peter shrugged his shoulders. "I thought you might like some backup. Guarding Christopher Sullivan and his family twenty-four seven can't be pleasant or easy—strategically it must be a nightmare. I could get a few guys from Vaughn Securities up from the New York office in less than two hours."

Scarlett paused with her cup an inch from her lips, eyes narrowing into slits. "In exchange for what? You always want something."

"I don't suppose you need a plus one for Caitlin Sullivan's wedding?" Peter asked. "I'd love to speak to the new governor about opening a Vaughn Securities office in Boston."

"Get out," Scarlett said. When he didn't move, she slammed the Starbucks cup down on the island, the lid flying off as coffee splashed in a circular arc. "Get *out*, and don't bother sending me money for the lock I'm sure you destroyed getting in here—I won't use it."

Peter sighed, and it was amazing how such an innocuous sound made Scarlett want to grind her teeth. "Fine, I'll go." He tossed the newspaper on the part of the island that wasn't wet and headed for the front door. "Call me if you change your mind."

"Like hell," she grumbled in response, her whole body taut like a bowstring until she heard the door close behind her father. She went to grab some paper towels to clean up the spilled coffee, and on her way to the trash can, the first part of the *Boston Herald*'s byline caught her eye. "Oh, come *on*."

Resigned to seeing another thing that would piss her off, she flipped the paper open with her trigger finger to read the whole thing: ***COPS STUMPED BY SNIPER AS PRIMARY DRAWS CLOSER: WILL THREAT OF VIOLENCE HURT SULLIVAN'S CHANCE AT NOMINATION?***

~***~

Lynette's was a specialty bakery on Broadway in Somerville, all bright colors and celebration shoved inside a corner storefront next to a Benjamin Moore, at almost exactly the midpoint between the railroad bridge and Powder House Square. Caitlin had informed Sebastian when he arrived with Constantin for the cake tasting that she'd chosen Lynette's not because they had stellar Yelp reviews (they did) or because they were willing to ship the cake a few hundred miles to the White Mountains for the wedding (they were), but because the owner was a cousin. And in the Sullivan family, you supported your cousins.

Sebastian hadn't been in many bakeries, nor had he ever seen this much cake in one place before. They were all seated on the same side of a long table, which was filled to the edges with cakes of all different sizes, heights, and colors, some adorned with intricate fondant designs and others covered in frosting. A card in front of each cake indicated the flavor combinations, and a perky woman in an apron—Lynette, he presumed—waited to serve their desired slices on tiny plates. Until a few minutes ago, Sebastian was operating under the (mistaken) impression that a cake tasting was less about actually choosing a cake and more a rite of passage for a soon-to-be married couple. Oh, how wrong he was.

"Why am I here again?" he wondered aloud, only to be elbowed in the ribs by Caitlin. On his other side, Constantin was frowning down at his phone. "Ow! It's a serious question!"

"You're here because we needed somebody who was impartial to help us try cakes," Ryan said, evidently taking pity on Sebastian while Caitlin *hmphed* and crossed her arms, like she was offended that Sebastian would dare question her motives (he questioned everybody's motives, that was his thing). "Besides, who says no to free cake?"

Sebastian knew when he'd been outmaneuvered, and ran a hand through his hair to get it out of his face. It was almost time for a trim. "No one sane."

"I was going to ask Jake to come too," Caitlin said. She paused the conversation while the various cakes were dished out, all of them getting a small slice of each flavor. "He never texted me back this morning. And I know he's still recovering from a huge trauma, but since he moved out of our place he's gotten distant."

Sebastian—a walking poster boy for how *not* to deal with traumatic events—took a bite of lemon chiffon and said, "I'm sure he'll come around. Maybe the change of scenery is doing him good."

"Maybe," Caitlin echoed, sounding unconvinced. She chewed thoughtfully on some chocolate cherry cake. "We saw you and

Jimmy on TV the other night at the Red Sox game." When Sebastian looked confused, she nudged him with her foot. "You know, *together?*"

Sebastian choked a little. "Oh no, Caitlin—Jim and I are only friends." When Ryan and Constantin both snorted in disbelief, Sebastian rolled his eyes. "I swear, there's nothing going on between us." *No matter how much I wish there were*, he added mentally.

Caitlin looked at him in a way that suggested she knew he was full of shit but was too polite to call him out on it. "Then you're blind, because Jimmy looks at you with giant dopey heart eyes whenever he thinks you're not paying attention."

Sebastian's phone buzzed with a text message, and he pulled it out of the back pocket of his skinny jeans. As if summoned by some supernatural force, the message was from Wolfe: *hey... are we going to the vet gala together? It's good cover unless you're busy.*

Before Sebastian could chicken out and give Wolfe a half-hearted excuse for why he couldn't come, Constantin looked up from his own phone long enough to say, "I have something I need to take care of tonight, so if you don't go to the charity gala tonight you'll wind up sitting at home alone."

"Go for it, man," Ryan encouraged. "What do you have to lose?"

Sebastian chewed on his lower lip, and his thumbs tapped out a response of their own volition: **sure, I'll have Constantin drop me**

off at the Sullivans. Almost as soon as he sent the text, his phone rang; it wasn't Wolfe calling, but Diana.

He pushed his chair back and placed a light hand on Caitlin's shoulder. "I'll be right back, I need to take this." He walked outside, the bell over the door tinkling, and leaned against the bakery's display window as he answered the phone. "Dijana—to what do I owe the pleasure?"

"Our father," Diana said without preamble. One thing Sebastian admired about his pseudo-sister was her intolerance for beating around the bush. "He is convinced that someone is trying to copy the Rapture formula. You wouldn't know anything about that, would you?"

Sebastian thought back to his encounter with Danh Sang at Ryan's Diner and the car chase after the baseball game, choosing his words with care. "Not directly. I have heard rumors that the Red Dynasty may have an interest in cutting Anton out of the Rapture business." He paused. "You should be careful. Sang is aware of more than previously thought—for example, he knows you work with David Wolfe. It is in your best interest that information does not get back to Anton."

Diana was silent for a moment, and Sebastian knew she didn't doubt the veracity of his information but compartmentalizing it for later use. "Thank you, *mali brat.*" *Little brother* in her native Serbian, something she hadn't called him since they were children. "I will not forget this."

~***~

Lacey lived in an apartment on Market Street in Cambridge that was smaller than Jake's former dorm room at Mass Art. The building was perfectly square and done in flat gray clapboards, everything about it screaming utilitarian; he wondered briefly who owned it, and if it was Danh Sang. He got the answer to that question when Lacey held down the buzzer in the vestibule and said something in clunky Vietnamese to make the door open.

Lacey glanced at Jake, a wry smile tugging at her lips. "Don't worry—this is where Sang stashes people he doesn't want getting caught up in police raids. Cops in Dorchester like to show up with battering rams when somebody sneezes. He doesn't come here much, though."

"Well that's a relief, since he hates me," Jake said, and he wasn't exaggerating. His testimony was the thing that got Sang sent to jail, and he couldn't imagine that had endeared him to the mob boss. "What are you doing working for him, anyway? You said on Twitter that once you were done with rehab you were going on tour."

She rolled her eyes. "If you believe everything you read on the internet, then you must buy *all* the shit they write about you." They got in an elevator that smelled like old beer and body odor, and Lacey hit the button for the top floor. "Last conspiracy theory I saw said you were in on all the killings and one of your brothers was the Mass Art Murderer." Arms crossed, she leaned against the railing at the back of the elevator and snorted derisively. "I mean, how cliché would *that* be? Sounds like the end of a bad novel."

A shudder ran through Jake that he couldn't control, but he hoped Lacey would write it off to the temperature change between the heat outside and the cooled interior of the apartment building. "You made your point, but you also didn't answer my question. Why are you working for Danh Sang when he almost got you killed?"

"Because I decided I liked getting high more than living in my dad's fucking shadow, okay?" Lacey snapped, any trace of a cordial demeanor suddenly gone. She shoved her sunglasses up on her head, revealing semi-manic eyes of a junkie. "You have no idea what it was like, trying to do my own thing with his name and his problems hanging over my head like an axe all the time! Maybe it's not the smartest solution, but I fuck Sang every other week and he gives me all the Rapture I want—and if he gets his way, pretty soon he won't have to buy it off that gypsy bastard who kidnapped me in the first place."

Jake didn't have a response for that, and evidently Lacey didn't expect one, because she was silent on the walk from the elevator to her apartment, which was the last door at the end of a poorly-lit hallway. She rattled some keys and opened three different locks, the door groaning on its hinges as she went inside, immediately crossing the room to kick the air conditioner into submission. The whole apartment was about the size of a storage unit, save for the bathroom, which was a sliver of moldy grout and bleach stink he could barely make out through a half-closed door.

Lacey went over to a scuffed-up coffee table near a couch that looked like it was older than Jake. The table was one of those that had a top that lifted up and off on metal supports so you could store stuff underneath, and from that compartment Lacey drew out a gallon-sized plastic storage bag that had apparently once been full of silvery Rapture vials. At that moment, it held exactly two.

"I know a place where we can get as much Rapture as we want and I won't even have to suck Sang's cock," Lacey said when Jake sat down on the couch beside her, handing him one of the vials. "There's a club downtown, but they only let in couples and I'm painfully single."

"So am I," Jake replied, cracking open the vial and taking the Rapture like a shot. It slid down his throat as sinuously as mercury and he relaxed back against the couch cushions, dirty as they were. "I'm also gay as hell. Doesn't mean we couldn't fake it, though."

Lacey pointed at him, drinking her own vial and tossing it in the direction of her kitchen sink. She rimmed it, but it went in. "Now *there's* an idea." She grinned, lipstick on her teeth and a wicked gleam in her eyes. "What are you doing tonight?"

~***~

David took the rented Toyota on his way to check out the shell corporation connected to Blakely Manor, and rather than use the highway, he chose to stick to surface streets. That meant the route to Medford took him through Somerville, and before his brain listed out all the reasons why it was a bad idea, he was making all the turns so he could drive by his old house on Putnam Street.

He and Angela bought the three-story new-age Greek revival before Josh was born, back when their respective jobs—trauma nurse and Army major—paid enough that they hadn't needed a mortgage. It looked almost exactly as David remembered it, the off-white porch columns and mansard roof paired with a new porch swing and red vinyl siding. The front lawn was still tiny like a postage stamp, and Angela must've kept up with her green thumb, because the garden near the retaining wall had just about doubled in size.

Nostalgia hit David like a punch to the gut as he rolled slowly by the property, and he meant to drive to the end of the street to parallel park and collect himself… but that wasn't what happened. Instead, he folded himself out of the Toyota and walked back up the sidewalk to his old house. He climbed the wooden steps to the side door, which still creaked like mad despite that some of the boards had clearly been replaced since he'd been gone.

Steeling himself, David hesitated for only a second before rapping on the screen door with his fist, one, two, three times.

Angela Wolfe opened the door a moment later, a dish towel thrown over her shoulder, her red hair tied back in a loose ponytail. In David's eyes, she hadn't aged a day, though in reality they were both different people than they had been all those years ago.

Angela's eyes went as wide as dinner plates. Her mouth moved silently for a moment, before she managed to breathe out, "David?"

David managed a crooked smile. "Hey, Angie. We need to talk."

~***~

Chapter Ten

Later in the afternoon, Scarlett arrived at Christopher and Melissa's house, a dress bag and Wolfe's covered uniform draped across her arms. She was barely in the door before she told Wolfe about what transpired between her and her old man. On the one hand Wolfe was surprised, because while he knew Peter Vaughn to be a Grade-A Dick, he didn't think he was brazen enough to break into his own daughter's condo while she slept. Christopher walked into the master bedroom, where the guys were getting ready; Melissa was holed up in her walk-in closet, and that was where Scarlett would be shortly.

"What's your dad's problem in life?" Christopher asked. "Isn't he that guy who owns the big private security company?"

"Vaughn Securities," Scarlett confirmed with an eye roll. "Trust me, he never lets you forget it." She handed Wolfe his stuff and added, "He offered us some goons in exchange for an invite to Caitlin and Ryan's wedding."

"That's... weird," Wolfe said. "What interest would Peter have in their wedding?"

"Probably not the wedding he's interested in," Kevin remarked as he came in the door next, a suit bag slung over his shoulder. "And speaking of the upcoming nuptials, don't you think it's strange that neither of them is having a party? I was *really* looking forward to drowning Ryan in a vat of tequila during his bachelor party! Isn't it tradition to have some kind of send-off from singlehood?"

"Hey, sometimes tradition's overrated," Wolfe pointed out, as Scarlett wandered into the walk-in closet and shut the door behind her. "I learned that when I kissed Billy O'Rourke when we were in Boy Scouts... which was also why I got kicked out of the Boy Scouts."

Christopher was lost: "But you're not gay."

"No, I'm bisexual," Wolfe said. When he got a blank look from Christopher, he added, "I like men and women."

"What? That's a thing?" Christopher asked, and Wolfe would've thought he was kidding except the expression on his face was a mixture of befuddlement and curiosity. "Wait, does that mean you think guys are hot?"

"Sometimes I do, yeah." Wolfe had to smother a laugh, especially since they were in the process of getting dressed and Christopher decided he needed to cover himself. "I don't want to sleep with everyone I meet—don't worry, you're safe."

At that moment Sebastian and Constantin arrived, but Wolfe only got a glimpse of Sebastian looking gorgeous in his fully black tuxedo before Constantin tugged Wolfe into the hall to speak with him. "You are aware your ass is on the line tonight, yes?"

Wolfe blinked. "You're going to cut my ass off?"

"And I will mount it on the wall above my fireplace if Sebastian gets as much as a scratch tonight," Constantin said, low and serious. His craggy face was lined with annoyance at Wolfe, but there was concern underneath it. "Not only that, but if Anton finds out I was not at this function as your chaperone he will skin all three of us."

"Constantin, I know you and I aren't best friends—" Constantin snorted loudly and Wolfe rolled his eyes "—but we both care about Sebastian." He put his hand on Constantin's shoulder, who looked at it like it was a cockroach. "Put your ass-cutting blade away. I'm not going to let anything happen to him."

Constantin regarded him for a moment before he nodded tightly. "All right. I'm trusting you. Do not make me regret it." He left, trudging down the stairs with heavy footfalls.

Wolfe ducked (literally, the doorways were short) back into the bedroom in time to hear Christopher say to Sebastian, "Are you okay with Wolfe being... bisexual? You know, since you two are dating?"

In unison:

"We're not dating!" from Wolfe.

"You're bisexual?" from Sebastian.

"Am I watching a soap opera?" from Kevin, pulling on his pants in the corner.

At that moment Melissa and Scarlett emerged from the walk-in closet. They were both dressed in full-length formal gowns, Mel's a conservative black satin number accented with diamonds in her ears, and Scarlett's an off-the-shoulder lace dress that was as red as her name, color-coordinated with her lipstick and a ruby pendant. They each carried little clutch purses, and Wolfe imagined Scarlett's gun was most likely strapped to her thigh, accessible through the slit in the side of her skirt.

"You boys ready?" Melissa asked. She looked at each of their faces—which ranged from confused to stupefied—before glancing at Scarlett. "I feel like we missed something."

Scarlett shrugged, touching her up-do and offering an arm to Kevin. "Probably nothing important. Let's go!"

~***~

The club Lacey knew was on Warrenton Street, which was less of a street and more of a scythe-shaped cut-through for Stuart Street and Charles Street South before it blended with Tremont. Warrenton was true to its namesake, an extremely narrow tunnel between tall buildings that resembled a rabbit warren. Incidentally, the street also ran directly behind the Courtyard Marriott where David and Diana had a room. Jake didn't know that, and even if he had, it wasn't like he would care; David wasn't *his* father, and there was nobody who was going to stop him from getting his next Rapture hit.

He'd hung out at Lacey's for the remainder of the day, and then she'd given him some of her ex-boyfriend's clothes to wear—leather pants and a patterned long-sleeved shirt to hide most of the scars. With his hair gelled into a spikey style and eyeliner ringing his green irises, it was doubtful anyone would recognize him as *Jake Wolfe*, and that was good enough for him.

A line started at the club's awning and ran to Stuart Street, but he and Lacey got there early enough that they were two-thirds of the way to the doors when they opened. The street wasn't what one would call well-lit, so it took ten minutes of holding Lacey's sweaty hand and pretending to be straight before Jake got close enough to the club to read the name embossed in golden script on the burgundy awning: *Balançoire*. He didn't remember much from high school French, but he knew *Balançoire* meant *Swing*.

Jake was reasonably sure it wasn't a swing-dancing club, which left a swingers' club as the alternative—a place where couples met to "switch spouses" and have sex with other like-minded individuals in a non-judgmental environment. He only knew what a swingers' club was because one had been a bone of contention (pun intended) in a divorce case that Misha's boss had taken to court.

Jake nudged Lacey with his elbow. "Who owns this place?"

Lacey swayed a little on her high heels, using her free hand to yank down the hem of her blue mini-dress. "Uh, duh? That French bitch who owns the wine shops?"

They moved up in line and were almost to the doors, but Jake no longer cared. He turned toward Lacey and grabbed her by the shoulders. "You mean Joanne Lavinge?" He kept his voice low, aware that a few people had turned to inspect the "couple" having an argument. He heard some cars turn down Warrenton from Stuart but didn't take his eyes off Lacey's mulish, confused face. "*She* owns the club?"

"*Yeah*, she does—Christ, what's your deal?" Lacey tried and failed to get out of Jake's grip; despite the broken bones and scarring, he had an artist's hands and they were strong. Her gaze drifted over his shoulder, eyes widening. "Hey, what are those guys doing?"

Jake turned and his blood ran cold at the sight of a dozen or so rough-looking guys with automatic rifles piling out of cars parked haphazardly in the middle of the road. A few of them had shaved heads or exposed biceps, and Jake glimpsed tattoos of a large four-leaf clover. That was the insignia of the Mahoney Mob, Boston's biggest Irish gang—much to the chagrin of Uncle Bobby and the boys from Winter Hill.

"Nothin' you need to worry about, sweetheart," said a guy in a windbreaker, a cigarette dangling from his lip and an AK-47 in his hands. He lifted the gun and riddled the bouncer with bullets in a frightening cacophony of sound that sent a lot of people running. The stragglers weren't so lucky. "Now, be nice hostages and get inside. We need to get Ms. Lavinge down here as soon as possible."

~***~

From a black Mercedes sedan parked near the curve where Warrenton Street met Charles Street South, Constantin saw the invasion of the Mahoney Mob unfold in his rearview mirror. He'd taken to keeping tabs on Lacey Stahl, for reasons he couldn't justify.

She was the approximate age of his daughter, but she wasn't *his* daughter; she was a drug addict who'd kick him in the balls if she found out the chief bodyguard for the guy who'd had her kidnapped was following her around.

Much like Lacey's Rapture addiction, this was a habit Constantin couldn't shake. Whenever he wasn't out with Sebastian or trying to sleep through blood-soaked dreams of Nicolae Ceaușescu's ruthless regime, he was tailing Lacey to different bars and shops. She liked expensive clothes and even more expensive liquor, and he'd seen her down vials of Rapture on more than one occasion. He figured if he couldn't reset her life to the point before she caught Anton's eye, he could at least make sure she got home safely each night.

Constantin was already out of the car when the Mahoney thug he belatedly recognized as Neal Joyce shot the bouncer outside Lavinge's club. The gunshot didn't surprise him, but the shine of copper hair he saw move under the club's outside lights did. Because of course Lacey wasn't at a swingers' club by herself, oh no—she was with Jake Wolfe. That didn't make sense at first, because Constantin knew Jake was gay (he had, after all, slept with Sebastian), but if he and Lacey *both* wanted a Rapture fix this was a no-brainer way to get it.

"*Rahat*," he cursed under his breath, drawing his Ruger and hitting the sidewalk in a crouch, crab-walking closer behind a line of parallel parked cars. Most of the gangsters had their backs to him, so once he was close enough he risked sticking a hand above the hood of a Prius in a wave and prayed silently that Jake was half as observant as his brother.

As Constantin watched, Jake made sure he and Lacey wound up as one of the last couples to get herded inside. By then there was only one Mahoney mobster left outside, lazily waving his AK at the shuffling hostages. Constantin nodded at Jake and aimed the Ruger over the hood, and right before he and Lacey were going to walk inside Jake spun on his heel and slammed a hard right hook across the last goon's jaw, making him stumble and fall to the ground. His fellow Mahoneys shouted curses but were trapped by the bodies of their hostages and couldn't get to Jake and Lacey before they scampered away.

They joined Constantin behind the Prius but there was no time for conversation before they made a bent-over run to the Mercedes, gunfire chasing them.

~***~

The Four Seasons was one of Boston's best-known and most expensive hotels, a sprawling monolith of brick and steel that took up half a block of Boylston Street in Back Bay and had spectacular views of the Public Garden. The night of the Delaney Veterans Center's annual charity gala also saw the end of the unseasonable heatwave shrouding the city, which was a blessing for everyone involved.

When Wolfe exited the limousine ahead of Christopher and Melissa he was pleasantly surprised that he didn't start sweating. He squinted against the camera flashes from the media gathered outside the doors to the hotel and turned to look at the street before waving for the others to get out. He felt naked without his gun, but the venue had a strict no-weapons policy except for their own armed security guards.

Sebastian emerged first and offered his arm to both Melissa and Scarlett so they didn't get tangled in the skirts of their dresses. Christopher got out next, waving to the reporters before taking Melissa's hand. Kevin tumbled out and Scarlett put her hand on his elbow, and Wolfe only hesitated for a split second before he grabbed Sebastian's hand.

Wolfe's phone vibrated in his pocket, but he waited until they were through the metal detectors to glance at the screen.

One text message from his mother: **we need to talk about your father**

"Shit," he muttered. David must've revealed himself to Angela, but why now? And why hadn't he told Wolfe *before* he did it? Since leaving his mom on read was never a good idea, Wolfe typed a quick *I'm sorry* before putting his phone away.

"Is everything okay?" Sebastian asked lowly. He'd stopped walking when Wolfe slowed down to check his phone, tugging them out of the flow of incoming guests. That allowed Christopher to mingle further ahead as they made their way into the ballroom. "You seem tense."

"It's my dad," Wolfe said, and Sebastian made a noise of understanding, because to say they both had issues with their fathers would be an understatement. Wolfe looked at Sebastian's face but only briefly, his eyes scanning the room for potential threats. Several people had brought veterans as guests, but he had the craziest amount of ribbons and medals—except for one man who was half-turned in their direction, a head shorter than Wolfe but built like a brick shithouse. "Flynn? Son of a bitch, is that you?"

Former Sergeant Flynn Walker laughed at the shocked look on Wolfe's face, coming over to shake hands and give him a slap on the back. Flynn was in his late forties but one wouldn't know it by looking at him, all barrel chest and brown eyes flecked with gold. His dark hair had gone salt-and-pepper around the temples and in his neatly-trimmed beard, but any lines in his face gave him character and there was plenty of muscle definition visible under his Army dress uniform. Where Wolfe wore the blue and green shield of the 75th Ranger Regiment on his jacket, Flynn carried the red arrowhead and dagger of Delta Force.

Wolfe returned the brief embrace before introducing Sebastian. "This is Flynn Walker, the only bastard crazy enough to get out of the Army alive and join up again after a stint with the CIA. What are you even doing here, man?" He paused, noticing the woman with Flynn for the first time. "And who are you?"

"Charlotte Tran," she answered, shaking his hand firmly. She was around Scarlett's height and age, with long black hair parted to the side in a smooth braid and dark angular eyes that were offset by the ochre of her skin and the burgundy of her lipstick. She wore a plum gown with a beaded bodice; her right arm was tattooed with an intricate gold and red dragon, the head resting on the wing of her shoulder and the tail curling around her wrist. Various other tattoos were scattered over both of her arms and her décolletage. "Please, call me Lottie. We're here for the open bar and to bid on sports memorabilia—if you know Flynn, then you know he loves the Bruins."

"Only because the Dallas Stars are shit," Wolfe said, absently echoing a statement from Flynn back when they'd run into each other in the Sandbox. Part of him didn't buy Lottie's excuse for a second—the part that remembered Flynn had spent his ten years separated from the Army working for the CIA. "Where's Devereux? I thought you two were attached at the hip."

"Oh, you know Dev," Flynn replied, waving a hand dismissively. His Texas drawl was barely detectable on a normal day, and nonexistent when he was working, so he and Lottie definitely weren't at the gala for fun. "He's always got a crazy project in the works, said he couldn't make it. Plus he hates shit like this."

Before Wolfe could agree with that sentiment, he caught movement out of the corner of his eye. A waitress dressed in an unflattering black suit worn by the catering company's staff was walking from the bar toward the back of the ballroom. Her hair was collected in a bun at the back of her head, but it shone a familiar shade of red under the yellowed light of the chandeliers.

"Excuse me," Wolfe said to Flynn and Lottie, and lower, to Sebastian, "I'll be right back."

He followed the redheaded waitress, trying to be subtle as he pushed his way through the crowd.

~***~

Flynn and Lottie moved on after Wolfe left, and Sebastian contemplated what they were really doing at the gala as he grabbed a flute of champagne from a passing waiter. Some kind of espionage, no doubt, but *what* kind? He took a sip and raised his eyebrows at the quality; he didn't know much about the Delaney Veterans Center, but evidently they were plying their donors with fantastic alcohol.

Sebastian walked the perimeters of the party, checking out the items up for auction and bidding on an autographed poster of Tom Brady that he thought Wolfe might like. The room was massive but warm with all the bodies in it, the scent of pricey perfumes and body odor mingling with shrimp puffs and some kind of *foie gras* that Sebastian wouldn't touched if he were paid. He kept an eye out for Scarlett and the others, but Christopher had no doubt surrounded himself with potential supporters, which made it hard to find them.

He stopped at the bar to deposit his empty champagne flute, and froze when he heard his father's all-too familiar voice behind him: "Sebastian? What the *fuck* are you doing here?"

Thinking nothing but a litany of Romanian curses, Sebastian turned around to face Anton. "Father," he greeted, inclining his head. "You're looking quite svelte this evening. Did you find a tailor to replace Otis?"

Anton got in his space immediately, standing close enough that their noses were only an inch apart. "Do not get smart with me, boy," he growled, one hand coming up to fist in the lapel of Sebastian's tuxedo jacket. "I asked you a question—and where is Constantin?"

"Not here," Sebastian spat, and before he knew what he was doing he was batting his father's arm away. "And get your hands off me."

Anton's face twisted, skin going puce. "You little—"

Sebastian never got to find out what little thing he was because before Anton could finish the thought there was a commotion near the front of the ballroom. The windows there faced Boylston, and right before their glass was dissolved by a hail of bullets, Sebastian caught a glimpse of the same black van that had terrorized Stela three nights earlier.

~***~

Scarlett was in the middle of taking a bite of mango and bacon bruschetta when the gunfire started. She threw down her delicious bread and pushed Christopher and Melissa until they bent double and ran them behind one of the buffet tables. Pulling her handgun from

169

the holster strapped to her thigh, she hip-checked Kevin to the floor to get him clear. Then she climbed on an abandoned cocktail table to look for Wolfe's ridiculous shoulder-to-waist ratio in the scrambling clusters of guests. Some of the ones in uniform were having PTSD episodes, while others were trying to herd those without combat experience away from the blown-in windows.

She spun a full three-sixty and didn't see Wolfe, but the added height allowed her to spot the dozen guys with black balaclavas over their heads trooping into the ballroom, some carrying sawed-off shotguns, others wielding battered M16s. Their tattooed bodies fanned out through the crowd, looking for someone—this was a different MO from the shooting at Stela, and Scarlett didn't like the implication of it one bit. She gripped the skirt of her dress near the split in the fabric and yanked up hard, ripping the seam and giving her mobility, then kicked off her pumps and grabbed them up, flipping them so the spiked heels faced outward.

"Need an assist?" a voice asked from below her, and she glanced down at a woman in a purple dress who had torn her skirt too, red-bottomed Louboutins gripped in her fists. She grinned at Scarlett, dark eyes shining with adrenaline. "Lottie Tran, nice to meet you."

Scarlett grinned back, sensing a kindred spirit. "You wanna go kick some ass?"

~***~

Wolfe experienced a strong sense of déjà vu as he chased Laine Parker through the Four Seasons, flashing back to the other night and his impromptu dead-sprint down Brookline Avenue. This was a much less crowded run and Wolfe was able to catch up to Laine, grabbing her shoulder when they reached the middle of the street behind the hotel. "Laine, I know it's you! Why are you doing this?"

Laine whipped around much faster than Wolfe anticipated and spin-kicked him in the chest, knocking him back a few steps. She stared at him with wide, haunted eyes, her scarred face ghoulish in the pale moonlight. "I… I don't know."

Before Wolfe could react to that, the unmistakable rapid-fire purr of a minigun firing on Boylston had him half-turning back toward the Four Seasons. *God-fucking-dammit, Bobby*, he thought.

Then he jumped out of the way as a beat-up Oldsmobile careened down the street, a young man with an enraged expression on his face behind the wheel. Wolfe half expected the driver to point a gun at him, but all he did was glare and put the pedal to the floor once Laine dove in the backseat. He had no hope of catching them, so Wolfe memorized the license plate even though he was certain the car was stolen.

He booked it back to the hotel, rushing through the kitchen and into the ballroom, which was a disaster of broken glass, trampled food, and ripped garments. Only a few people were inside—Lottie and Scarlett, along with Anton and a couple of his bodyguards. The rest of the guests must've stampeded out when the shooting started, probably through one of the side doors or the emergency exits.

"Hey, are you okay?" Scarlett asked. She was barefoot and her dress was torn, stray pieces of hair falling down around her shoulders. "I had your buddy Flynn take Christopher and Mel and Kevin outside—I'm gonna guess from your hangdog face that you didn't get her?"

"Close but no cigar," Wolfe said, and he did another scan of the ballroom, because someone was missing. "Where's Sebastian?"

"Gone," Anton practically spat, crossing his arms over his chest. "They took him."

~***~

Chapter Eleven

Sebastian was jarred back to consciousness in time with the rocking motion of the panel van. His skull throbbed in time with his heart, the source of the pain a lump above his left ear. A vague memory of balaclava-clad bruisers surrounding him in the midst of the chaos at the Four Seasons emerged from his sensory fog. He'd stabbed one in the arm, but he'd only gotten hit over the head with the butt of a gun and kidnapped for his trouble.

Opening his eyes to slits—an old trick from when he'd been whoring for his father and wanted to spy on clients when they thought he'd passed out—he glanced around as much as he could. He was on the floor of the back of the van, which had had all the seats removed save for the front two; he could feel through his tux that the vehicle-grade carpet had been removed as well, leaving behind cool steel and plastic. The masked men from the hotel were crouched around him, leaning into the turns and bumps of the road, their guns propped between their knees.

There was something warm and hard pressed against Sebastian's right arm, and it took him a moment to work out what it was: the minigun. Or the base of it, which was bolted into the floor of the van itself. It was a mean-looking thing, and he supposed that was appropriate, given the job it was created to do. Coiled next to it was a belt of ammunition, equally menacing.

They passed under a streetlight at exactly the wrong moment, when Sebastian was moving his gaze back toward the men. One of them saw the reflection of the whites of his eyes, and kicked Sebastian back unconscious with a booted foot.

~***~

"I don't know who you know, but it's somebody pretty goddamn important," Detective Jeff Kamienski said by way of greeting, as he and Silent Mark walked into an unmemorable conference room on the second floor of the Four Seasons. He was looking not at Wolfe or Anton, but at Lottie and Flynn, the latter of whom had joined them after handing off Christopher, Melissa, and Kevin to Frankie when he arrived in his squad car. "What are you, Feds? NSA?" He waved for Scarlett to put her bloodied shoes on when she was ready to hand them over as evidence. "You can keep those, Vaughn, we don't need them. These two got you off the hook."

"How the hell did you do that?" Scarlett wondered.

"We have connections," Flynn said, and glanced at Wolfe in a way that was subtle enough that nobody but Wolfe himself caught it. "Let's keep it simple and say we work for a portion of the government that doesn't exist."

Kamienski snorted. "That's an oxymoron—there's no such thing as simple when it comes to spooks."

Silent Mark tilted his head in a way that indicated he found the oxymoron humorous.

"Call us whatever you'd like," Lottie said, regarding Kamienski with an unimpressed expression. "The pressing issue is Wolfe's missing date."

Anton turned toward Wolfe with the slow grace of someone who was fully prepared to kill another human being. "*Date?*" he repeated, the single word sounding like it shriveled up and died in his mouth. "He's supposed to be weaseling information out of you, not sucking your cock."

Much like during their first meeting, Wolfe fought the urge to break Anton's nose. "He's our intern," he said flatly, and beside him Scarlett shifted, like she was ready to either keep Wolfe from launching himself at Anton or hold him down while Wolfe beat in his face. "And my friend, so watch your fucking mouth." He took two quick steps with his long legs and bridged the gap between himself and Anton so fast that neither the mob boss nor his bodyguards had time to react. "You want information? Here's some: I know you made a big donation to Christopher's campaign, along with Big Mike's and probably some others. What I don't get is why you hired Laine Parker to blow his head off—seems kind of counterintuitive to kill the guy you want to get elected governor."

Anton was silent for several beats, staring into Wolfe's unwavering eyes with a hard set to his jaw. "You have no idea what you are talking about. Where is Constantin?"

Wolfe's phone vibrated in his pocket with an incoming call, and he backed off a half-step to see who it was—speak of the devil. "Constantin?"

"Wolfe, we have a problem," Constantin said. For a wild moment Wolfe thought he meant what had happened to Sebastian, but it turned out Constantin had his own shitshow to deal with. "It's a long story, but the short version is I pulled your brother and Lacey Stahl out of Joanne Lavinge's swingers' club as it was getting raided by the Mahoney Mob, and—"

Anton snatched the phone from Wolfe's hand and started speaking into it in rapid Romanian, too fast for Wolfe's infantile knowledge of the language to follow. Instead of eavesdropping he told Kamienski and Silent Mark about his second encounter with Laine Parker and the man driving the stolen car. They pulled aside a passing uniform and asked them to see if they could get security camera footage of the incident from the back of the hotel.

Anton hung up and tossed Wolfe his phone in a careless gesture. "Constantin will bring Jake to your mother's house. He is, as my head bodyguard so artfully put it, 'high as balls'."

Wolfe realized that Constantin didn't mention Lacey being with Jake to Anton and filed that piece of information away for later. He refused to thank Anton for anything, so he looked at Kamienski and asked, "Are we free to go? Do you need statements? Because if not, we need to find Sebastian."

"I don't suppose you'd like some official help with that," Kamienski remarked dryly, like he knew it was pointless to suggest it. He looked at Anton and crossed his arms over his chest. "You know, Mr. Codreanu, it's getting harder and harder for me to believe that you're just a restaurateur."

While Anton brushed Kamienski off and tried to get out of an interrogation, Wolfe watched Silent Mark receive an evidence bag from another uniformed officer. Through the clear plastic Wolfe saw the bulky casing from a .50 caliber round and felt his stomach drop into his shoes—his fucking Uncle Bobby was the one who took Sebastian. He thought about telling Kamienski but discarded that idea for a few reasons, not the least of which was that despite his idiocy Bobby was still family, and he'd wind up in jail if Wolfe got BPD involved.

Silent Mark caught his eye and gave him an almost imperceptible nod.

Wolfe mouthed *thank you* in his direction and grabbed Scarlett's arm, and they slunk out of the conference room with Lottie and Flynn while Anton and Kamienski argued.

~***~

About a half-hour later, Wolfe sat at the dining room table in his mother's house on Putnam Street in Somerville. It was the same table he'd watched Sebastian fight for his life on three months ago, and now he drank a cup of coffee with his mom, his dad, Scarlett, Lottie, and Flynn. Wolfe and Flynn had stripped off their uniform jackets and ties and were left in their shirtsleeves, and Lottie and Scarlett had chopped off what was left of their skirts so they draped to the knee instead of the ankle. Constantin was in the living room with Jake and Lacey, and the only thing he'd done when Wolfe told him about Sebastian's kidnapping was shut his eyes and swear under his breath. Since Christopher and Melissa's kids were being babysat by Patrick and Maureen at their house across the street, Frankie took Christopher and Melissa there along with Kevin and volunteered to stay with them until Wolfe and Scarlett found Sebastian.

After they finished telling David what happened at the gala—and Wolfe mentioned the .50 cal round—he practically slammed his coffee mug down on the table and pulled out his cell phone. "Let me see if I can get Bobby, I'll be right back."

He went out on the porch, and Wolfe asked Angela if they could speak in private. They went into the kitchen and Wolfe bent down to hug his mother. She returned the embrace and he buried his face in her shoulder. He'd honestly been worried for a moment that by not telling her about David he'd broken something fundamental in his relationship with his mom.

"I'm sorry," he said quietly, pressing a kiss to the side of her head before he pulled away. "I wanted to tell you, and I should've, but Dad—"

Angela cut him off by placing her small but strong hands on his shoulders. "Your father explained everything. I may not agree with some of his choices, but…" She took in a deep breath. "As pissed off as I am, I understand that he was trying to protect us. I don't agree with it, but unless you have a time machine we're also not going to change it." She looked up into Wolfe's face and whatever she saw there made her forehead crease, one of her hands moving to cup his stubble-covered cheek. "You're going to find Sebastian, Jimmy. And when you do, please give Bobby a swift kick in the ass for me?"

Wolfe was helpless to do anything but smile. "Sure, Ma. I can do that."

~***~

In the living room Scarlett stood over Jake where he was lying on the smaller branch of the L-shaped couch, her arms folded across her chest. "What the hell is wrong with you? And why—" she flapped a hand toward Lacey, who was passed out on the big part of the couch "—are you hanging out with Lacey Stahl?"

Jake looked up at her with a glazed expression, his lips pale and stained silver. He shivered with the comedown from his last hit of Rapture, disfigured fingers tapping with no rhythm against his thighs. "None of your business," he sneered, right before his eyes rolled back in his head and he joined Lacey in the land of the unconscious.

"Fantastic," Scarlett muttered, and turned to face Constantin. He sat in the recliner near the television, staring aimlessly at his reflection in its black screen. "Hey… why were you following Lacey? Was it for Anton?"

"I have a daughter," Constantin said after a moment, so softly that for a second Scarlett thought she'd misheard him. She came closer and crouched down next to the chair. "I have never met her, but she would be around Lacey's age, I think."

Scarlett looked at Constantin with pale green eyes full of curiosity. "I had no idea. Were you married, or…?"

"*Dumnezeule*, no," he replied, chuckling at the thought. "Her mother was a woman I met at the *Palatul Parlamentului*—" the Palace of the Parliament, Scarlett recalled from Frogger's research on Anton, was in Bucharest and it was the seat of parliament in Romania "—while I was standing guard for Anton during his meetings. She was a secretary, and unlike the majority of the women there she did not walk faster when she saw me." He smiled, craggy face lifting at whatever memory was playing in his head. "She was so beautiful, and very well-spoken. I often felt—what is that expression? Tongue-tied, when I talked with her? I did not have much free time during Ceaușescu's regime, but I hung around her office whenever I could."

Scarlett smiled too, but she suspected this story didn't have a happy ending. "What happened?"

"She discovered she was pregnant." Constantin rubbed at his eyes, and Scarlett pretended she didn't see the tears glimmering in them. "I was ecstatic at the idea of becoming a father, but Dumitra… she did not see things the same way. She feared that my job, my association with Ceaușescu—with Anton—would be a danger to our child. And her point was only proven when Vladimir was killed instead of Ceaușescu. It wasn't long after that when the government began to crumble, and the Codreanus fled Romania. I begged Dumitra to come with us to America, but she refused. I don't... for all I know she died in the riots and never even gave birth."

Scarlett was silent for a moment as she absorbed Constantin's story, chewing on the inside of her cheek. "I don't know what it's worth," she said slowly, "but in my opinion, I don't think you'd be following Lacey around if you *didn't* have a daughter. Your fatherly instinct is there, Constantin—I see it with Sebastian all the time." She stood up and put a hand on his shoulder, shaking him a bit for emphasis. "If you want to find Dumitra and your daughter, we'll help you. Let's deal with our current multiple-crisis situation first, and then maybe we'll take a trip to Romania."

~***~

Aiden and Laine dumped their second stolen car in the parking lot at the Mattapan T stop and walked back to their apartment in the dark. Laine trembled the whole way, her borrowed catering company jacket too big for her shoulders even when they were hunched up to her ears. Aiden could hardly stand to look at her as they passed under streetlights and dodged around the odd drunken bum, and by the time he was unlocking their door his hands were shaking with barely-contained rage.

As soon as they were inside, Aiden crowded Laine into the nearest corner. He raised his hand but didn't strike her, and she lurched away from him with wide eyes. "Why the *hell* are you such a fuckup?" he hissed, vision going red at the edges. "That was our *chance*, Laine, and you couldn't even get that fat bastard Big Mike drunk before you ran away?" If one of Aiden's coworkers hadn't texted him that they'd seen his sister bailing on her temp job, he would've watched her get hauled away in a squad car.

"I saw—" Laine started to speak but her voice broke, one hand holding the side of her head where her scar began. "I've seen Jim Wolfe twice now, Aiden, he—he knows me, from before, from when I was…" She trailed off, squinting and breathing hard, and Aiden was reaching for the drawer in the little table by the door where they tossed the mail and their keys. "Aiden, *why* am I doing this? Why am I trying to—?"

Aiden yanked the drawer open and pulled out a vial of Rapture, popping out the stopper and jamming it between Laine's open lips. He tilted it up quickly before throwing it aside and clamping her mouth shut. She let out a closed-mouthed scream and tried to fight him, but he jammed a thigh between her legs and pinched her nose shut until she swallowed. The drug began to take hold in under a minute, and she slumped barely conscious in Aiden's arms. The doses Aiden kept on hand for Laine were stronger than what the average consumer could get, and he was grateful for that as he dumped her on the couch.

Pulling a burner phone out of the coffee table, Aiden turned it on and pressed the only speed-dial number. His call went straight to voicemail, and after the beep, he left his message: "Codreanu, it's me. I think my sister needs a tune-up—I'm bringing her to Blakely."

~***~

Chapter Twelve

It was past midnight in Somerville's Winter Hill neighborhood. In a run-down laundromat on Pearl Street, Sebastian Codreanu opened his eyes. He knew it was a laundromat right away from the smell, detergent and old socks and the sharp tang of bleach for the machines between customers.

In his experience a lot of laundromats also offered dry cleaning, and he'd been with Constantin on a number of occasions when clothes needed to be picked up. He seemed to be in some kind of back room, maybe a storage area? There were lots of shelves and not much light, just some from the street outside seeping in through a high window. His head hurt worse than it had in the van and his arms and legs were tied with rope to a wooden chair.

Sebastian realized he couldn't feel his phone or his wallet in his pants, and since they'd taken his tuxedo jacket he no longer had the switchblade concealed in the inside pocket. The fixed dagger he kept strapped to his ankle was gone too, but they evidently hadn't looked closely at his shoes. There was a hidden blade in the toe of his right loafer, one of those *just in case* things that Constantin insisted on but Sebastian never thought he'd use. So much for that.

The door to the room opened, and a man walked through it. He was easily as tall as Wolfe or David, but unlike them he carried a beer belly and a slight limp. He was around Constantin's age and looked it, with bad skin and prominent wrinkles around eyes like craters in his skull. He dressed like someone who bought their entire outfit from a golf catalogue, and two generic thugs (most likely picked from the crop left standing after the shooting at the Four Seasons) trailed behind him like lapdogs. "Mr. Codreanu, how do you feel? I told the boys not to be too rough with you."

Sebastian worked his jaw and spat blood on the floor, his tongue stinging raw from where he'd bitten it. "Well, I know you're not a Mahoney—they would never be this foolish."

The goons exchanged a look with their boss, and then the bigger one took two quick steps forward and punched Sebastian in the gut. Air escaped his body in a harsh wheeze, but he disguised his gasp of pain as a mocking chuckle—he was sure Anton would be proud.

"Let's get something straight here," the man in the golf clothes said, his accent all urban Boston, reminding Sebastian of slamming screen doors and Moxie. He walked around Sebastian's chair in a slow circle, coming to a stop in front of him. "This can be civil or it can be bloody, I don't care. But you're going to tell me where your old man is hiding the Rapture formula, one way or another."

The question spiked fear up Sebastian's spine because he didn't know the answer, but he couldn't let these *idioți* know that or he'd be leaving the laundromat in a garment bag. "If you're not Mahoneys, then what are you?" he mused aloud, looking up at Golf Clothes and his weathered face with a mocking half-smirk. "Winter Hill Gang, perhaps? Or whatever is left of it." The man's expression soured, and Sebastian knew he'd hit a nerve. "What makes you think I'll tell you what you want to know, hmm? I've been tortured before."

He earned himself another punch for that, this time on his cheek. It was hard enough to make stars burst behind Sebastian's eyelids, but it also rocked him back in the chair, which gave him an idea of how strong the wood was and how much force it would take to push it over. He forced out a laugh and spat more blood on the floor, making sure the edge of the spray caught the shoes of the goon who'd just hit him. All he had to do was keep them talking. Someone—be it Anton or Wolfe—would come for him eventually. He hoped it would be Jim.

~***~

"David, question," Scarlett said from the backseat of his rented Toyota Camry. She was squished between Constantin and Flynn, neither of whom were small in the shoulders; Lottie was perched on Scarlett's knees, hands tucked under Scarlett's thighs to keep her balance. "Did you rent the smallest car in existence, or do you moonlight as a circus clown?"

"I don't think circus clowns drive cars," Flynn mused. He tried and failed to give her more room by pressing himself against the door, and stuck out a hand to catch Lottie when David took the turn on to Summer Street too hard. "Aren't the ones that have the little cars usually the ones who do birthday parties?"

"Is this guy for real?" Frogger wondered over Wolfe's speakerphone. She was trying to help them out by tracking the GPS on Sebastian's cell phone. "Seriously, is *everybody* who's been in the Army crazy?"

"You have to be kind of crazy to sign up for a job where people shoot at you, Frogger," Wolfe replied, grunting when Constantin kicked the back of his seat. "Any luck finding Bash?"

"Not with that number—phone's either off or it got smashed." Some keyboard-clicking sounds. "You got anything else you want me try?"

"What about Bobby's phone?" David asked. He was driving slowly since they didn't have a destination yet, and thankfully it was late enough that traffic was cooperating. "Try his number."

Wolfe gave it to her, and a moment later Frogger made a triumphant sound. "Got it! According to his GPS, your uncle's in a laundromat on Pearl Street… which isn't that far from where you are now. Less than a block, maybe?"

David jerked the wheel and turned up Walnut Street, took that to Highland Avenue, and veered on to Route 28. Wolfe thanked Frogger and ended the call, and a moment later they parked across and down the street from a shitty-looking place with an awning that said it was Pearl Street Laundry. The big windows that were typical in the front of a laundromat were papered over, but not well enough that it hid the fact that were lights on inside. A dozen members of the

Winter Hill Gang milled around outside, all armed with handguns or poorly-concealed M16s.

Scarlett let out a low whistle. "That's a lot of firepower, and I doubt they've been told to ask questions first and shoot later."

Lottie craned her neck to see around the building. "Looks like there's an alleyway along the side. I would imagine there has to be a back entrance or a loading dock of some kind." Wolfe had heard her speak a few times now and he couldn't pin down her accent; it was a mix of California English and the precise consonants that came as a result of parents who spoke their native Asian dialect at home. "What's the plan?"

"I say we kill them all," Constantin suggested.

"I'm okay with that," Flynn agreed.

"Let's try diplomacy first," David said as he got out of the car. "Jimmy, you're with me. The rest of you scatter behind the cars parked on the street—I'm pretty sure you'll know if we need you."

Wolfe followed his father to the laundromat, and when it became clear to the gangbangers where they intended to go they all raised their weapons. David and Wolfe raised their hands over their heads, slowing their pace but not stopping.

"Not any further unless you want your brains turned to mush," a big guy with a red beard said, his M16 pointed dead-center at Wolfe's chest. Not exactly his brain, but close enough. "Who are you and what do you want?"

"My name is David Wolfe—Bobby's my brother." David was calm and collected, like he was having a conversation over a game of gin rummy, minus the rifle. "I need to speak with him right now. It's urgent."

Beard Guy snorted. "You hear that, boys? Not only is this asshole pretending to be a dead guy, he needs to speak with the boss *right now*!" The group of goons chortled like this was a hilarious joke. "You know what I need you to do, asshole? I need you to go fuck yourself."

A low buzz started at the base of Wolfe's brain, adrenaline warming his chest and spreading outward to his limbs. His body knew what was coming next, remembered it like an old friend. Some part of him, deep down, even *liked* the violence, because it allowed him to *do* and not *think*, sliding into the mindset of the cold-blooded killer the military had manufactured.

David sighed. "So much for diplomacy," he said, and grabbed the barrel of Beard Guy's M16, twisting it to the side before he drove it back into Beard Guy's face and smashed his nose into pieces.

Gunfire erupted, and the buzz in Wolfe's brain turned into a roar.

~***~

As soon as he heard the commotion outside the laundromat Sebastian moved, throwing himself backward in the chair. It splintered apart under his weight when it hit the floor, and he smacked his right heel against the linoleum, which made the spring-loaded blade inside his loafer burst forth. He kicked and caught one of the goons in the shin, blood spurting everywhere as Sebastian elbowed the other one in the balls and then delivered an uppercut to his chin.

They both went down groaning, and Sebastian grabbed a gun from the one closest to him—a cheap revolver with blued metal—and was up and pointing it at their boss while he was still fumbling for his weapon. "Put your fucking hands up," he said, flicking the hair out of his eyes with a well-practiced head motion. The snub-nosed barrel of the gun pointed at the fat man's heart. "I won't tell you twice."

The door to the room opened again and Sebastian went a little weak-kneed with relief when he saw Wolfe on the other side of it. He stepped inside when he saw Sebastian had the situation under control, hopping over the man who'd gotten his nuts destroyed and putting his hand on top of the revolver so Sebastian would lower it. "I know this is probably hard for you to believe, but you don't have to worry about him."

Sebastian trusted Wolfe enough that not only did he lower the gun, he turned his head to look at him with one wry eyebrow raised. "Considering he had me kidnapped and was about to have me beaten until I gave him information I do not have—yes, I *do* find that hard to believe."

David Wolfe entered the room next, scowling at the mob boss on the floor. "Bobby, you stupid son of a bitch, I *told* you to stay out of this!"

"You ain't the boss of me, David," the fat man—Bobby, apparently—snapped back, and he sounded like a petulant child. He seemed to process something, and his gaze shifted to Sebastian again. "Wait, you really don't know where your old man keeps the Rapture formula?"

"No." Sebastian tossed the revolver on the remnants of his chair and put a hand over the bruises that were no doubt forming on his abdomen. He allowed his eyes to trail over Wolfe's profile, taking in his strong jaw, the hard look in those normally soft gray-green eyes. "Who is this idiot, anyway?"

"My uncle," Wolfe replied grimly.

Sebastian suddenly and fervently wished he was still unconscious.

~***~

"Let me make sure I have this correct," Sebastian started about ten minutes later, once they gathered out in the front part of the laundromat, he was told the story, and the bodies were dragged into the alley. This wasn't the type of neighborhood where the residents called the police over a little shootout, at least not right away. "Danh Sang wants the Rapture formula for himself, and he tried synthesizing it from the product they sell at Lavinge's shop. When that didn't work he paid you—" he pointed at Bobby "—and the Winter Hill Gang to kidnap me, *after* you'd already shot up my father's restaurant in some kind of revenge plot—and you just *happen* to be Jim's uncle?"

Bobby was handcuffed to a radiator behind the rickety cash register stand, his expression equal parts embarrassed and dejected. "Yeah, that's more or less the size of it."

"And?" David pressed, looking at his brother imploringly.

"And I'm sorry," Bobby muttered, staring at the metal of the radiator like he wanted to burn holes in it with his eyes. "I didn't know you weren't clued in to Anton's operation, okay?"

"Well, this is the first time a mob boss has ever apologized to me," Sebastian said, "so I suppose I can forgive you." He glanced over his shoulder at Constantin. "That means you can't shoot him, *cavalerul meu curajos*."

"Pity." Constantin's smile was all teeth. "I saved a bullet just for him and everything."

Lottie performed a perfect reverse roundhouse kick, the bottom of her shoe less than an inch from Bobby's nose. "Speak for yourself. I could bash his head in if you want."

Scarlett looked at Lottie like she'd hung the moon. "We're best friends now," she declared, and looped their arms together. "I like you."

Wolfe put a hand over his heart, mock-offended. "I'm hurt, Scar," he said. "Did that friendship necklace made from half a beer cap and some string that I gave you mean *nothing*?"

Scarlett cocked her head and grinned at him. "That was a necklace? I thought you just wanted me to have your trash."

Flynn looked first at Lottie, then at David, exasperation and amusement in the lines around his eyes. "And here I thought our team was bad—these guys are a nightmare."

Constantin pulled out his phone. "I will call Anton, tell him I found Sebastian." A wry smirk. "By myself, of course. Should get my ass out of the fire and keep you all out of this." He clasped Sebastian's shoulder briefly before he walked outside to make the call.

Wolfe took the break in the action to pull Sebastian aside, one big hand curved around his elbow through the fine material of his ruined dress shirt. His hair was a mess, matted with blood near his temple, and a bruise bloomed purple on one sharp cheekbone—all of that combined made Wolfe's eyebrows draw down in concern. "Are you sure you're okay?"

"I'm all right, Jim," he replied, looking up at him with those eyes, the ones Wolfe was careful to only think of as *gorgeous* when he was alone. "A little banged up, but I have had worse." He blinked, long lashes casting shadows under the cold tone of the fluorescent lights. "Thank you for coming to get me."

"Of course," Wolfe murmured, and he drifted closer to Sebastian as they talked. He felt his face morphing into a soft, fond expression that he usually reserved for Scarlett or Jake. "From the looks of things, it seemed like you had the situation under control."

Sebastian shrugged, but the tilt to his mouth showed he was pleased. "Just waiting for my opportunity to shine."

David wandered over, hands in the pockets of his jeans. "Hey, Sebastian, can I ask you something?" When Sebastian nodded at him dubiously—David *was* the man who'd murdered Sebastian's brother, Wolfe recalled with a wince—he continued, "I was wondering if you'd heard of a place called Blakely Manor. You aren't the only person in your father's circle who's gone missing recently. Do you know a man named Otis Webber?"

"I have never heard of Blakely Manor," Sebastian said, his diction slowing with each word, gaze narrowing in David's direction. "As for Otis, he was my family's tailor. His wife passed away recently, so he closed his shop and moved back to Germany— or at least that is what my father told me. I am going to assume from the look on your face that is not the case?"

"It's not," David confirmed. "He's dead. Your sister and I had an unfortunate encounter with Otis a few days ago. From what he described, it sounded like he was brainwashed somehow at Blakely Manor."

Wolfe's brows furrowed. "What were you doing with—wait, is Diana a *spook*?"

Sebastian snorted. "Well of course she is. She's always had more freedom that me, and she's been spying on our father for years now. I figured she wanted blackmail material, but being a CIA agent is a better fit." He glanced at Wolfe, one corner of his lips twitching up in amusement. "The twist is that she's your father's partner. I did not see that coming."

"Believe me, the irony is not lost on either of us," David said, rubbing at his forehead. "Diana was recruited to the CIA shortly after your father brought her to the United States. She already possessed a... useful skill set. I was assigned to train her, and eventually we became partners."

Wolfe was working through new information, turning it this way and that way to try and make sense of things. "So when she drugged me and ransacked your office—" which had ended Wolfe and Diana's six-month-long relationship "—she *knew* you were alive? And just... didn't tell Anton?" Something else occurred to him, and he felt like an idiot. "That's why she was in my apartment *and* why she offered to walk you home the day Jake was in surgery."

David nodded. "She's been playing both ends against the middle for years now, and she's damn good at it." He looked at Sebastian again. "As soon as your father chose to immigrate to the United States he was flagged on several watch lists, but over the years other agencies lost interest in him when he appeared to go legit. I couldn't let it go because I was terrified he'd go after my family even if he thought I was dead, and then Diana came into my life and it was almost like fate. It didn't take much to convince the CIA to let us keep an eye on Anton as long as we were putting up numbers elsewhere. We even got to assemble our own team of… unique intelligence assets." He gestured toward where Flynn and Lottie stood, looking at something Scarlett was showing them on her phone. "You've already met two of them."

"You sent them to the gala," Wolfe said—a statement, not a question. "I can't decide if I want to hug you or hit you for that."

"I realize I don't have a lot of privileges as your dad right now, but I'd like to think one I've retained is being able to worry about my son. With all the near-misses you and Sebastian have both had recently, I thought a little extra firepower couldn't hurt." David shrugged his shoulders. "Besides, Flynn told me you met him and Dev in the Sandbox, so I figured you wouldn't be suspicious… at least not right away."

Wolfe gusted out a sigh and scratched at his beard. "I saw something about Blakely Manor when I was looking up Laine Parker—she's the sniper from Fenway, and I saw her again at the gala, posing as a waitress." He looked at Sebastian, apologetic. "I ran off to try and talk to her, but she got away again. If I had been in the ballroom…"

Sebastian reached out and squeezed his arm. "We can't change what's already happened, Jim. All we can hope to do is figure this out before more people get hurt."

"He's right, Jimmy," David said, earning a surprised glance from Sebastian. "Was Laine a patient at Blakely? The place is some kind of mental institution, at least on paper."

"It was her last known address, so I'd guess yes." Wolfe was hyperaware of Sebastian's touch against his skin, and the moment before he took his hand away seemed like it lasted an age. He forced himself to focus. "That was all I was able to see in BPD's records before Kamienski got shifty about letting me look."

David pulled out his cell phone and opened an app that required him to input a long string of numbers and letters before he was allowed access. "Let's see what else we can find." He sat on top of a washing machine, and Wolfe and Sebastian did the same thing on either side of him so they could both see the screen. "This is a highly classified database and you two never saw me use it in front of you—clear?"

"Yep," Wolfe said. "What is this, Lexus-Nexus for spooks?"

His dad smiled. "Something like that." He typed Laine's name into the search bar, and a bunch of results popped up. "There's her birth certificate, military record—and here's an arrest by the Boston Police Department."

Sebastian raised an eyebrow in Wolfe's direction. "You'd think that would've come up first instead of her last known address."

Wolfe snorted. "You'd think." He read the first portion of the report made by the arresting officer and blinked in confusion. "She was homeless after she got discharged? That woman's a war hero."

"Unfortunately, you know as well as I do that the Department of Veterans' Affairs is significantly lacking in most areas," David said, scrolling down. "Apparently she was arrested for attacking a civilian and resisting arrest. Interesting that the civilian's name isn't in the record, and the case never made it to jury trial. Almost like somebody didn't want it getting out to the press."

Sebastian pointed at the judge's ruling. "So she was sent to Blakely Manor for rehabilitation instead of serving jail time?"

"It looks that way." David closed the app, put his phone away, and turned his head to look at Sebastian. "I'll be blunt: I think your dad's involved with Blakely Manor somehow. If not on paper then in principle, and whatever they're doing over there can't be good if this Laine woman wound up becoming a gun for hire."

"I will look into it when I can," Sebastian said, exchanging a glance with Wolfe that said *I'm not doing this because I like your father*. "Probably while my father is chewing out Constantin for not being with me. I'll let you know what I find out."

~***~

Laine Parker woke up with her head pounding and her mouth dry, and she didn't know where she was at first. Wherever it was, it was cold… not just the air around her, but the steel table under her back and the manacles around her wrists and ankles were all freezing. It didn't help that the only thing she wore was a thin hospital gown that wasn't tied at the back. A suspended lamp on an adjustable arm hung over her head, and its bluish-white cast made her eyes hurt.

A door slammed and her eyes snapped toward the noise. It was a heavy steel thing, and she heard it lock from the outside as a woman in a lab coat approached her, flanked by two large, mean-looking men dressed like orderlies. The room around them was shaped like a box and covered in beige tile, and when Laine glanced down she noticed a large drain set into the center of the floor.

"Laine?" the woman in the lab coat asked, her voice tinged with some kind of accent—Russian, maybe? "I am Doctor Ivanova. Do you remember me?"

A bead of sweat trickled down Laine's temple. "No," she whispered, and she shook hard enough to rattle the manacles. Why was she shaking if she couldn't remember? *Why* couldn't she remember?

The noise that Doctor Ivanova made was one of disapproval, and she put a checkmark on the clipboard she carried. "Oh, don't worry, *dorogoy*," she said, and motioned to one of the orderlies. He went around behind Laine, and then something heavy and hard was clamped around her head—some kind of helmet? "You may not remember me, but I am in your mind somewhere. We will just have to search until we find that place, *da*?"

The other orderly shoved a clunky rubber mouth guard between Laine's lips, a leather strap covering her lower jaw a moment later. The next thing she knew, electricity coursed through the helmet and into her head, peeling her brain apart like onionskin. If she screamed, she didn't feel it, and nobody heard her.

~***~

Chapter Thirteen

Flynn and Lottie were left in charge of taking Bobby home and threatening him some more, and Constantin and Sebastian departed the laundromat in a car that Anton sent over as the sun came up. Scarlett and Wolfe decided to go back to Angela's to have breakfast so Wolfe could have a heart-to-heart with his errant little brother—whatever was going on with Jake needed to be addressed pronto. Since David drove them to the laundromat he brought them back to Putnam Street but declined the invite for pancakes.

Jake was still curled up on the couch under one of Maura Sullivan's quilts when Wolfe brought him a cup of coffee. The other part of the L was empty, so Wolfe's first question was, "Where's Lacey?"

"Left as soon as she could stand up," Jake replied, mumbling his thanks when Wolfe pressed the warm mug into his scarred, crooked hands. His hands had once been so elegant, and now Wolfe knew Jake could barely hold a paintbrush without being in pain; it reminded Wolfe of Sebastian and his piano, and not in a good way. "Go ahead and yell at me, Jimmy. I know I deserve it."

Wolfe sighed as he took a seat next to him, scrubbing a hand over his face and wondering if he looked as tired as he felt. "I'm not gonna yell at you, but I need you to talk to me. How in the hell did you wind up doing Rapture with Lacey Stahl, let alone going to a swingers' club with her?" Jake told him the story in halting pieces—

from his near-breakdown in the parking lot at Caruso's to now—and by the time he was done Wolfe felt like the worst brother in the world. "God, Jakey, I had no idea. You were doing so well when you were staying with Caitlin and Ryan, I just thought…"

"That's because I didn't have to *do* anything when I was at their place, except go to physical therapy or my shrink appointments," Jake said. He took a sip of his coffee and tentatively met Wolfe's eyes. "So… you're not mad?"

Wolfe chuckled. "Of course I'm mad. But as long as you swear to me that you're not going to pull something like this again—that you're done with the Rapture—then I'll get over it, and more importantly I won't sic Ma and Caitlin on you." He hesitated for only a second before he slipped an arm around Jake and bit the inside of his cheek to stave off tears when Jake leaned into him. Ever since the Mass Art Murderer, Jake had been, well, *touchy* about people touching him, for good reason… and that almost made Wolfe want to ask Jake if he was absolutely sure he didn't remember that monster's face, or voice, or *something*.

That train of thought was derailed by Scarlett from the kitchen: "Jimmy? You should come see this."

Wolfe gave Jake's shoulder a gentle parting squeeze and got up, walking back into the dining area to stand at the window with his mom and Scarlett. Three black Cadillac SUVs rolled up in front of the Sullivans' house, along with Nikki Shaw's Volkswagen Beetle. The SUVs, Wolfe noted, all bore a startling resemblance to the ones that had tried to overtake him and Sebastian on Comm Ave after the shooting at Fenway.

Only one of those vehicles had made it out unscathed, so the other two had to be replacements—but he still couldn't put a motive to the car chase, at least until Peter Vaughn got out of the lead vehicle. Scarlett was out the door and Wolfe was hot on her heels, taking the stairs down two at a time to catch up. He realized absently that they both probably looked crazy—her in her cut-down gown, and him in the shirtsleeves and pants from his dress uniform, both of them bloodstained from the fight outside the laundromat.

Scarlett reached her father first and from her posture, it looked like she stopped just short of punching him in the nose. "Dad, what the hell? I told you we didn't need your help!"

"Turns out that's not up to you," Peter said, hooking his sunglasses to the front of his Ralph Lauren polo. He spotted Wolfe and grimaced. "Ah, the illustrious Jim Wolfe. Still don't know how to use a razor, I see."

"Mr. Vaughn," Wolfe said, and made a point to smile in a way that reflected his namesake. "Still an asshole, I see. Was there a particular reason you tried to kill me and my date after the shooting at Fenway Park the other night, or do you just commit vehicular homicide on the side for kicks?"

Peter's grimace deepened, and to Wolfe's surprise he didn't try to deny the accusation. "I apologize for that. Vaughn Securities was asked to shadow you—"

"By who?" Scarlett interjected.

"Me," Nikki said, walking over from her car. Her black hair was in a loose bun and her lipstick was so perfect Wolfe wondered if it was tattooed. "It was Christopher's idea to hire you, not mine, and he never said I couldn't put someone more competent on the payroll."

"Ouch." Wolfe nodded like he agreed with her. "I can see how a former Special Forces operator and an ex-NYPD detective would be *way* less experienced than—I'm sorry, Peter, what shady military contracting group did you start post Nine-Eleven to take advantage of two war-torn countries and soldiers with PTSD who didn't know how to stop fighting?"

"As I was saying…" Peter sounded like he was trying hard not to burp or Wolfe had struck a nerve. "I *did* authorize three cars for that operation, but my second in command decided to take matters into his own hands when he saw you leave the ballpark. He thought Scarlett was with you, not Sebastian Codreanu. Things got out of hand when you took off, and I apologize."

"I thought Walters was your second," Scarlett said, crossing her arms over her chest. "*And* I thought he had working eyes in his head—I don't know if you've noticed, but Sebastian and I don't look the same."

"Walters was a schmuck," Peter deadpanned. He mirrored Scarlett's pose. "Fleischer's my second now."

Scarlett's eyes went wide like saucers before they flashed with anger. "You made my *ex-boyfriend* your *second in command*?"

"Is Keane Fleischer the same ex-boyfriend who turned out to be spying on you for your dad and was one of the reasons you left New York? The one with the weird Irish *and* German accent?" When Scarlett and Peter both glared at him, Wolfe raised his hands. "Sorry, I just like to know who I'm mad at."

By now, Christopher, Melissa, Frankie, Maureen, and Patrick were all on the front lawn, along with a dozen well-armed, well-suited gentlemen of various races with crew cuts and bad attitudes. They were all packing heat—Wolfe could tell from how they carried themselves and the tailoring of their jackets—and they all sported earpieces and non-reflective sunglasses.

Scarlett's gaze flitted over the bodyguards before returning to her father, her face hard like stone. "So if Keane's your second, where is he?"

"With the rest of the boys, securing the venue for the governor's chili cook-off in Nahant." Something pithy and smug wafted through Peter's expression like a bad stench. "Which you won't be attending—at least not as Christopher's security detail."

"You're fired," Nikki clarified, shoving her hands in the pockets of her blazer. "If you want to help, the best thing you can do is stay out of the way."

Wolfe looked at Christopher, who met his gaze briefly before glancing away. "I'm sorry, Jimmy," he said, and while he sounded genuine the words rang hollow in Wolfe's ears. "I have to protect my family. They come first."

The Sullivans and Nikki were ushered inside by Peter save for Melissa, who hung on to Frankie's arm. "I'll stay with her," Frankie said to Peter's men. When they didn't budge, he gestured toward Wolfe and Scarlett, who had crossed the street to stand in Angela's driveway. "She wants a minute to talk to them, okay? I'm a cop, I'll bring her back in one piece."

The Vaughn Securities goon squad took up positions inside and outside of Patrick and Maureen's home. Wolfe stood close enough to Scarlett that he practically felt her vibrating with outrage, so he put a hand flat against her back, between her shoulder blades. She relaxed in increments under his touch, the pink flush that had started creeping up her neck receding. Right before Frankie and Melissa joined them she glanced at Wolfe and inclined her head, a wordless thank you. He just smiled back—as far as Wolfe was concerned, Scarlett never needed to thank him for anything.

"I want to hire you," Melissa declared without preamble, smoothing out the wrinkles in her long black dress. In the daylight, she looked eerily like an old-style widow attending a funeral. From her clutch purse she pulled out a checkbook and a pen. "Not to protect us, but to investigate. You can go places police detectives can't, not without everybody clamming up." She scribbled out a check and handed it to Scarlett, who raised her eyebrows at the sum and tilted it so Wolfe could see. "Can you find out who's trying to kill my husband?"

"We can certainly try," Wolfe said, and while the retainer she gave them was enough to pay the rent for a few months, he felt kind of skeevy taking it. "Mel, you don't need to—"

"Yes, I do," she insisted, snapping the clutch closed again. She handed it to Frankie, who held it in both hands like it was a brick instead of a purse, and reached out to put a hand on Wolfe's arm. "I believe in you. Just do your best."

~***~

Over in Mattapan, Kamienski and Silent Mark parked their unmarked cruiser across the street from Aiden Parker's apartment building. The place was derelict even by Mattapan's standards, a five-story brick box on Blue Hill Avenue stained with bird shit and within spitting distance of the Neponset River. Kamienski was thankful the stretch of abysmally hot weather had broken. This wasn't the type of place that had air conditioning and the temperature went up ten degrees as soon as they stepped into the vestibule that led to the stairs.

"You know I've sweated through every work shirt I own in the past month?" Kamienski griped, yanking at his tie so it felt less like a noose. "It's pleasant as fucking punch outside and in here it's a goddamn Easy Bake oven, because this is where we *have* to be."

Silent Mark didn't look remotely uncomfortable.

Five flights later, Kamienski rapped on Aiden Parker's door. It was little more than plywood painted brown, plastic decals from the hardware store indicating the number. Aiden slid back a bolt lock and pulled the door open a few seconds later. Late twenties, a muscular six-foot-five with close-set hazel eyes and buzzed-down red hair. He wore basketball shorts and a Linkin Park t-shirt, and a quick peek behind him showed a run-of-the-mill bachelor pad, with a fan oscillating mercilessly in the background. "Hi. Can I help you?"

"Aiden Parker?" When he nodded, Kamienski showed his badge in unison with Silent Mark. "We're Detectives Kamienski and Hale, Boston Police. We'd like to ask your sister, Laine, a few questions about the shooting down at Fenway Park the other night. Have you seen her recently?"

"Can't say as I have," Aiden replied with a frown. He leaned a beefy shoulder against the doorjamb. "Is she in trouble?"

"We have reason to believe she might be involved somehow—an eyewitness puts her in the area at the time of the shooting," Kamienski hedged, watching Aiden's face for tells. The kid was good, not even a twitch of a lip or an eyebrow. "Do you know where she might be?"

"Last I heard she was going back to Blakely Manor for some kind of outpatient treatment." Aiden scratched the back of his head before he shook it a little, like an idea had evaded him. "We don't talk much. I'd check with them." He stepped away and added,

"Good luck finding her," before he shut the door in their faces, the bolt sliding back into place.

Kamienski waited until they were down in the cruiser to speak: "Well, that was hokey as hell. I can't believe I'm saying this, but I think Wolfe's right—they're in on this together and Aiden's covering for Laine. The question is, how do we prove it?"

~***~

Sebastian had expected his father to go ballistic as soon as he and Constantin walked through the door of Anton's Beacon Street brownstone, but it didn't happen.

Anton sat at the head of the dining table when they arrived—solid cherry, polished to a glossy sheen and big enough to seat twenty guests—sipping his morning coffee and reading the finance section from the *Boston Globe*. The rest of the paper was set off to the side along with a half-eaten plate of scrambled eggs; Sebastian tried to remember the last time he'd seen his father eat and found he couldn't.

When he saw them in the doorway, Anton snapped the newspaper shut and almost smiled, a spasmodic twitch of his mouth. "Sebastian, *baiatul meu*! Come in and have a seat."

Sebastian was shocked but did as he was told, sitting down at his father's right hand in an antique Victorian dining chair. He felt more than saw Constantin come to stand behind him, back to the wall, no doubt as perturbed by Anton's cheeriness as Sebastian was.

"Father… forgive me, but I did not expect you to be in such a good mood."

"After the debacle at the veterans' gala last night, neither did I," Anton admitted. "But you getting kidnapped worked out better than I could have predicted. Not only has Bobby Wolfe been castrated as the leader of the Winter Hill Gang by his nephew, but Danh Sang has one less weapon in his arsenal to attack us with to get the Rapture formula."

"So… you are not upset that I went to the gala with Jim?"

"Why would I be?"

"You were last night," Sebastian pointed out, resisting the urge to pinch himself under the table to make sure he wasn't dreaming. He felt like a gymnast poised on a balance beam, one misstep away from a broken leg… or a broken neck.

Anton shook his head, taking another sip of his coffee. "You misunderstood my ire, Sebastian. I was angry that Constantin chose to spend time he was supposed to be guarding you chasing down that Stahl girl at one of Lavinge's little side projects. Which I hear is no longer under her control, thanks to the efforts of the Mahoney Mob."

Sebastian glanced through the windows that looked out on the bustle of Beacon Street for a moment, thoughts racing. For the first time in months, his teeth itched for a line of cocaine. "You… you didn't plan the raid on Lavinge's club," he said, watching Anton's face for his reaction. "But you put the idea in Mahoney's head, didn't you?"

"You did not honestly think that fool decided to do that on his own, did you?" Anton asked with a chuckle. He folded his hands in his lap and nodded toward the door. "Get out of here. I need to speak with Constantin. Alone."

Reluctantly, Sebastian stood. He traded a glance with Constantin on his way out, and hoped the fact that his father and Constantin had been best friends since childhood still held some sway. Other bodyguards had been killed for much less grievous offenses than letting Sebastian attend a party alone. Even if Sebastian hadn't *actually* been alone… he's been with Wolfe, which was endlessly more complicated.

He stepped out of the dining room into a walnut-paneled hallway, but instead of going back upstairs to his bedroom, Sebastian checked around to make sure no house staff or guards were watching before he wandered further down the corridor. Toward the back of the house near the kitchen was what had once been a library; it now functioned strictly as Anton's office, and the door was always locked.

To Sebastian's knowledge, the only person who had a key was his father, and not even the housekeepers were allowed inside without Anton's supervision. Reaching into the back pocket of his tuxedo pants, Sebastian pulled out his lock picks and got to work. It didn't look as cool as it did on television, but he was able to get the door open and slip inside. This was uncharted territory, and he took a slow three-sixty turn inside the space.

Floor-to-ceiling bookshelves filled every wall, making the two cutouts for windows look like long, despondent eyes in a bumpy face. The windows were covered with blackout shades, even during the day. An ornate, heavy-looking desk took up the middle of the room, much like the one that had occupied the closet-sized office Anton had had in the back of Seams. There were no visitors' chairs or any other furniture, and the only things on the desk were a laptop computer, a green-shaded lamp, and a neat stack of pay-as-you-go cell phones still in their packaging.

The obvious target was the laptop, but Sebastian knew his father better than that. He only kept what records were absolutely necessary, and never on a computer; technology was too fallible and an easy way to get caught. That was part of the reason the CIA and other federal agencies had had such a hard time pinning any kind of crime on Anton for all these years. Unlike his counterparts, he hadn't kept up with the times—with the exception of the burner phones, a necessary evil after the death of the payphone.

Sebastian was about to start snooping when there was the barest whisper of a noise in the hallway. He froze, hand stopped mid-reach for one of the drawers, but the tension drained from his shoulders when Diana came inside and shut the door quietly. "Sister—you damn near gave me a heart attack."

"David told me what happened at the gala," she said, coming to stand next to him behind the desk. Her hazel eyes were ringed lightly with coffee-colored liner, and her black hair hung wild down her back. "I'm glad you're okay."

Sebastian inclined his head. "Thank you." He pulled open the drawer he'd been reaching for and raised his eyebrows when he saw it contained a pile of pens and notepads. "David told *me* you're looking for information on Blakely Manor. I do not think he expected you to break into Anton's office."

"Probably not. I rarely have an opportunity to sneak into the house without an audience with our dear *tata*—" *daddy* in Serbian, said sarcastically "—but somebody had to do it." She was watching his face for something, but Sebastian couldn't figure out what. "I did not realize that David had… confided in you."

"I doubt he wanted to, but after last night he didn't have a choice," Sebastian replied, and realized with a start that Diana was *nervous*. It was an emotion he'd never seen her exhibit before, which was why it took him a moment to place it. "Relax, Dijana. Do you think I care that you work for the government? You are probably the best position out of any of us to take Anton down."

Diana frowned mulishly at the use of her true name. "I do not want to take you down with him," she said, which surprised Sebastian. He knew she cared for him on some level, but until now he didn't think it went beyond her own self-interest. "Please try to stay out of this. Help me find the information on Blakely Manor and then get the hell out of here."

They started opening drawers, checking underneath and behind them, and it wasn't until Sebastian picked the lock on the bottom left-hand drawer that they found something interesting. It was an old datebook, and stuck inside its pages was a newspaper clipping. It was three and a half paragraphs of praise for the work of a clinical psychologist named Elena Ivanova was doing at Blakely Manor… and Boston social magnate Anton Codreanu had donated a significant sum of money for restorations and improvements to the facility.

"Ivanova," Sebastian murmured, and Diana made a questioning noise, leaning in to read over his shoulder. He tapped at the newspaper clipping with his index finger. "Isn't the Russian gang Anton does business with run by a man named Ivanov?"

"Mikael Ivanov," Diana confirmed, tucking her hair behind her ears. She wore simple earrings, a little silver hoop in each lobe. "*Moskovskiy volk*—the Wolf of Moscow. Never had the pleasure but I've heard he is a real bastard. You think she is a relation?"

"We both know Anton is like a spider—he weaves webs between people, and if they suffocate slowly, that's not his problem." Sebastian held the clipping out so Diana could take a picture of it with her phone, then returned it to the datebook and the datebook to the drawer. "It is more likely than not that this Doctor Ivanova is behind the production of Rapture."

Diana cocked her head. "But I thought Anton said Rapture was being manufactured in Russia and then shipped here. That was why he needed the warehouse from the Mahoney Mob, the crates of wine from Lavinge..." Her eyes went wide, and she shifted her weight like she was getting ready for a fight. "He's moved production to the United States, and he wants to cut out the middlemen."

"That's why he helped Mahoney with his raid on Lavinge's swingers' club," Sebastian said, and when Diana raised her eyebrows he realized she didn't know about that. He told her, then started ticking off salient points on his fingers. "Lavinge and the Mahoneys are distracted, which makes it easier for him to kick them out of the operation. He needs the Russians for their chemical supply, Blakely Manor, and Doctor Ivanova, but only until he locates his own supply of chemicals and another place to make them into Rapture. Danh Sang wants the formula because he sees the writing on the wall—Anton doesn't need Sang's connections at the wharf anymore."

Diana swore under her breath in Serbian. "This is bad. If Anton monopolizes the entire Rapture operation he will be nearly impossible to pin down. The money he'll pull in without having to give cuts to the other gang leaders will be enough to grease any palm in the city."

Sebastian agreed with that sentiment, but before he could say so out loud, his phone vibrated in his pocket. He checked the screen and frowned. "It's Jim. Is Anton still ripping Constantin a new asshole?"

Diana went to the door and put her ear to it. "Yes, he just said something about Constantin being a goat-fucking imbecile."

"Wonderful," Sebastian said, and answered the call. "Jim? I'm in the middle of searching my father's office."

"Oops, sorry." Wolfe sounded truly apologetic, even for such a small inconvenience. It was one of many things Sebastian lo—*liked* about him. "I've got good news and bad news. Good news is we're still getting paid, but the bad news is we got shitcanned by Nikki and Christopher."

Sebastian blinked. "Then... how are we getting paid, exactly?"

"Melissa—she wants us to investigate and figure out which of the candidates hired Laine." Traffic noise in the background, including Wolfe leaning on his horn and cursing. "Sorry again, some asshole in a Miata cut me off and I thought about crushing his little tin-can car. Anyway, the first thing we need to do is look into Governor Halliday, and conveniently enough, I know where he's going to be today."

"A chili cook-off in Nahant," Sebastian said, and smiled a little when Wolfe sputtered. "I got an invitation to that but never RSVP'd... do you suppose they'll be upset if I show up with a couple of guests?"

Wolfe chuckled. "I was hoping you could sweet-talk us in, but this is better. If you, me, and the fencepost—" meaning Constantin "—are busy in Nahant, who's gonna go with Scarlett to Big Mike's book signing a couple hours from now? He's our other prime suspect, and while he's not as hard to get to as Halliday, he needs to be... baited properly. And I'm being a concerned partner and not a misogynistic douche when I say I don't want her going alone. She's at her place getting ready now."

"I can help," Diana said from where she'd appeared at Sebastian's side like a ninja, and eavesdropped on his conversation through his phone's tinny speaker like... well, like a sister might. "Big Mike likes pretty ladies, yes? I think Scarlett and I can handle that."

Wolfe's response was surprised but grateful: "Thank you, Diana. I'd appreciate that."

The front door slammed, the reinforced reverberation of it echoing through the house. Ten seconds passed, and Constantin opened the door to the office a crack and peeked inside. "Get out here, both of you!" he hissed. "Anton read me the riot act and left, but I do not know how long he will be gone."

"Perfect timing," Wolfe said, and Sebastian heard the Mustang's engine in stereo, over the call as well as out on the street. "I'm here to eat donuts and detect shit, and I just ran out of donuts."

~***~

Chapter Fourteen

After the incident at the laundromat, David drove out to Petersham on Route 2. It took him about two hours, and once he arrived, the closest he could park his rented Corolla to Blakely Manor without arousing suspicion was the dirt lot outside the Petersham Gun Club. The gun club was directly across from Blakely Manor, which was denoted by a long, twisting driveway that led away into a thick cover of trees. A chain-link fence topped with curls of barbed wire cut through the forest, connected to a tall gate that crossed the driveway; next to the gate was a call box and a rotating surveillance camera.

It didn't rotate far enough to catch David hunkered down behind the steering wheel in full stakeout mode. His baseball cap was pulled down low and all his windows were down for maximum air flow. He was in the middle of sipping sparingly from a large iced Dunkin' coffee when his phone rang. "Hey, D. What's up?"

"You're out at Blakely, right?" When David made an affirmative noise, Diana continued, "I will not be able to join you. Your son needs my help with something." She explained what she and Sebastian had found inside Anton's office, and pitched Sebastian's theory about Anton cutting the other players out of his game. "My brother may be right."

"Son of a bitch," David said, and shoved half of a glazed donut into his mouth. Spies were different from cops and private investigators in many ways, but their choice of breakfast food was not one. "We've gotta figure out a way to nail Anton before he gets his hands on that kind of cash flow." The first thing Diana told him registered. "Are you trying to get back in Jimmy's good graces?"

Diana made a disparaging noise, her BMW purring in the background of the call—probably on her way to pick up Scarlett, David presumed. "You think I give a shit what Wolfe thinks about me? I only want us to be civil at Caitlin's wedding."

"Speaking of the upcoming nuptials," David said, and if he wiped his suddenly sweaty palm against the leg of his jeans, nobody was around to see him. "I... need a date."

"What about Angela?" Diana asked, honking her horn a few times. In Boston traffic, that sound was more common than the *click-click* of a turn signal. "You texted me that the two of you talked, and I just assumed—"

"She's going with Constantin." *And you were my first choice anyway*, he thought but didn't say. "Please, D? Don't tell me you were going stag."

He practically heard her roll her eyes. "Fine. But you better not step on my feet like that time in Prague."

"Hey, the dancefloor in Prague was *collapsing*, which was *Dev's* fault—wait a minute." David glanced at the road and did a double take, because passing right in front of him was a car he'd seen photographed countless times: a black-on-black Mercedes SUV with tinted windows and Massachusetts plates. It didn't turn at the gun club, but instead pulled to a stop in front of the gate to Blakely. He put the call with Diana on speakerphone and opened his phone's camera to take pictures. "Holy fuck—Anton's here, in his personal car."

Diana was as surprised as she ever got, which was fifty percent less than most people. "Is he alone?"

"It was him driving," David said, watching as the SUV was admitted through the gate. "This could be how we get him. If we found some kind of proof of whatever's going on at Blakely, he'd be done for."

"That would be nice," Diana agreed. "But somehow I do not think it will be that easy."

~***~

The first thing Laine heard in… hours or days, she didn't know, was Dr. Ivanova's voice from a great distance away, like she was trapped underwater: "Thank you for coming, Mr. Codreanu. I have some concerns—"

"And as I told you on the phone, those concerns are unfounded," a man's voice said, his tone snappish. "You have precisely one job, Elena, and that is to figure out how to get our weapon under control. We will not even discuss the fact that you killed Otis behind my back."

"I did not have a choice!" Ivanova snapped. "He left the facility and the failsafe mechanism was activated—and as for this wretch, she is hardly an ideal candidate! We have given her twice the recommended dosage of Rapture, and the electroconvulsive therapy is too dangerous if the levels are any higher."

Laine blinked, a slow, deliberate motion that brought her shadowy world into focus. She was in a cold room, strapped to an even colder table, something heavy over her mouth. She wasn't sure she could've spoken even without the gag; her entire body felt heavy and useless. Ivanova and the man were vague outlines near the door, along with a couple of white-clad orderlies. Everything smelled like burned hair and ozone, the slightest tang of urine and some kind of cleaning solution present as well. The room was familiar to her... and so was the man's voice, especially when it went from annoyed to irate.

"Give her the Rapture intravenously," he barked, "and turn the ECT up to maximum. She's useless to me if I do not get the results I require... and so are you."

Ivanova was silent for a moment. "What about the brother? Won't he object?"

"Her brother is no longer a viable handler," the man (*Anton*, the back of Laine's brain whispered) said, and she heard the squeak of his shoe on the floor as he turned to walk away. "Make sure she listens to me. Leave no trace of Aiden behind."

The man left, and Ivanova let out a long sigh before she came over to the table, muttering as she adjusted dials and instructed the orderlies in terse Russian.

Laine's last thought before they put the helmet on her head and the needle in her arm was clear as a bell: *who is Aiden?*

Hours later, when they took the helmet off and the needle out, her first thought would be: *who am I?*

~***~

The smallest municipality in Essex County, the town of Nahant was the bulbous end of a peninsula that jutted off the southeastern edge of Lynn. Arguably most famous for the thin strip of white sandy beach that followed the eastern side of the peninsula road, Nahant was home to around three thousand people. While Wolfe was reluctant to categorize any area as resembling a loaf of Wonder Bread—he was from a city touted by many as most racist in the country—the label fit the little island community well.

The drive from Anton's brownstone in Back Bay took about an hour thanks to construction on Route 1, and by then it was close enough to lunchtime that even Constantin grumbled about being hungry. Sebastian mostly spent the ride looking out the passenger's window, seeming especially enraptured as they drove down Nahant Road past the beach. That made Wolfe wonder if Sebastian had ever been to the beach, or done anything else remotely fun.

The governor's chili cook-off slash campaign rally was held annually at the home of a local real estate mogul who had his face plastered on every billboard, bench, and bus from Billerica to Brookline. About ninety percent of the guests were the same shade of white as Wolfe, though he and Sebastian weren't the only same-sex couple holding hands—wait, holding hands? When had *that* happened?

As soon as they were through security Constantin made a beeline for the chili smorgasbord, which was a series of long collapsible tables sheltered under a rented tent. The wind blew in furiously off the water, making the ladies hold on to their hair and the men squint into the salty air and remark on how a gust like this would screw up a hypothetical golf game.

To blend in, Wolfe ordered them a couple of local pilsners from the bar and they walked along the edges of the crowd. "You know we're not being paid to… to look like a couple anymore, right?" He raised his voice enough to be heard above the stiff breeze. "You don't have to hold my hand if you don't want to."

Sebastian took a sip off his beer and made a face like he'd just sucked on a lemon. "What if I *do* want to? This tastes like skunk piss, by the way—brace yourself."

Wolfe thought he might be exaggerating and took his own sip, barely resisting the urge to spit it back out. "Jesus fucking Christ, why does everyone and their brother think they can make beer in their basement?" The first part of what Sebastian said filtered through his brain and Wolfe stopped walking, tugging Sebastian to a stop too. "Are you serious?"

Sebastian looked up into Wolfe's eyes, that one always-errant section of dark hair breaking free from his otherwise perfect styling. "I would say 'as a heart attack' but I have always found that phrase to be… morbid." He took in a deep breath, fingers tightening both around Wolfe's hand and the beer bottle. "Jim, I—"

"Sebastian!" a voice exclaimed from nearby, and Wolfe glanced up to witness none other than Governor Halliday heading straight for them. "Wasn't expecting to see you here—how's your father?"

Checking in at a lanky 6'7", Roy Halliday was a former NCAA star who went on to study law at Harvard and was one of few people Wolfe had to crane his neck back to lock eyes with. He was B-list actor handsome with a smile full of Chiclet teeth and a thick head of sandy blond hair cut and combed to hide a scar from an unfortunate encounter with a basketball hoop. Watching him shoulder his way through a cluster of semi-inebriated people holding soggy paper cups of chili was truly something to behold, like a giraffe trying to shove aside a dozen warthogs and look civilized while doing it.

"Oh, you know him, always busy," Sebastian replied, releasing Wolfe's hand to shake Halliday's when he drew close enough. The smile on Sebastian's face looked real to most people, but Wolfe had spent enough time with him now to see behind the mask; he didn't like Halliday but didn't want the governor to know. "Governor, this is Jim Wolfe, he's a—"

"Private investigator," Halliday interjected, holding out one of those giant hands to Wolfe next—it felt dry and weak around the thumb. "Heard a lot about you over the past few days, including that Christopher's campaign fired you this morning." The Chiclet grin. "Makes me wonder what you're doing here, Mr. Wolfe."

Fuck, they'd been made. "I've been hired by Melissa Sullivan to look into the attempt on her husband's life," Wolfe said, and he knew this wasn't going to end well. "I was just wondering if maybe you'd heard something I hadn't."

"All I'm hearing is you insinuating that I had something to do with an assassination attempt," Halliday snapped, any façade of good humor vanished. "I know nothing about that beyond what's been reported on the news and the briefings from my security team. I would ask you kindly to refrain from asking anybody else here about this, or you will be escorted out. Have a good day, gentlemen."

~***~

"Okay, I kept my mouth shut on the drive here because I thought you'd get into a fiery car crash to avoid talking to me," Scarlett began, squinting into the sun at Diana and pulling down the hem of her faux-leather skirt. Paired with a red bustier top with a large bow pinned between her boobs and a pair of six inch heels, she felt like a weird cross between Emma Stone in *Easy A* and Meghan Markle when she opened briefcases on that game show. "But now I can't help myself—why the hell are you helping me seduce Big Mike?"

They stood outside the Barnes & Noble store off Route 1 in Saugus in a line of a hundred people that spilled from the doors into the parking lot. That didn't seem safe to Scarlett, but who was she to judge? If some Big Mike fanboy waiting to pay too much for an autographed copy of his crappy book got run over, that wasn't her problem. If she was out here long enough that she started sweating, however, that *was* her problem, and the only thing she'd be seducing would be a bonus-sized tube of Secret Clinical.

Diana folded her arms across her own inflated chest and raised an eyebrow. "Is it so hard to believe that I simply wanted to do you a favor?"

"Yeah, it is." Scarlett blinked mascaraed lashes, mirroring Diana's expression and pose. "You're a spook—that kinda automatically means you don't do favors for people. Not only that, but you screwed over Jimmy in, like, the *worst* way with that whole 'I'm only dating you so I can get access to your dead father's old office but I know he's alive and you don't' thing. You *always* play both ends against the middle. Why? What's in it for you?"

"I…" Diana trailed off, her shoulders slumping. "You're right. I do not know how to do favors, or make friends, or have any kind of social interaction that's remotely genuine."

"See, that's what I—wait, what? You *agree* with me?"

"I don't want to, but the truth is the way I was raised was not to make friends. All I saw was competition—for my next meal, a blanket, a sliver of soap."

"Orphanages in Serbia are that bad?"

"Ones where they train child killers are, yes."

Scarlett blinked again. "Are you shitting me? You're a real-life Natasha Romanoff?"

"Minus the red hair and fake breasts," Diana quipped. "Does that make David the bird-man with the bow and arrow?"

"Nah, he's more the Nick Fury type." Scarlett smiled, and she nudged Diana's shoulder with hers. She didn't doubt for a second that Diana's backstory was just as convoluted and tragic as she'd implied, but Scarlett didn't want to push for more info. "I could be your Hawkeye if you want."

Diana looked at her for a moment before smiling back. "I would like that." They were inside and almost to the front of the line, so copies of Big Mike's autobiography that they were expected to purchase were shoved into their hands by store associates. She flipped it to the back cover and barely suppressed a grimace when she saw Big Mike's headshot. "Why did he think wearing a fedora for this picture was a good idea?"

"Why does anyone ever think a fedora's a good idea?" Scarlett wondered aloud, right before she plastered on a fake smile and stood across a table from Michael "Big Mike" Draymond. "Oh wow, it's really him!"

When it came to nicknames, the person they applied to often didn't match the descriptor—for example, a gangster called "Tiny" would turn out to be the size of a Honda Odyssey. That was not the case with Big Mike, because while he was barely taller than Scarlett (and as Jimmy liked to point out, Scarlett was *not* tall) he was as wide as a surfboard was long. In person, much like in the photograph on the back jacket of his book, his face reminded Scarlett of Leonardo DiCaprio if somebody sat on his head. He wore a dark blue button-down shirt tucked into a pair of black Wrangler jeans and a pinstriped tie that was too short.

His close-set eyes went wide like saucers when he saw Scarlett and Diana, and the way he clenched his pen in his hand so hard it stood up straight was probably a good metaphor for something else. "Yes, ladies, it's me. Can I sign that for you, miss…?"

Scarlett forced a giggle out of her throat and handed him her copy of the book. "Scarlett, and this is my friend, Diana." She linked elbows with her Eastern European companion, who flipped her hair and batted her eyelashes in a perfect imitation of a Valley Girl. "We were wondering something, Mr. Draymond… but it's a little embarrassing."

His manager pointed to his wristwatch and then to the line, but Big Mike waved him off. "Oh, please, call me Mike."

"Okay, Mike," Diana said, her voice high, vaguely Midwestern, and completely false. "Would you, um… maybe come out back with us?"

The question was dripping with sexual innuendo, and Scarlett swore she heard Big Mike's hard-on hit the bottom of the table. He was up out of his chair and fumbling to prop up a sign that declared he was taking a bathroom break; his manager flapped his arms halfheartedly but otherwise didn't seem invested in his employer's business. The best part was that Big Mike didn't have any security personnel to follow him around, which made things easier on the femme fatale front.

Scarlett took one of Big Mike's clammy paws in her own and led him to a fire door. She slipped two fingers between the red push-bar and the door and pinched off the wire that triggered the alarm, then shoved the door open. They emerged into the loading dock area behind the building, and Scarlett led Big Mike a few paces to the right before she allowed him to push her up against the wall. They were in a security camera blind spot, and he seemed to have forgotten about Diana.

That was a mistake.

One of Diana's hands clamped down on Big Mike's right wrist, yanking his arm behind his back at an awkward, painful angle; her other hand held a double-sided combat knife, which she held across his windpipe. "Step away from her and put your back to the wall. Do not do anything stupid—you scream, I slit your throat."

"Okay, goddamn!" Big Mike yelped, doing as instructed, his face gone blotchy purple with shock and fear. When Diana released her grip on his wrist he smacked both his palms flat against the brick at his sides, watching her and Scarlett like a gazelle eyeballing a pair of cheetahs. "Holy mother of Christ, what do you want?"

"We've got a couple of questions for you, Big Mike," Scarlett told him, wiping residue from his damp hands off her shoulders. "You either tell us what we wanna know, or the footage from the camera hidden behind this atrocious bow on my top can go viral on Twitter in under ten minutes. Your choice."

Big Mike's eyes went so wide she was afraid they'd fall out of his head. There was no hyper-masculine posturing or bargaining, only fear. From the pictures Scarlett had seen she thought Big Mike's wife was capable of crushing a tree trunk between her thighs, so his reaction matched the possible outcome. "What…" His voice cracked, and he cleared his throat to try again. "What do you want to know?"

~***~

David had contorted himself in every way possible behind the wheel of the Camry, but after almost two hours of watching Blakely Manor for any more activity he couldn't feel his ass and one of his legs. His phone buzzed in the cup holder, and when he glanced down at it he wasn't surprised to see it was Dev calling—what surprised him was that it was a video call. "Hey, blondie," he said after he answered. "Make any progress on the chip I pulled from Otis's brain?"

Adam "Dev" Devereux shot him a crooked smile from the other side of the call, and David realized when Dev's long-fingered hands came into the frame that it was Flynn holding the phone while his partner worked. With a youthful face and big blue eyes, Dev looked less like he was pushing thirty and more like he should be at college orientation, but David knew better. He was the best explosive ordnance disposal technician the Army ever had and a literal genius in a lanky, kind-hearted, and occasionally smart-mouthed body.

"Would we be calling if he hadn't?" Flynn countered, panning down to Dev's workstation and showcasing the dismembered parts of the chip. "Tell him what you told me, hoss."

"As far as I can tell, this chip wasn't much more than a glorified battery," Dev said, the tenor of his voice surprisingly deep when paired with his boyish features. He held the outer casing of the chip—which was plastic and almost completely melted—in a pair of tweezers, and moved it closer to the phone. "See this? The circuitry was overheated intentionally, and the resulting current drove the chip straight through Otis's spinal cord."

Based on what David saw in the moments leading up to Otis's death that tracked, but he was still confused. "How did his killer get the chip to overheat remotely?"

"That's the interesting part." Dev put down the outer casing and picked up a tiny circuit board with the tweezers, its surface charred black. "At first I thought this was from a long-range radio, but it's got the wrong kind of wiring. I showed it to Flynn, and he said—"

"That it looks an awful lot like a timing device," Flynn interjected, elbowing Dev good-naturedly. "Which is funny considering *you're* supposed to be the bomb nerd."

"And is it?" David wanted them to speed this along in case anything interesting happened across the street, but also because he had to piss and he wasn't about to whip out his Dunkin' cup in front of them. "A timing device, I mean."

"Yes it is," Dev confirmed, putting the tweezers down and taking the phone from Flynn. He raked a hand through his shaggy blond hair. "My best guess is that this chip was planted in Otis while he was at Blakely Manor and the timer started counting down when he left the property. It was probably insurance in case whatever they did to try and make him forget what he knew about Anton didn't work." His expression twisted sympathetically. "There was nothing you could've done for him, David. I know that doesn't make it better, but…"

"You're right, it doesn't make it better," David said, rubbing his jaw and sighing. "But at least now we know what happened. Thanks for the info, guys."

~***~

Wolfe, Sebastian, and Constantin met up with Scarlett and Diana at the Dunkin' off Central Square in Lynn, across from the elevated tracks for the Newburyport/Rockport T line. The train roared by at the same time the five of them sat down at a big table in the rear corner, a box of a dozen donuts open for sharing. They were the only people in the shop besides the workers, and would be until the folks experiencing their afternoon caffeine crashes stopped in around three o'clock.

"So get this," Wolfe began, taking a seat with his back to the wall, across from Scarlett. She'd changed out of the outfit from the picture she'd texted him earlier (with the caption "send help my boobs hurt") into a Thin Lizzy t-shirt and aquamarine short-shorts. "The governor got super cagey as soon as he figured out why we were at the chili cook-off—"

Constantin snorted out a mouthful of donut crumbs. "That event is an insult to chili connoisseurs everywhere."

Wolfe shot him a look. "*Anyway*, I expected him to have a less than positive reaction... but it got me thinking about something. Why would Anton want the candidate he's been backing to die? It doesn't make any sense."

"I hate to make this more confusing," Scarlett said, "but Big Mike says he was paid to get into the race... by Anton. He has several mistresses—shocking, I know—and it takes a lot of moolah to keep them all happy." She glanced at Sebastian. "Plus he said your father was very convincing. I have the feeling there may have been some blackmail involved."

"It would not surprise me." Sebastian had one hand wrapped around a large iced coffee so full of cream and sugar it was almost white. His other hand rested on his thigh, and looked *awfully* tempting to hold... Wolfe forced himself to pay attention to the conversation, and shoved a donut in his mouth. "As well all know, my father has many ways of manipulating people. I have a hard time believing he is not in bed with the governor in some capacity, even if it is not through his reelection campaign."

Diana drummed her fingers on the tabletop. "Big Mike was coerced by Anton into running for governor, Christopher has received large donations and public support from Anton, and we suspect but cannot prove that he was or is involved with Governor Halliday." She looked around at each of them. "What's the endgame? How do these things further Anton's ambitions?"

"I'm not sure," Wolfe admitted, licking some stray chocolate off his thumb. Dunks made a decent donut (was there such a thing as a *bad* donut?), but in his book nothing beat Kane's. "And I think the only way we're gonna find out is if we can take a peek at Halliday's finances."

"Time for a visit to Frogger?" Constantin asked, taking the lid off his coffee (he was the only one who'd ordered hot) and blowing in a vain attempt to cool it to an ingestible temperature. "I like her. She's tough."

"Yes, she is," Diana agreed, and pulled out her cell phone. "I believe she and I have a mutual friend who may be able to assist us further. Let me see if she is available."

~***~

The asset stood in an alleyway somewhere in Malden that stank of garbage and feces, a silenced pistol held down along her leg. She stared straight ahead, aware of the bad smells and the sun beating on

234

the top of her head, but she was focused on one thing: her handler. He was on her left side, one hand in the pocket of his trousers, the other one holding a lit cigarette. He brought it to his mouth and took a drag. He took six more before the redheaded man arrived, silhouetted like a target a shooting range with the street at his back.

"Lainey?" The man took a hesitant step forward and then he saw her eyes. She had seen them too, in a mirror at Blakely Manor while an orderly watched her get dressed. They were blank and hard, like twin sapphires set into her face. "Anton… what did you do to her?"

Her handler's lips quirked upward, and he dropped his cigarette on the pavement and stubbed it out with the toe of his loafer. "I improved her, Aiden. She is not your sister, not anymore—she's better."

The man took another step, quickly, but the asset was quicker to raise her weapon and aim it at his heart.

"That's close enough," her handler chided, sliding his second hand into his pocket to match the first. "She doesn't know who you are, Aiden."

The man—Aiden, evidently—stared first at the asset, then at her handler, his expression morphing from disbelief to fear. "Why? Why would you go to all this trouble to assassinate a fucking gubernatorial candidate?"

"Stupid boy," her handler spat. "It was never about Christopher. He was the bait, and you and your sister were so caught up in hating him that you didn't see my trap. I could not have predicted those idiots from Winter Hill would strafe my restaurant, but as it turns out, it saved me the trouble of convincing Christopher to hire his sister's ex for protection. I knew as soon as Laine saw Jim Wolfe she would miss her shot, and I took advantage of the resulting downward spiral. Now I have an assassin that is totally in my control, and will not tire until she kills Christopher… and then the man who ruined my life."

"You're crazy," Aiden said, his voice quaking. He held out a hand toward the asset and took a half-step in her direction. "Lainey, please—"

She dropped her arm and fired a warning shot at his feet, a loud pop issuing from the silencer. He danced backward, away from the bullet where it had struck near his shoe, and looked at her like a wounded dog, mangy and confused. The asset looked back at him, dull but steady and fully prepared to put her next shot in his chest.

Her handler waved dismissively. "You should go, Aiden. We would not want you getting hurt, after all." He turned and headed for his car, which was parked at the other end of the alley. "Come along, *ucigaş*."

The asset followed him and did not look back.

~***~

Chapter Fifteen

Frogger owned a house on Sanborn Avenue in West Roxbury, equidistant between Millennium Park and Bellevue Hill, both beautiful green areas that saw plenty of use by the locals. Her house was partially hidden from the road by several tall oak trees, a gravel driveway leading to a little two-bedroom bungalow with a dark-shingled roof and green siding. The windows were open, curtains fluttering in the breeze, and a car Wolfe didn't recognize sat in front of the garage next to Frogger's Toyota 4Runner. It was a Corvette, but unlike Scarlett's it was brand new and bright orange. Wolfe presumed it belonged to the mutual friend Diana mentioned back at Dunkin'. He parked the Mustang and got out with Sebastian and Constantin, Diana and Scarlett exiting the Beemer at the same time.

They approached the house as a group, and Wolfe could hear women laughing before he got through the screen door. "Started the party without us, huh?"

Frogger left her seat on the couch and her laptop on the coffee table to hug him, standing on her toes to wrap her arms around his neck. "Sorry, Sarge, but Tara and Lottie beat you here."

Lottie Tran sat in a bright purple wingback chair, a Bugs Bunny mug full of coffee balanced on her knee. Her hair was braided down her back and she wore no makeup; instead of a ball gown, she had on a loose button-down blouse and skinny jeans tucked into combat boots. She twiddled her fingers in a wave. "Hey, boss lady."

"For the last time, Lottie, I am not your boss," Diana said, rolling her eyes in a good-natured way. She walked over to stand next to the third woman in the room, who had a hacking rig propped in her lap. "Everyone, this is Tara Byrne. Tara, this is... well, everyone. I'm sure you've done background on them all."

Tara smiled at them, a lip ring glimmering at the corner of her mouth as she pushed a pair of square-framed black glasses up her nose. She was around Frogger's age, with straight blonde hair that hung to her shoulders, blue eyes, and a square jaw. She wore a strappy white dress patterned with palm fronds and a pair of worn-out Chuck Taylors, and sat in a manual wheelchair that had been spray-painted blue, pink, and white. "Only one deep dive on everybody—I tried not to be too invasive." She tapped at her keyboard with nails painted pastel yellow. "Now, when it comes to Governor Halliday's finances, that's a different story."

"Tara and I were friends back at MIT," Frogger explained, bringing over a serving tray piled full with coffee mugs, creamer, and an honest-to-God sugar bowl. And even though they'd just gotten done slugging down large coffees at Dunks, everybody grabbed a cup and made the necessary adjustments to it before finding a place to sit down. "Of *course* she winds up working for a super-secret intelligence agency and I'm still doing freelance."

"Emphasis on the super-secret, please," Lottie said, shifting in her chair. "Technically we're on the books as a think-tank."

Scarlett raised an eyebrow from where she was squished into the loveseat between Sebastian and Constantin. "Are think-tanks actually a thing? I thought that was a bullshit job people had in movies."

"I did too, but you'd be surprised how many people buy it without asking a single follow-up question," Tara said, tapping a few more keys before she glanced at Wolfe. "Are you cop friends going to get here soon? I'd rather only explain this once if I can."

With the perfect timing that only police officers and background dancers possessed, Detectives Kamienski and Silent Mark arrived, their unmarked cruiser spitting gravel as it blocks the end of Frogger's driveway. They were inside and set up with coffee a moment later, and Wolfe made quick introductions between them and Tara.

"Alrighty, so here's what we found," Frogger said, leaning forward with her elbows on her thighs, hands clasped between her knees. "Before he got elected governor, Halliday was the namesake CEO of a major pharmaceutical company. While that's not a secret—it was all over the news in the last election cycle—it's relevant to us because one of Anton's shell corporations had investments in Halliday's business."

"Interesting, but not illegal," Constantin said, crossing his arms over his chest. "You would not have stopped there."

Tara snorted. "Not hardly. This is where it gets a little difficult to follow, but I'll bullet point it for you: the governor was supposed to give up control of Halliday Pharmaceuticals before he took office. He no longer manages the company nor does he own stock, but that doesn't mean he's not involved—on the contrary, it turns out the new CEO is Halliday's college roommate, and the biggest shareholder? Anton's shell corp, Morningstar Holdings."

"Shit." Diana pinched the bridge of her nose, which was as close to stressed as Wolfe had ever seen her. "Morningstar Holdings owns Blakely Manor. David was out in Petersham this morning, and he saw Anton's car go through the gates."

Kamienski shook his head in disgust. "Guess we know why all those zoning changes and other laws Anton used the Mass Art Murderer to get through never got any pushback from the governor's office." He snapped his fingers and pointed at Wolfe. "He *wants* Halliday to win the election, doesn't he? But he can't be too obvious about it, so—"

"He puts money on every horse in the race," Wolfe said, picking up on the idea. "And in the case of Big Mike, he drags the horse out of the goddamn stable. No one would suspect Anton was involved, because he has enough ways of disguising his wealth that it's hard to trace back to him."

Scarlett jumped in next, coffee sloshing out of her mug in her haste to set it down. "I bet everything was peachy-keen, until Christopher's campaign started gaining too much momentum. The shooting at Stela made things worse for Anton because it played the sympathy card in Christopher's favor... but all the sympathy in the world is worth nothing if you're dead."

"And then Halliday has zero competition and he wins reelection in a landslide," Frogger finished, glancing around at all of them over the tops of her glasses. "Problem is, all of this is circumstantial at best and illegally obtained at worst. It won't help you put this puppeteering motherfucker behind bars—no offense."

"None taken," Constantin assured, rubbing his chin in thought. "What made him choose Laine? He could not have known about her connection to Wolfe, so she must have one to Christopher. What could it be?"

Lottie spoke for the first time in a while: "I don't know, but the primary is tomorrow. You guys should probably figure that out."

The ping of a text message bounced around the room, and everyone checked their phones. It was Sebastian who looked at his the longest, and when he stood up Wolfe saw his knees shake momentarily before he got control of himself. "I'm sorry, but Constantin and I need to leave." He flashed a smile that was stiff like cardboard. "My father has requested my presence, and the last thing I want to do is arouse his suspicions."

The two of them hustled outside with Constantin plastering his phone to his ear to order a ride, and after a split-second hesitation Wolfe got up and followed them. He made up the distance between them with a few long strides and put his hand on Sebastian's shoulder. "Bash, hey, wait a second. What does your dad want?"

Constantin kept walking toward the curb—he was likely trying to give them some privacy, but he'd never admit it. When Sebastian turned to look at Wolfe, there was something worn-down to the sharp edges of his face. "He wants me to visit Danh Sang and his men," he said, and the implication behind the words made Wolfe's blood run cold. "There is a shipment of Rapture coming in tonight and apparently the Red Dynasty is… dissatisfied about something."

"I don't understand," Wolfe said, a catch in his voice that he had to work to clear. "Anton hasn't made you… *visit* anyone since that night you almost died. What changed?"

The faintest hint of amusement made Sebastian's mouth quirk up. "It seems like an odd coincidence, does it not?" He brought his hands up to rest flatly against Wolfe's chest, as if he wanted to push him away but couldn't make himself do it. "I have to go, Jim. If I do not, Anton may start looking in places we do not want him to."

Wolfe made a slightly hysterical sound. "Bash, do you think I give a damn about that?" he asked, and of course he did, but all of it paled in comparison to how much he hated the thought of Sebastian having to degrade himself on his father's orders, *again*. He didn't know how but the hand he'd had on Sebastian's shoulder had wandered to his face, and Wolfe was amazed at how perfectly his jaw fit into his palm. "You have to know I'd drop everything in a second, that I'd burn this goddamn *city* down to—"

Sebastian's crooked fingers grasped the material of Wolfe's t-shirt tightly and pulled him down so he could press their mouths together in a kiss. That did two things: it stopped Wolfe's romantic monologue in its tracks and it broke his brain because *Sebastian was kissing him*. He kissed back, of course, and while it wasn't nearly as bad as that time his and Caitlin's braces got stuck together and Patrick had to use a wire snips to cut them free, it wasn't Wolfe's best work. Sebastian didn't seem to mind, making a sound in the back of his throat and pressing closer when Wolfe tilted his head to deepen the kiss, with one hand touching Sebastian's face and the other holding his side.

When air became a necessity, Wolfe pulled back enough to stare into Sebastian's eyes. They were even prettier up close, little starbursts of aquamarine scattered throughout the azure of his irises. "I've wanted to do that for so long," he admitted quietly, thumb stroking over Sebastian's cheekbone. "But I was terrified you'd think I just wanted sex, or that I'd scare you away."

"I could never be afraid of you, Jim." Sebastian's voice was soft but firm, and he dropped a feather-light kiss at the corner of Wolfe's lips before he stepped back. The expression on his face was... something else, a depth of emotion that Wolfe knew immediately he didn't deserve but would guard with his life. "I like you too much for that." A black Mercedes pulled up to the curb and he moved toward it, allowing Constantin to open the back door for him. "Please check in with my mother. I need to know that she's okay."

"I will." Wolfe had to force those two words out, a burst of affection in his chest making it hard to breathe. "And Sebastian? I like you too. Be my date to the wedding?"

This time when Sebastian smiled it was a bright, genuine thing. "Of course, Jim. I'll see you soon."

~***~

Jake was allowed to go back to the house in Cambridge only after he swore to Angela on a copy of *Good Housekeeping* that he would never do drugs again. He'd been there for a few hours when the doorbell rang. He waited for Misha to answer it before he remembered his roommate was in classes all day—and now whoever was out there was holding down the doorbell like a five-year-old. He glanced down at his t-shirt and sweatpants and decided he was too exhausted and disgusted with himself to give a damn if the idiot on his porch had a problem with his scars.

Jake opened the door and was shocked to see Frankie Sullivan on the other side. He wore his BPD uniform sans his gear belt and hat, and his cruiser sat in the driveway behind Jake's Camaro. He held a twelve-pack of orange soda in one hand—Jake's favorite—and in the other he had a greasy paper bag from the Jewish deli in East Somerville they used to walk to together on Fridays after school… at least until senior year. "You still like corned beef, right?"

"Yeah, I'm not a fucking heathen," Jake answered, and after a moment's hesitation he stepped aside. "What are you doing here, man?"

Frankie set the food and drink down on the kitchen island, turning to face Jake and running a hand through his curly brown hair. "I'm here to fix things with my best friend, if you're willing to try."

Jake crossed his arms over his chest, barely suppressing a wince when the motion snapped an adhesion built up on his shoulder. "I'm not *un*willing, but why the change of heart?" The last time he'd really talked to Frankie was during the Mass Art Murderer's rampage, when his friend Alana Bach had been kidnapped. "A few months ago you figured I was a suspect in the most vicious serial killings since the Boston Strangler and now you're bringing me corned beef?"

"And matzo ball soup," Frankie said, which was enough to get Jake to come closer and take a peek inside the bag. "Look, I know I screwed up in senior year—"

Jake snorted as he unpacked the containers of soup and paper-wrapped sandwiches. "Screwed up? You outed me to our entire school, Frankie—which meant you outed me to all of Somerville *way* before I was comfortable being gay." He got out silverware and glasses, which he filled with ice and soda, and they took the whole mess over to the second-hand IKEA dining table Misha had picked up at a garage sale. "Not even my mom knew, and I wasn't the one who told her, Father Donahue did."

Frankie's eyes went wide. "Shit, I didn't know that."

"Yeah, well, you can imagine how the local Catholic parish felt about one of their former altar boys turning out gay. His words were... not kind." Despite how traumatic the whole episode was, the next part always made Jake chuckle. "Ma broke Donahue's nose and she hasn't been to church since."

Frankie choked on part of a matzo. "That's awesome. I mean, it's not, but the mental picture of your ma boxing that old bastard is something else." He put his spoon down. "Jakey, listen… when you told me you were gay, I was totally blindsided. I didn't have a problem with it, but back then a lot more people thought it was wrong. I was scared of what might happen if you told anybody else… and then I did something *real* dumb."

Jake chewed on corned beef and sauerkraut and made a rolling motion with his free hand. "Go on."

"You remember Zara Rialto from biology class?"

"She's pretty hard to forget, between the bull ring and the shaved eyebrows."

"Right, well, I kinda… slept with her a couple times? I got Kevin to buy me beer and we hung out at her place when her dad wasn't home."

"How does this relate at all to you outing me to all of Somerville?"

"I'm getting there!"

"I bet that's what Zara Rialto said to you."

Frankie laughed at the cheap joke and nudged Jake with his shoulder. "You're a giant dick." He drained the last of his soda. "The third—and last—time she and I did the whole drink a little, screw a little thing… it was same day you came out to me. And I had a couple more beers than I normally would've, and later, during the pillow talk—"

Jake held up a hand. "Wait, did you just say *pillow talk*? Is that a real thing real people say?"

"Whatever, man, let me finish."

"… I bet Zara Rialto said that too."

"Oh my *God*," Frankie lamented, rolling his eyes. "She kept needling me, saying she could tell something was wrong… and I sort of blurted out that you'd told me you were gay. She didn't really react, which should've been a huge red flag, and then the next morning…"

"'Jake Wolfe is a fag' was spray-painted on the front of the school, yes, I remember," Jake said dryly. He kicked Frankie's ankle. "Why didn't you tell me what happened?"

"I was embarrassed as hell." Frankie shrugged, fiddling with his spoon. "Plus I thought you'd think I was lying, and even if I wasn't, it was a piss-poor excuse for fucking up your last year of high school. I'm so sorry, man."

"Well, you're right—it *is* a piss-poor excuse," Jake started, and when Frankie looked at him with hazel eyes full of hurt he smiled and kicked his ankle again. "But it's also the truth, and I accept your apology." He put his sandwich down on the wrapper and opened his arms. "Come here, you big stooge."

Frankie hugged him hard, the badge on his chest biting into Jake's shoulder. He smelled like sweat and the peculiar blended stench of the inside of a police cruiser, and Jake felt grounded in a way that he hadn't in years. "I missed you, Jakey," Frankie muttered near his ear, a little catch in his voice indicating he was close to doing a Sullivan Ugly Cry. He didn't comment on the scars, didn't seem to mind the way they felt when his hands brushed Jake's biceps.

"Missed you too, Frankie," Jake replied, and when they broke apart, an idea struck him. "Hey, do you have a date to your sister's wedding yet?"

Frankie made a face. "No, and Caitlin's been all over my ass about it." Their eyes met, and it was like they hadn't spent any time apart—Frankie could still read him like a book. "You thinking what I think you're thinking?"

Jake grinned at him, so hard his face hurt. "I'm thinking if we go together, we can get those cool couples' drinks at the open bar without any awkward small-talk."

~***~

Sebastian and Constantin arrived at the Ramada in Dorchester right as rush hour peaked on the Southeast Expressway, bumper-to-bumper cars trying to leave the city in a mass exodus less than fifty feet from the swimming pool behind the motel. Just down the road was The Rainbow Swash, a brightly-colored paintjob over a 140-foot tall liquefied natural gas storage tank owned by National Grid and the largest copyrighted work of art in the world. Sebastian caught a glimpse of it as they pulled into the parking lot, but it was soon obscured by peeling siding and single-pane windows.

Constantin ordered their driver to wait for them to return, and they were halfway to the entrance of the motel when someone whistled at them from the far corner of the lot, close to the chain-link fencing and the traffic. Sebastian turned his head to locate the source of the sound, and at first he didn't see anything, the shadows lengthy in that area. Then he nudged Constantin in surprise when he spotted none other than Danh Sang leaning against the front bumper of a midnight-blue Lexus, Thanh Ngo standing next to him with his hands clasped behind his back.

He and Constantin switched directions, heading for the Lexus instead. "This is… unexpected," Sebastian said, not bothering with formalities. "My father told me your men requested my company."

Sang inclined his head in acknowledgement. "That is the lie I told him in order to get a meeting with you. And do not look so tense, Sebastian—I have a proposition for you, and if you accept, you will not be required to snort coke or fuck my men anymore."

Constantin opened his mouth—probably to tell Sang to go to hell—but Sebastian held up a hand for silence. "I'm listening."

"You already know Anton's preparing to cut the Red Dynasty and the other gangs out of the Rapture trade." It was a statement, not a question, but Sang waited for Sebastian to nod before he continued. "If that happens, your father's power will have little limitation and he will eliminate any potential competition. That is the kind of bloodbath no one wants to see, not even yours truly. Here is my offer: you steal the Rapture formula from Anton, and I will kill him and make sure it cannot be linked back to you. He'll have an... accident."

Sebastian went completely still. A thousand responses flashed through his head as his pulse ratcheted up, but only one made it out of his mouth: "You're serious."

Sang brushed at some invisible lint on his suit jacket and raised a brow. "Are you interested?"

"Sebastian," Constantin said, low, and serious, and it was enough to get him to glance in his bodyguard's direction. "*Amintiți-vă de fabula rusă.*"

Remember the Russian fable.

The Russians had many sinister stories, but Sebastian knew the one of which Constantin spoke. *The Scorpion and the Frog* was a tale that had fascinated him as a child, not because it involved animals, but because he couldn't understand why a creature would hurt another when it was against their best interest. There were a few versions, but essentially it went like this: a scorpion asked a frog to carry it across a river, and the frog hesitated, afraid of being stung by the scorpion. The scorpion argued that if it stung the frog they would both drown, so the frog agreed to transport the scorpion. The scorpion climbed on to the frog's back and the frog began to swim, but midway across the river, the scorpion stung the frog and doomed them both. The dying frog asked the scorpion why it stung, to which the scorpion replied, "I could not help it. It is in my nature."

Sang was a scorpion if Sebastian had ever met one, but Anton was a miserable bastard, one that had caused Sebastian and countless others so much pain to fuel his own selfish desire for power. This was an opportunity not to knock him off the metaphorical chess board, but to upend the entire game. Even though David and Diana had good intentions, if they hadn't found a way to charge Anton with *something* by now, it wasn't going to happen, so perhaps… perhaps this was the only way. And if it looked like an accident, then Sebastian would still have influence with his father's associates and could dismantle his operation from the inside out.

"I cannot steal the formula now," Sebastian told Sang, watching his face carefully for a negative reaction; the only thing Sang showed was that he was listening. "My father's guard is too high, and he will suspect it was someone close to him if it happens now. I have a wedding to attend later this week, but after that… I think we could make a deal."

Sang grinned, sharp and full of teeth. "Excellent."

~***~

Chapter Sixteen

Primary Day in Massachusetts dawned bright and beautiful, not a single cloud in the sky, and Wolfe and Scarlett waited outside Wolfe's polling place on West Dedham Street so that he could vote. Scarlett had voted in her district before picking up coffee for both of them and meeting Wolfe in line; in front of them was an Indonesian couple arguing in their native language, and behind them was a woman who kept pushing her baby's stroller back and forth to try and keep the little guy from exploding into sobs. There had to be two hundred people on the sidewalk and more inside. The high turnout was unusual for a primary election, but given how polarizing the race was, Wolfe wasn't surprised that people wanted their voices heard.

And speaking of voices Wolfe wanted to hear, he switched his Starbucks cup to his left hand so he could thumb open his phone with his right. No new messages from Sebastian, so Wolfe took a burning swallow of his coffee and watched Scarlett from the corner of his eye. "What's up with you? You seem... twitchy."

"Kevin texted me last night and asked me to be his date to the wedding," Scarlett said, tugging on the end of her ponytail as she watched the traffic on nearby Tremont Street. "And I figured it was fine, we get along okay and nobody wants to go stag to something like this. But I think he might be more invested in it than I am and I don't want to hurt his feelings, you know?" She glanced at him curiously. "Do *you* have a date for the wedding?"

"I do," Wolfe told her, rolling his eyes when she gasped theatrically. "I asked Sebastian to go with me and he said yes. Now if he'd just text me back, I'd feel a lot better about—"

His phone buzzed with an incoming message from Sebastian: *I'm fine, but we need to talk in person ASAP. Meet me at the office.*

He and Scarlett both read the text, and when Wolfe met her gaze she raised her eyebrows and said, "Well, that's ominous."

Wolfe glanced up at his polling place before leaving the line to head to the Mustang. The democratic process would have to wait.

~***~

At the office on Boylston Street, Sebastian paced the length of the room and spun on his heel to face the door when Wolfe and Scarlett came through it. Before Sebastian could so much as muster the breath to apologize for not texting sooner he was crushed to Wolfe's chest in a too-tight hug; after a split-second hesitation he hugged him back, burying his fingers in the soft cotton of Wolfe's t-shirt. He smelled like laundry detergent and gun oil, and before now Sebastian had never known a person's scent could be so comforting. He closed his eyes for a moment and breathed, pressing his face against the piecemeal muscle of Wolfe's bad shoulder and feeling the knot of scars there under his cheek.

"I'm glad you're okay," Wolfe murmured into his hair, one large hand stroking down Sebastian's back. He leaned back to look at Sebastian's face, no doubt checking for bruises or other injuries. "Where's Constantin?"

"He dropped me off. I think he went to try and talk to Lacey, make sure she didn't get herself into more trouble after she left your mother's house."

"Okay, so what did Sang want? Was it... what you thought it was?"

"Not at all," Sebastian said, staring up into Wolfe's eyes. "He used that as cover so he could talk to me without my father getting suspicious." He took a deep breath, glanced at Scarlett—who watched them from the doorway, a small smile on her face—and continued, "Sang wants to make a deal. If I get him the Rapture formula, he'll... he'll kill my father."

"Holy shit!" That was Scarlett, stepping into the office and shutting the door behind her. "Are you serious?"

Sebastian chuckled. "That was what I asked him, and he most definitely was." He glanced up at Wolfe again before looking down at the toes of their boots, too afraid of what he might see. He noted that while his feet were smaller than Wolfe's by at least two sizes, they both preferred to wear lace-up boots with steel toes. He wondered if Wolfe liked to keep a knife strapped to his ankle too. "Jim, I know this probably doesn't sit well with you, but—"

"Do you believe him?" Wolfe interjected. One of his hands came up to touch Sebastian's cheek lightly, getting him to make eye contact again. "Do you believe he'd hold up his end of the bargain?"

"I have no reason to think he wouldn't," Sebastian replied, an image of the scorpion riding on the frog's back forming in his mind's eye. He shrugged it off, saw the look that Wolfe and Scarlett traded—one of those silent exchanges where they seemed to read each other's minds. "Wait, are you… you aren't going to talk me out of it?"

Scarlett put her hands on her hips and raised her eyebrows. "Why should we? Your old man has been making our lives hell for months—look what he had done to Jake, for Christ's sake. It's about time he got a taste of his own medicine."

"I agree," Wolfe said, and for a second Sebastian saw not the private detective, brother, and friend, but the soldier he tried so hard to bury. The one who'd made hard choices when no one else would, who pulled the trigger and lived with the consequences. "Anton is never going to stop trying to corrupt this city. Sang is a bad fucking guy, but at least he's predictable—he also makes mistakes, like he did in Chinatown a few years back. If he ran the Rapture operation, it would be much more likely that the BPD could take him down." He sighed and scratched at his stubble-covered chin. "It has to be after Caitlin's wedding."

Sebastian nodded, slightly stunned. "I already told Sang, he was amenable. You actually want to do this?"

Wolfe chuckled, but it was a bitter sound. "Want to? No. But I'd like to think I'm capable of reading the writing on the wall, and it says that if we don't take your father out of the picture soon he's going to poison this whole city—figuratively *and* literally." He folded his hand around Sebastian's, squeezing lightly, mindful of his fingers. "And between the shit he did to my brother and to you... he needs to pay. We could have some big moral debate about whether it's up to us to play judge, jury, and executioner... or we could just do it."

Scarlett held out her fist, and Wolfe bumped it. "Amen to that, babe."

At that moment Wolfe's phone rang, the opening lines of The Clash's "I Fought The Law" exploding into the office. "Ah shit, that's Kamienski." He answered after one ring, putting the call on speaker so Sebastian and Scarlett could listen. "Detective, to what do I owe the pleasure?"

"Hey, Wolfe," Kamienski said, his tone unusually flustered. "We don't have time for our usual song and dance. Remember how that Aiden Parker kid said he didn't know where his sister was when Silent Mark and I visited him yesterday? He came in to report her missing, and you need to get down here ASAP."

~***~

Across town, David and Diana walked out of the John F. Kennedy Federal Building after getting their asses reamed by their boss, Special Agent in Charge Dwight Whitney. He called the meeting to tell them the brass was ending the years-long mission to bring Anton up on charges in exactly one week if they couldn't find a new lead. That would look bad not only for Diana, David, and the Boston CIA field office, but for Whitney in particular, since he was gunning for a promotion to the Pentagon.

Whitney claimed he had nothing to do with the decision—the pointy-heads were looking at budget cuts and the fact that Diana had been in deep cover since she was a little girl. She knew a liar when she saw one, and Whitney had been doing his best not to sweat while she glared at his trembling mouth. He wanted to distance himself from any operations that weren't performing or he wouldn't get the position in D.C., and that meant cutting them off at the knees.

They sat down on the wide brick stairs on Congress Street, the ones that faced the Public Market and the Holocaust Memorial. When David looked at Diana his expression was as hopeless as she'd ever seen it. "What the fuck do we do now?"

"I don't know," she replied, staring at the traffic zipping by on either side of the divided road without seeing it. "This mission, David, it's all I've ever known besides the orphanage." She had her hands on her knees and squeezed them involuntarily, to the point where the joints creaked in warning. "I... I can't go back to being what I was before."

David put one of his larger hands over both of hers. "And I won't let that happen," he assured softly, and Diana wondered if she was the only one who felt a spark every time their skin touched. "You're a good person, D. You just… had to do some bad things to survive. It's not any different from what I've done, or Jimmy, or anybody who's life hasn't been all picket fences and apple pie."

One corner of Diana's mouth turned upward. "Do Americans really eat that much apple pie? I only see it at Thanksgiving."

"I have no idea." David thumb rubbed back and forth over her fingers in what she was sure was an unconscious gesture… right? "I'm more of a pumpkin guy myself."

Diana chuckled and shook her head, watching as a drag queen held the door for a couple of elderly Asian ladies before they all went into the Public Market. "I think the only option we have left is to infiltrate Blakely Manor. If I cut and dye my hair, I can use one of my aliases to get admitted—Diana Johnson has no history of psychosis, but Dajana Jagr does."

"I remember." David pulled his hand back, and she missed it for a moment before snuffing the feeling out like a lit candle. "Wasn't she the one who destroyed an entire liquor store with a baseball bat?"

"The very same." Diana heard the wry humor in her own voice. "I'm sure Tara can craft something convincing and have me get picked up in a van with no windows."

"After the wedding." If she didn't know him so well, Diana wouldn't have seen the concern shimmering in David's eyes. "I still need a date."

~***~

Aiden Parker had attempted to file a missing person's report at the Boston Police station that served Back Bay, the South End, and Fenway. An arched-front brick building on the corner of Harrison Avenue and Plympton Street, it was across from public housing apartments, next door to a dialysis company, and within hollering distance of Boston Medical Center.

Scarlett, Wolfe, and Sebastian stood on the observational side of a two-way mirror with Kamienski and Silent Mark, and Wolfe glanced into the interrogation room where Aiden was. He sat at a metal table that was bolted to the floor and appeared to study his hands, occasionally picking at a cuticle. He looked like he hadn't showered in a couple of days, and his clothes were rumpled and dirty.

"When he came in earlier he told the officers here that he would only speak to me," Kamienski said, rubbing at his temple like he was fighting off a headache. "I drove like a bat out of hell across town, and when I got here he told me that yesterday he had an encounter with your father—" he nodded at Sebastian "—in an alley in Malden, of all fucking places. Like who goes to *Malden*? Anyway, he spun this batshit yarn about how Anton's got Laine under some kind of mind control, and she didn't recognize him at all... and then he asked me to call you. Said he had more to say, but he'd only talk to Wolfe."

"Me?" Wolfe wasn't surprised, not exactly, but he hadn't been sure that Aiden knew about his connection to Laine. "She must've told him what happened in Iraq."

"Evidently, yeah." Kamienski walked with him into the hall and unlocked the door to the interrogation room. "Good luck."

Wolfe stepped inside and took a seat across the table from Aiden. He felt oddly naked without his gun—it was locked in the Mustang's glovebox, since cops didn't like it when people who weren't officers carried weapons inside police stations—but he wasn't afraid. Aiden was the size of a mature oak tree, but Wolfe was no slouch in that department and with his Ranger training he was confident in his ability to disable him if things got ugly. "I don't suppose you want to apologize for almost running me over the other night."

Aiden looked at him with red-rimmed eyes, his cheeks puffy and splotched from crying. "I wanted to see you because you're the only one that might be able to get through to my sister before she does something horrible."

Wolfe leaned back in his chair and folded his arms over his chest. "More horrible than attempting to assassinate a gubernatorial candidate with a long-range sniper rifle?"

"Lainey already wanted to kill that asshole, and so did I," Aiden told him, venom behind the words that Wolfe wasn't expecting. "Do you know what he did to her? The video was all over the internet and Sullivan paid off all the media outlets before this election to make it go away."

"Doesn't ring a bell. Why don't you tell me?"

"Sullivan was a state rep before he ran for governor, and he liked to pretend he was just like the rest of us. Every day when he went to work he'd take an MBTA bus from Somerville to the State House on Beacon Street. And every day, he walked by my sister. She was homeless back then, and liked to set up near the stairs into Boston Common—lots of foot traffic, plus she could be in the sun if it was cold. She had a sign saying she was a vet, and a coffee can that she used to collect money."

Wolfe knew his next question was a futile one, but as an investigator he had to ask it: "The VA couldn't help her?"

Aiden snorted. "The VA couldn't find their way out of a paper bag with a flashlight and a fucking map." Something envious and ugly crossed his face. "Did they help *you*?"

Wolfe's memory flashed back a decade ago, when he'd stumbled off a plane at Logan Airport with newly-healed scars over shifting shrapnel and a mind that wasn't his own anymore, that had been twisted by war and pain and death. He'd tried going to the VA, but between the lack of staffing and the subpar care, it was easier to ask Caitlin for help. "No, they didn't. Go on."

"Laine was homeless for a few months before the day she tripped Sullivan," Aiden said, exhaling a gusty breath before chuckling mirthlessly. "You'd think there'd be some big punchline, right? That she did something so *terrible* to him that public ridicule was necessary retribution—but no, he didn't see her fucking foot on the sidewalk and when he tripped he spilled his six dollar latte." His cheeks reddened with agitation to match his hair. "Sullivan lost his mind, started screaming at my sister while tourists and commuters filmed him. He called her trash, told her she was a disgrace to the country she served, spewed all kinds of bullshit. She took a swing at him when he spat on her, and suddenly she was the bad guy."

"Was that how she wound up at Blakely Manor?"

"Yeah, court-ordered rehabilitation, and Sullivan had the gall to be pissed she didn't get jail time. Now Rapture's the only thing that keeps her stable… or at least it was until Codreanu messed with her head this time around."

Wolfe sat forward, bracing his arms on the table too. "Rapture can be used for psychological manipulation?"

"It's worse than that," Aiden said, his voice dropping to a whisper. Tears welled in his eyes, and while Wolfe thought Aiden Parker was just as guilty of manipulating Laine as Anton, there seemed to be some genuine love in him too, as warped as it was. "She didn't know who I was, and she was… blank behind the eyes. Like a snake, or a puppet." He met Wolfe's gaze. "I don't know what Codreanu's planning, but you should watch your back."

~***~

Chapter Seventeen

Jake got startled awake at eight in the damn morning—not by a nightmare for once, but by his phone chirping with alerts on the nightstand next to his head. The first thing he saw was a news blurb from WBZ that Christopher Sullivan won the Republican gubernatorial nomination in a landslide and would face down incumbent Democrat Roy Halliday for the highest office in Massachusetts in November. Following that was a slew of text messages in the Sullivan/Wolfe-plus-Scarlett-and-Sebastian group chat, most of which were from Caitlin.

He scrolled back to the top to read the saga. The band she'd hired for the wedding cancelled on her, citing the fact that their lead singer had apparently literally thrown up her vocal cords on the stage. This was a problem because not only was the wedding in two days, but today they were traveling up to Mount Washington, which meant Caitlin and Ryan didn't have time to look for a new musical act.

Jimmy had tried and failed to calm Caitlin down and Sebastian volunteered to play the piano but got shot down. He was already doing it for the ceremony and Caitlin didn't think it was fair to ask him to play for the reception too. Kevin offered to bust out his drum kit—Jake hadn't seen him play since middle school—and it was that suggestion that gave Jake an idea of his own.

What about Lacey and her dad? he sent to the group, and text bubbles popped up immediately.

That's a great idea!! Kevin sent, then amended, **If she's not high as balls I mean.**

I'll take high over no band. Caitlin was, as usual, very direct. **Jimmy, do you have Samuel's #?**

Regrettably, Wolfe sent after a moment's delay. **If this goes sideways, I blame my brother.**

Jake found himself smiling as he put his feet to the floor and got ready to leave town.

~***~

Everyone coming up from Boston for the wedding carpooled the best that they could (Patrick and Maureen had the luxury of walking across the street) and ditched their cars in Angela's driveway at two o'clock sharp. About five minutes later a luxury bus—complete with oversized leather seats, charging ports, and an actual bathroom in the back—came rolling down Putnam Street to pick them up. It had a capacity of fifty-six people and it was full by the time it chugged its way over to Interstate 93 and headed north.

Wolfe knew everybody on the bus, but that didn't make sharing a confined space with them for an almost three-hour ride any less daunting. Mercifully he got to sit between Scarlett and Sebastian, and once they were on the road he took in the familiar faces. Caitlin sat with her parents since Ryan and the rest of the Murphy clan needed their own bus; various Sullivan relatives Wolfe had met at barbecues and birthday parties were scattered here and there; newly-minted primary winner Christopher sat with Mel and their kids, along with Scarlett's old man and her ex, Keane; Lacey and Samuel Stahl had answered Caitlin's emergency call; Kevin, Frankie, and Jake crowded together in a row; Constantin sat with Angela and Frogger, who cracked a joke about being the lonely lesbian without a date; and finally, David and Diana were in conversation with Flynn and Lottie.

Caitlin frowned when she saw there were only two extra guests. "David, I thought I told you to invite your whole super-secret spy team?"

"I did, but Dev and Eileen are busy with a project at headquarters, and Tara went to help them out," David replied, and Wolfe was disappointed he wouldn't get to hang out with Dev—the kid was nothing short of brilliant, if a little socially awkward. "They all said thanks for thinking of them."

Lacey waited for her father to put in earbuds before she twisted around in her seat to get Jake's attention. She had a soft guitar case braced between her knees, and the zipper was open enough that Wolfe saw the telltale shine of her Gibson Les Paul Standard in Blue Mist—it was the guitar Constantin had saved for her in a storage unit. He was glad it was back with her, and even happier when he heard her speak to Jake: "Hey… I want to apologize for the other night. Sorry for dragging you into that mess at the swinger's club."

Jake smiled a little, leaning forward to talk to her. "That's okay, Lacey. I wasn't in the best place mentally—I should've been trying to help you."

"Well, in a weird way you *did* help me," Lacey told him. When Jake's eyebrows rose, she explained, "Getting shot at scared me straight, and I haven't done Rapture since. After the wedding I'm packing up my shit and moving back in with my dad."

They kept talking, but Wolfe tuned them out. As long as Jake was okay, that was all he cared about. He put his hand over Sebastian's where it sat on the armrest between them, smiling when Sebastian threaded their fingers together. It took Scarlett about two seconds to notice, and she went from glancing at them out of the corner of her eye to turning in her seat and smacking Wolfe in the shoulder. "Ow! What the hell was that for?"

"You pulled your heads out of your asses and you didn't tell me?!" Scarlett exclaimed, reaching around him to flick Sebastian's ear. "You know I shipped you two from day one, right?"

"I do not know what that means and I do not want to," Sebastian groused, rubbing at his cartilage. "But if that is your fucked up way of congratulating us, I accept."

Scarlett stared at him for a moment before grinning wide. "Good, because I'll be standing up for Jimmy when you two get hitched and it'd be awkward if you thought I didn't approve."

Wolfe cleared his throat loudly. "I think we're getting ahead of ourselves, don't you?" He felt his cheeks heat up and not for the first time he cursed his Irish relatives, snow-white and freckled as they were. His blushing only intensified when Scarlett and Sebastian both started snickering. "We just started dating! I'm not ready to propose!"

"If you change your mind, don't drop down on one knee during my reception," Caitlin said, and threw an empty bottle of water at his head for emphasis.

Frankie looked at them and frowned. "I thought you guys were already dating? You looked awfully convincing during that baseball game."

"Oh my God, can we *please* change the subject?" Wolfe slumped down in his seat, but he had to hide how pleased he was that this bout of familial nonsense made Sebastian laugh. "I'll pay someone to talk about *anything* else. Or beg, I can do begging." Everyone found that hilarious for some reason and they started laughing too—except for Peter, of course, because he was incapable of amusement. "You're all the worst and I hate you."

~***~

Built by Italian artisans at the turn of the 20th century, the Mount Washington Hotel was a grand Y-shaped resort with 200 guest rooms and many amenities, including multiple restaurants, a couple of golf courses, and a full-service spa. It was also a National Historic Landmark, and its twin-peaked red roof and white curved balconies were practically synonymous with New Hampshire's White Mountains. Nestled against a picture-perfect backdrop of forested peaks that were starting to show hints of fall color, it was hard to imagine a better venue for a wedding… especially one with almost 300 guests.

Since the #SulliMurphShakeup (Caitlin no doubt regretted allowing her teenaged cousins to choose the wedding hashtag) had taken over the entire hotel, room assignments were nonexistent. Originally Wolfe had planned on sharing with Scarlett, but once she found out about him and Sebastian she abruptly decided to bunk with Frogger. Angela had all but dragged Constantin off to a single king room—there was something going on there beyond attending a wedding together, and Wolfe wasn't sure he wanted to know about it.

Sebastian didn't seem perturbed by the change in arrangement, depositing his bag on the bellhop's cart along with Wolfe's before they got in the elevator. He looked at Wolfe out of the corner of his eye, a dimple appearing near his mouth. "Didn't expect them to bail on us, huh?"

"I knew Scarlett would," Wolfe said, rolling his eyes when he pictured the shit-eating grin she'd flashed in his direction before blowing him a kiss and saying she'd see him at the rehearsal dinner. "But my mom and Constantin? What's up with that, anyway?"

"I'm not sure." Sebastian tilted his head in thought. "Constantin has not mentioned your mother to me once in the time they've known each other. That in and of itself is a red flag."

Wolfe cocked an eyebrow as they got off the elevator and went hunting for their room number. "Him not talking about her is a red flag? How?"

"When something is truly important to Constantin, he does not speak of it," Sebastian explained, flashing Wolfe a smile when he unlocked the door and held it open for him to walk through first. Their room had one king bed and a rustic yet elegant feel, with a plaid-patterned pullout couch and crown molding at the ceiling. "I believe it comes from his time under Communism. If you valued something, you did not tell others about it because it would be taken away or stolen."

"Oddly enough, that makes me feel better," Wolfe said, turning around to tip the bellhop when he dropped off the bags. Then he did what everyone does when they stay at a hotel: he went to the window to check out the view. It was nothing but lush mountains and blue sky, and he let out a low whistle of appreciation. "This place is really stunning." He thought of Laine and felt his expression darken briefly. "I just hope we don't have any problems while we're here."

"Me too," Sebastian agreed, his tone low and solemn. He came over to stand next to him at the window and touched Wolfe's shoulder lightly. "I know you were embarrassed earlier, on the bus, so if you would like to swap rooms with someone so people don't talk—"

"People are gonna talk no matter what, Bash." Wolfe shifted his stance to look down at him without getting a neck cramp. That errant piece of hair was back, falling over Sebastian's forehead, so Wolfe brought up his hand and pushed it back in place. "I don't care about that, especially when it's my family—they mean well. And I want this… this thing between us to work, and I don't care who knows about it." He hesitated. "I know your track record with guys and hotel rooms isn't great. I'd be happy to sleep on the couch if that's what you want."

Sebastian shook his head, but there was gratitude in his eyes. "I trust you, Jim. That was never a question." He reached for Wolfe's hand and squeezed it. "Let's worry about sleeping arrangements later and just try to make it through the rehearsal dinner in one piece."

~***~

About an hour later, the wedding party milled around outside one of the hotel's ballrooms, waiting for the staff to put the finishing touches on the rehearsal dinner setup. The rest of the guests were free to dine in any of the restaurants, but since Christopher and Melissa's daughter Sarah was the flower girl they were at the rehearsal too… along with Scarlett's dad, and her ex-boyfriend. If that wasn't a plot point for a terrible primetime sitcom, Scarlett didn't know what was. *My Mental Breakdown is filmed in front of a live studio audience!*

She saw Keane approach from the corner of her eye, but in front of her there was a kerfuffle about to happen between Wolfe and Christopher. Scarlett knew Wolfe was going to confront Christopher about what Aiden said as sure as she knew the New York Jets would always suck major dick. Of the two options her job was much more favorable than rehashing old hurts with someone she knew hadn't changed.

Unlike Keane, Wolfe was solid and dependable. He grabbed Christopher's elbow and said something near his ear; whatever it was made him blanch, and Scarlett followed them when they made their way toward a utility closet. And when Peter attempted to do the same thing and tried cut her off, she curled her hand into a fist and cup-checked him without breaking stride, smirking when she heard him wheeze and grab himself.

The three of them slipped into the utility closet, and Scarlett batted a thin chain out of her face, then yanked it to bathe them in the dull white glow of a single incandescent bulb. "You better have a damn good explanation for why you publicly embarrassed a decorated war hero," she said to Christopher. "Otherwise we're just standing in a dusty box in semiformal attire, and I'm not enough of a comedian to come up with a joke from that."

"Wait… you guys think the person who's been trying to kill me is that woman who used to beg across from the State House?" Christopher asked, his tone incredulous in the way only the privileged could be. "Last time I checked you guys were all hot to trot about some big conspiracy with Anton and the governor."

At Scarlett's shoulder, Wolfe exhaled hard. He was visibly agitated, which wasn't something that happened often; her partner prided himself on being a calm, objective person, but this whole case had pushed all of his buttons and he was at his limit.

"You're an asshole," he said, taking a half-step forward until he was in Christopher's face, or more accurately towering over him. "You're a self-absorbed smiling *asshole* and you think you're hot shit because you went to law school and have a wife and two-point-five kids. You believe you're better than everyone else but you never once stop to think that part of the reason you get to live your life however you want is because of people like Laine Parker, who risked hers to help others and protect this country. And if I had the dismal amount of integrity that you do, I'd *want* her to shoot you—or I'd do it myself."

Wolfe glared at Christopher for a moment after he finished speaking, and then he turned away, exiting the closet after jamming his broad shoulders through the doorway. Scarlett stayed for a half-second longer just to savor the dumbstruck look on Christopher's face before she went after Wolfe, hurrying to catch his much longer stride. Being in four-inch stilettos put her at a disadvantage, but she'd been hightailing after Wolfe for a long time and had an idea of where he was going anyway.

The nearest balcony was down a corridor—why were the hallways in this building so *long*?—and through an ornate set of double-doors filled with stained glass. Scarlett pushed her way outside, a lock of blonde hair coming free from her ponytail as she looked around for Wolfe. She spotted him a few feet away, leaning against the railing with his head in his hands. As she got closer she noticed a fine tremor running though his whole body, like he'd been hooked up to a livewire, and she made sure her heels clacked against the tiles so he heard her coming.

"I'm proud of you, big guy," Scarlett said, setting a hand on Wolfe's shoulder. Not for the first time she was struck by their size difference, and thought that it was only fitting that someone who was so huge would have such a big heart... but why did it have to get battered all the time? "I would've broken his nose."

Wolfe didn't look at her, but he made a sound—half laugh, half sob. "I thought about it," he told her, fingertips digging into his scalp. "But he'd look like shit for the wedding pictures and I'd never hear the end of it from Caitlin."

Scarlett snorted. "Oh, I don't know about that. She's not a fan of his shit." She heard the doors open again, and was surprised to see Melissa coming their way. "Hey, Mel. You in the mood to kick your husband's ass?"

"Give me a couple glasses of wine and I'll get there," Melissa replied, taking a deep breath and blowing it out like a dragon breathing fire. She actually resembled the one tattooed on Lottie's arm since she wore a burgundy rehearsal dress, platinum hair spread across her shoulders like shiny scales. "Jimmy, I am *so* sorry. We should've told you and the cops about that video of Christopher and Laine, but it was so long ago..."

"For you, maybe," Wolfe said, truthful but not unkind. He lifted his head, dragging the heel of one hand across his damp cheeks. "For Laine I bet it feels like yesterday."

"You're right, and if I could turn back the clock and keep Christopher from acting like a fuckhead, I would." Melissa pursed her lips into a frown and leaned her elbow on the railing, reaching out with her other hand to touch Wolfe's arm. "Be honest with me… is she going to come after him here?"

"We don't know," was Scarlett's answer, and that was the truth—or a version of it. It was more likely than not that Laine would take the wedding as a golden opportunity to kill Christopher, especially if Aiden was to be believed and she was under some kind of MK-ULTRA mind-control courtesy of Anton. "But if she is, the worst place we could be standing is on a fucking balcony. Come on, let's get dinner over with."

She put a hand on both Mel and Wolfe and ushered them inside, glancing over her shoulder at the rest of the hotel and the woods beyond it.

The binoculars watching them were too far away to be noticed.

~***~

Chapter Eighteen

Sometimes when Jim Wolfe slept, he dreamt of the dead dog in the middle of the road, the blast that took the lives of his men, and the way it felt to have his organs exposed to the desert air. And for all the times that dream had shifted and changed on him from what it had been in reality, it had never borrowed the people he loved to fill in other roles until this particular night.

The world caught on fire, the blast threw him, and the bodies fell around him like angels with charred wings. All of that was familiar and expected, but one of his fallen comrades had long blonde hair and held a Colt pistol; another was scarred and clutched a paintbrush; a pair of sightless bottle-blue eyes stared at him, crooked fingers extended; and yet another wore scrubs instead of a uniform, brown curls spilling into a pool of blood. It was horror after horror everywhere he looked, a solider who'd had his own family that loved him replaced by Wolfe's like some grotesque attempt at masquerade.

A shifting shadow in his peripheral vision, and somehow Wolfe turned his head even as he choked on his last breaths. Laine Parker stood above him, but not the one with the medic patch who had saved his life. This was the Laine Parker of today, the one with the scar bisecting her face and the hate in her eyes.

Laine held a gun, and Wolfe recognized it as his own Glock 22 as she aimed it at his head. She leaned down until their faces were inches apart, the red of her hair a waterfall of blood that wouldn't stop flowing. Her breath was hot and pungent in his nose, and he felt the kiss of the gun muzzle between his brows, saw her well-calloused finger close around the trigger.

"You should've died out here, Jimmy," she reminded him. "You should've died with them."

And then she shot him.

~***~

Wolfe woke from his nightmare to the brief sensation of falling, and then his back hit the floor of the hotel room and punched the breath from his lungs. He laid there gasping like a dying fish for a moment before Sebastian's face appeared above him, his normally carefully-styled hair mussed with sleep and a pillow crease on one of his cheeks. He was still stupidly gorgeous, but Wolfe couldn't tell him that since, as previously mentioned, he couldn't breathe.

"You threw yourself out of the bed," Sebastian said, squinting at him, dangling an arm down so he could touch Wolfe's chest with his fingers. "Nightmare?"

The fact that Sebastian was comfortable enough with him to initiate such casual contact made Wolfe's heart flutter. He sucked in some oxygen and managed to sit up, leaning his back against the nightstand. A glance up at the alarm clock told him it was almost seven in the morning, which was around when they'd planned to get up anyway. "Yeah... it's one I've had before, but this time it was different. I'm just hoping it wasn't an omen."

One of Sebastian's eyebrows rose. "You believe in omens?"

"I believe in the past coming back to bite me in the ass." Wolfe smiled when Sebastian's hand moved to pet his head absently, like he was a spooked puppy and not a full-grown man. "It does it every day. Maybe it's just my conscience telling me I should feel bad about what happened to Laine. I wouldn't be here without her."

"Mhmm… what happened to her is awful, Jim, but it is not your fault." Sebastian folded his other arm underneath his head and used it as a pillow, blinking at Wolfe through a shaft of light coming through the curtains. "I would imagine that when you came back from the war you were barely holding yourself together. It's doubtful you would've been able to do the same for someone else, at least not then."

Wolfe impulsively pressed his forehead into Sebastian's palm and shut his eyes. It wasn't absolution—it was reassurance, which was better. "You're the second-smartest person I know," he said, opening his eyes and smiling again when Sebastian's other eyebrow rose to join the first. "If I bumped Scarlett out of first place she'd kill me."

"Duly noted." Sebastian chuckled, scratching his nails over Wolfe's scalp briefly before pulling away. "How about we go down to breakfast and you can reassure her that I'm not moving in on her territory?"

Wolfe pushed himself to his feet, ignoring the burn when an adhesion in his side decided to split and bending to kiss Sebastian on the mouth. "You have the second-best ideas."

He got hit with a pillow for that.

~***~

After the #SulliMurphShakeup destroyed the buffet and omelet bar, it was announced (read: shouted) by Caitlin that the men and women would be splitting up for the day. The ladies had reservations for an all-day spa package followed by dinner, and the guys were taking the kids on the Cog Railway up to the summit of Mount Washington for a picnic and hike before dropping them off to head to an adult-beverage bachelor celebration at the bar.

There were a bunch of children in the group ranging in age from toddlers to teenagers, and they were all excited to go and ride the world's first mountain-climbing cog railway. This was a pleasant surprise for Sebastian, who'd expected at least some of them to be unimpressed in the way only a middle schooler could be. Everyone was coated in sunscreen before they got on the bus which took them to the train station, where they learned that because of the size of their party they had an entire biodiesel locomotive to themselves.

The views were spectacular, the types of autumnal-cusp images Sebastian had only seen on postcards sold at Faneuil Hall. He'd never had a chance to spend much time outside Boston, so travelling through the peaks of the White Mountains was a new experience. He found he enjoyed it immensely, especially since he got to sit next to

Wolfe for the whole ride, trading glances and ducking their heads like schoolchildren with their first crushes.

And if he'd thought the views from the train were something special, he was blown away when they reached the summit and stepped outside. While some of the others unloaded picnic supplies, Sebastian joined the children in looking at the sprawl of blue-green mountains below them. He felt a presence at his side, and a glimpse from the corner of his eye showed him red hair and freckled skin… but at the wrong height to be Wolfe.

Jake glanced at him and smiled a little. He shoved his hands in the big front pocket of his sweatshirt and rocked on his heels. "Expecting somebody else?"

"Yes, but don't worry about it," Sebastian replied, returning the smile with a touch of hesitancy. "Actually, we should probably talk."

"That's what I figured." Jake stared at the rolling peaks spread in every direction, travelling until they met the clear cobalt of the sky. "I'm presuming you're serious about Jimmy? Because I know you weren't serious about me when we slept together. I'm not gonna stand here and pretend that didn't hurt… but I want my brother to be happy."

Sebastian chewed on his lower lip, shutting his eyes briefly. "I am sorry, Jake, for everything that happened," he said, the words quiet but sincere. "I know it probably doesn't mean much, and it does not bring your friend back—"

A hand touched his shoulder, the back gnarled with scars and the fingers just as crooked as his own. "Sebastian, it's... well, it's not okay. I'm not sure it'll ever be that, but I forgive you. Your old man's a real shithead, and you've had to deal with that for years. *He* had Matt killed, not you." Vivid green eyes looked at him, much older than they should have been. "Just treat Jimmy right, okay? Don't hurt him. That's all I'm looking for."

"I... I'll try my best," Sebastian whispered, and felt a weight he hadn't realized he was carrying around slide off his back. "I promise, Jake."

"Sweet," Jake said, squeezing Sebastian's shoulder once before letting go. "Now let's go get some of those sandwiches before they get annihilated."

~***~

One of the reasons Caitlin chose the Mount Washington Hotel for her wedding venue—besides the one-of-a-kind views and the storybook tranquility of the honeymoon suite—was the full-service spa. They did everything from hot stone massages to mud baths, and the whole thing with her brother's campaign combined with her own stress over flowers, leg waxing, and whether or not the priest would show up drunk meant she needed all the relaxation she could get. Short of getting married in Cinderella's castle at Disney World, it was perfect.

After getting all of the kinks worked out of their backs and receiving facials, the girls gathered to get their nails done. And while

Caitlin was no detective she also wasn't blind, and she'd noticed how the tall dark-haired gentleman in the expensive suit tailored to conceal a gun had been watching Scarlett all day. He tried to be subtle about it, but his eyes followed her through every room they entered, a permanent frown etched into his aquiline features.

Caitlin made sure Scarlett was in the pedicure chair next to hers so she could ask her about it while tiny fish ate all the dead skin off their feet: "Who is that guy? I know he works for your dad, but it seems like he has the hots for you."

Scarlett made a gagging sound. "Oh God, no. That's my ex, Keane." She glanced at him and he immediately turned away, pretending to be occupied with scanning for threats through a window; the other bodyguard had evidently noticed the same behavior Caitlin had, because he rolled his eyes. "He started working for my father after we broke up—you know, taking the job that my old man insisted I couldn't do."

Caitlin felt her eyebrows furrow. All Scarlett had ever said about Peter Vaughn was that he ran a private security company and the divide in their relationship stemmed from Scarlett's desire to be a police officer. But now it sounded like after she'd gotten forced out of the NYPD, Scarlett went to her father for a job and got turned away. "He didn't want you to be a cop... and then he didn't want you to work in the private sector?"

Overhearing their conversation, Melissa chimed in by asking: "Is it a sexist thing?"

Lottie rolled her eyes. "Of course it's a sexist thing."

"That, and the fact that he changed after my mom died," Scarlett said, wiggling her toes once they were free of the water and in the hands of a pedicurist. "He got super overprotective, but at the same time he wanted nothing to do with me. Said I looked too much like her, that it was painful to look at me."

"Jesus Christ—who says that to a kid?" Frogger wondered, unknowingly echoing what Caitlin was thinking, and reached over to squeeze Scarlett's hand. "I'm think I speak for everyone here when I say I'm sorry your dad's such a prick."

"Thanks, you guys," Scarlett mumbled, ducking her head in an uncharacteristic show of shyness. She cleared her throat and tried to change the subject: "So Caitlin, on a scale of Tom Brady before a Super Bowl to a male praying mantis after sex, how nervous are you about the wedding?"

"I'm past the male praying mantis and well into the owner of a china shop when a bull walks in," Caitlin replied. She shivered, and it had nothing to do with the temperature of the polish being applied to her toenails. "Just thinking about it gives me the heebies *and* the jeebies."

Diana squinted at her. "Are these heebies and jeebies some sort of illness?"

Maureen patted Diana's shoulder reassuringly. "No, honey, she's fine."

Melissa glanced at Scarlett and said, "Personally, I'd feel a lot better if we knew where the heck Laine Parker was."

Scarlett quickly explained what she and Wolfe knew about Laine's motives and what Anton had allegedly done to control her.

Stela swore profusely in Romanian—Caitlin didn't understand a lick of it, but she knew cursing when she heard it. "There are days I regret marrying that man. What an ass."

"But it's not like she knows where the wedding is," Angela piped up. "You guys didn't put an announcement in the paper or anything."

Caitlin nodded and tried to relax—it was the last time she'd get the chance until the reception. "I guess we just have to hope for the best and plan for the worst."

~***~

When evening arrived, the boys dropped off the kids in their hotel rooms, entrusting the teenagers with the duty of babysitting in return for anything they wanted from room service and as many PG-13 movies as their little hearts desired. Everybody grouped up again after a quick shower and change of clothes to head down to the bar near the lobby. Wolfe had informed the staff ahead of time about Ryan's bachelor party, and they'd decorated with an absurd amount of glittery streamers and a spread of appetizers and finger foods that ran the length of the bar.

"Damn, that's a lot of chicken wings!" Kevin exclaimed. He'd traded in his usual frumpy sweaters and slacks for a blazer and some jeans. "And look, Frankie—they have boneless ones, so you can't choke like you did at the last family reunion!"

Wolfe smiled as Frankie grumbled good-naturedly, more than used to the Sullivan family's banter. While Kevin seemed okay, Wolfe wanted to know how things were between him and Scarlett, so he waited until the bartender was free and snagged a couple bottles of Sam Adams. Then he made his way through the gaggle of partygoers to Kevin, who'd snagged a stool at the far end of the bar, along with a sizable plate of fried pickles.

Wolfe set a beer down in front of him and took a seat, nodding toward the food. "Those all for you, or can I have some?"

"Knock yourself out," Kevin replied. "What's up, Jimmy? I sense a heart-to-heart coming on."

"Scarlett told me you asked her to be your date to the wedding." Wolfe decided there was no sense in beating around the bush, not when it came to two people he cared about. "For what it's worth, I think she likes you. Usually I'm the only guy she can stand being around for more than five minutes at a time—after that she tries to bash their heads into a solid object."

Kevin chuckled into his beer. "I'll take that as a compliment, I guess." He looked at Wolfe from behind his glasses with uncertain eyes. "Do you think I have a hope in hell of impressing her? I mean, she's... *Scarlett*, and I'm... me."

"Hey, don't sell yourself short," Wolfe said, nudging him with his elbow and sniping a fried pickle. "You're a cool dude, Kev—I should know, I grew up with you. Just be yourself and see what happens."

"Easy for you to say," Kevin muttered, looking Wolfe up and down in a way that was confusing until he continued, "Must be easy to get dates when you're afflicted with chronic hotness."

Wolfe laughed so hard he spit out his beer.

~***~

There wasn't much Diana liked about herself, but one of the traits she possessed that she found most useful were her observational skills. Not only were they good for her job, they aided her in figuring out what to do in social situations—no amount of training would erase her Serbian heritage, and American women were *very* different from their Eastern European counterparts. For example, at a Serbian wedding there would be no bachelorette party… and if there were, it would certainly not include watching the bride-to-be get carried around on her chair by a bunch of male strippers.

"This is the weirdest bat mitzvah I've ever been to!" Lottie exclaimed over the din of women screaming and pop music thumping through the speakers. "And I've been to, like, fifty of those!"

Diana smiled at the joke, but her eyes followed Caitlin. She was grinning and laughing, the Shirley Temple in her hand sloshing as the strippers took their final turn around the room. Thankfully they were in the same dining hall from the rehearsal dinner and not an actual restaurant, or someone would've tripped over a table and died. That was common sense, not Diana's observational skills—no, what she'd *observed* was that Caitlin hadn't imbibed a single drop of alcohol all day.

Plenty of people didn't drink for a variety of reasons, including but not limited to medical conditions and religious beliefs. Diana didn't fit either of those criteria and had always enjoyed a beer or a nice glass of wine. She knew that Caitlin had a similar nature because she'd observed it at a couple of Sullivan-Wolfe get-togethers David brought her to over the summer.

Why wouldn't she at least have a flute of champagne the night before her wedding? There was only one answer Diana thought of, but she wasn't sure if she should say anything. She knew through Wolfe that Caitlin saw Diana as two-faced and untrustworthy, but she had no ulterior motive, and she had some… experience in the area of pregnancy. Before things had gotten bad in the village, she brought in money for the orphanage by working as an assistant to a midwife. That was before they'd had to count every mouth they had to feed… before Diana was forced to do things that made her wake up screaming as recently as yesterday.

She was broken out of her thoughts by Caitlin's chair getting put back down on the floor, and the bride-to-be patting the nearest stripper on his bare chest in thanks before heading for the buffet. It had everything from a fresh fruit and crepe station to a section where you could barbecue your own steak, and Caitlin was snatching up toppings for a burrito bowl when Diana approached her.

"Are you pregnant?" Diana asked quietly, and she was unable to hide a smile when Caitlin nearly dropped the bowl and looked at her with wide eyes. "Congratulations."

"Thank you," Caitlin responded, the words no doubt automatic because of her excellent manners. She grabbed Diana's elbow, squeezing a little too tightly. "How the hell did you know that?"

Diana took in a slow breath and fought her training, which told her to slam the burrito bowl into Caitlin's face in order to break the hold on her arm. "Would you believe me if I said it was womanly intuition?"

Caitlin continued to stare. "Not for a second."

"You didn't drink any alcohol today," Diana said. "Not a mimosa at breakfast, no tequila sunrise at lunch… I could go on." She tilted her head. "When did you find out?"

"Last night." Caitlin removed her hand from Diana's arm and was going to rub her stomach but thought better of it. "I've been getting sick the past few mornings, but I thought it was wedding jitters until I took a pregnancy test. I haven't even told Ryan yet—I didn't want him to freak out and refuse to go out with the guys today, which is totally what he would've done."

Diana felt one corner of her mouth lift. "He's a good man. A little excitable, perhaps, but he's good all the same." She reached for her leather handbag where it sat on a nearby table. Bypassing the gun and her lipstick, she pulled out a small silver drink charm shaped like the state of California. "A gift from David when he was late to exfil once. Perhaps you can use it to order something virginal and blend in a little better?"

Caitlin contemplated the charm for a moment before taking it out of Diana's palm. Then for the first time that Diana could recall, Caitlin smiled at her. "Thank you, Diana. That's... really nice. Just... could you please not tell anyone? I want to at least tell Ryan first before I announce it to the world."

Diana returned the smile, and felt it not just on her face but in her heart. "Your secret is safe with me, Caitlin."

~***~

Chapter Nineteen

When Wolfe woke up at five o'clock in the morning—an autonomic function from his time in the military—instead of rolling over and going back to sleep, he had two thoughts. The first one was: *Your ex-girlfriend is getting married today and you're her soon-to-be husband's best man.* The second one was: *Your maybe-boyfriend isn't in bed with you.*

He sat up and glanced around, but the hotel room was quiet and still. Some light stretching worked out the kinks in his neck and shoulders from lying down, and a peek between the curtains showed him Sebastian was outside supervising as some workers moved the grand piano on to the courtyard's flagstones. The ceremony wasn't until the afternoon, but the hotel staff were already setting up the flower-covered archway and using a laser level to make sure the chairs for the guests were in perfect rows.

By the time Wolfe threw on a sweatshirt and some flip-flops and got downstairs, Sebastian was sitting at the piano, hands gliding over the keys as he warmed up and checked the tuning. Constantin watched him from the glass double-doors that led into the hotel's daytime dining area, a steaming mug of coffee in one hand and a folded-up *Boston Globe* under his robed arm. When he saw Wolfe he raised his cup in silent greeting, then nodded toward the hot drink bar for him to get his own.

Once he had a cup for himself dwarfed in his giant hands, Wolfe nodded toward Sebastian and said, "I can't get over how talented he is."

"It is something to see," Constantin agreed. He glanced at Wolfe, icy blue eyes burning a hole in his cheek. "You are good to him, yes?"

"Constantin, we haven't even been on a date yet," Wolfe replied, but when that made Constantin glare harder he sighed. "I think I am. To be honest with you, I have no idea what I'm doing."

"What do you mean?"

"I've known I was bisexual for a long time—it's actually why I got kicked out of Boy Scouts, remind me to tell you that story sometime. Anyway, I... the only girlfriend I ever had was Caitlin, and I've never had a boyfriend. I've dated people here and there—"

"Like Diana."

"Not the best example, but sure. I guess what I'm saying is I'm sort of... flying blind? Since my last successful relationship was in high school with someone of the opposite sex."

To Wolfe's surprise, Constantin's expression softened into something sympathetic. "Sebastian has never had a boyfriend either, and to my knowledge all the dates he's been on were... work-related." He said that part with a scowl, and just the thought of Sebastian going out with some skeevy guy on his father's orders made Wolfe's blood boil. "He is… fond of you. Fonder than I have seen him become of anyone else. Do not misuse that fondness."

Wolfe smiled into his coffee. "Or you'll kill me?"

Constantin patted him on the shoulder. "Perhaps you are not as dumb as you look after all."

~***~

Scarlett stood in front of the full-length mirror in Caitlin and Ryan's suite and smoothed down her skirt, then grabbed the hairspray to tame a flyway from her braided bun. She and Frogger had elected to pair their emerald dresses with beige pumps, and even their makeup matched—red lips, a little eyeliner and mascara, and a touch of blush.

If she shifted her gaze, she could see the reflection of Melissa and Lottie putting the finishing touches on Caitlin's hair, fitting the veil into her elaborate crown of curls. Maureen and Angela had been adamant that no security personnel would be in the room while the women got ready, but Peter was hovering out in the hallway and no doubt had Keane following Christopher around like a guard dog. There was a knock at the door, followed by Peter sticking his head inside.

When he caught sight of Scarlett, something that was almost a smile passed over his face. "Are we almost ready, ladies? You look beautiful, Scarlett. Just like your mother."

Since she intended to follow the bride downstairs so they could assemble with the rest of the wedding party, Scarlett froze in a half-turn toward Caitlin. Peter *never* brought up his late wife… unless he wanted something from his daughter and couldn't think of another way to get it. It was the worst kind of manipulation, and exactly the reason why Scarlett didn't trust him further than she could throw him—and right now she was thinking about throwing him all the fucking way back to New York.

She spun around and took three quick steps toward her father, putting her hand flat on Peter's chest, shoving until his back hit the door of the room across the hall. "You don't get to talk about her," she hissed, acrylic nails digging into his skin through the material of his dress shirt. "I'm done with your bullshit, old man. Tell me what you want, *right now*, or I'm going to put your head through this goddamn door."

Peter didn't beat around the bush, less out of concern for his head and more for his designer suit: "I want you to move back home and work for me."

Anger flared through Scarlett. "Are you kidding me? I *begged* you for a job after I left the NYPD, and you said—"

"Things were different then," Peter said, his tone infuriatingly placating. "You had a lot of your mother's impulses—" read: she travelled alone because he was always busy and cheated on him for the same reason "—but I can see you're different now, in a good way." He put his hands on her shoulders. "That, and… Marshall Raider. He's out of prison."

Hearing the name of her mother's murderer made Scarlett reel back in shock, yanking herself out of her father's grasp. Instead of falling on her ass, she was caught by Diana and Frogger. Her heart pounded in her chest so hard she thought it was trying to escape her body, and she stared at Peter, struck not for the first time by how calm he always was when he discussed her mother's death. As if it had been something inconvenient like a scheduling conflict and not a life-altering trauma.

"Stay the fuck away from me," Scarlett choked out. "I'm not gonna move, I'm not gonna work for you, and I certainly don't need you to protect me from Marshall Raider or anybody else." She pushed past him, adding over her shoulder: "It's not like you were able to protect Mom."

She held her head high as she walked away and knew without looking back that her friends were following her. She didn't give a damn if her father did or not.

~***~

The ceremony was beautiful and went off without a hitch. After Caitlin and Ryan were officially married and the wedding party posed for pictures—taken by Frankie, who was a closet photography nut—they all moved to the hotel's ballroom for the reception. For Sebastian it was akin to just about every party or gala he'd ever been to… except everyone was *happy*.

It didn't take him long to find Wolfe once the crowd spread out between the dance floor and the buffet. He stood near the gift table, watching as Caitlin danced with her father for a song before Ryan cut in, mouth curved in a faint smile. Sebastian didn't miss the edge of sadness to it, and wondered not for the first time how different Wolfe's life—and consequently the lives of many people in the room—would've been altered had he decided against joining the military.

When Wolfe saw Sebastian that sadness melted away, replaced by an affection that left Sebastian feeling breathless. He even sounded a bit winded when he spoke: "You were an excellent best man. I would give you five stars on Yelp."

Wolfe ducked his head and chuckled, hands in the pockets of his dress pants. "Well, your piano playing was pretty incredible."

Sebastian raised an eyebrow. "Are you referring to when Caitlin walked down the aisle… or this morning, when you and Constantin were spying on me?"

"You, uh… you noticed that?" A faint blush colored Wolfe's cheeks, making the freckles on his skin stand out. "He gave me the shovel talk, in case you're interested."

"I would expect nothing less," Sebastian said wryly, resisting the urge to roll his eyes. "In case you hadn't noticed, he is a *tiny* bit overprotective." He noticed some hotel employees rolling out the wedding cake and nodded toward it. "I hope you're in the mood for marbled vanilla and chocolate cake with a light buttercream frosting and fresh raspberries."

Wolfe looked perplexed for a second before he smiled again. "That's right—Caitlin had you come to the cake tasting." He paused. "Wait, did *she* give *you* the shovel talk?"

"No." Sebastian smiled back. "Jake did that."

"Of course he did." Wolfe offered Sebastian his hand to hold. "Can I buy you a drink at the free bar?"

Sebastian twined their fingers together and grinned so hard his face hurt. "I'd love that."

~***~

Scarlett waited until Wolfe and Sebastian were done being adorable near the bar before she approached Kevin, thumping his shoulder lightly as she sat down next to him. "What, you didn't order me a tequila sunrise too?"

"Didn't know you were coming over here," Kevin replied, giving her a small but genuine smile. "The ceremony was beautiful—I was surprised by the lack of bloodshed."

She knew Kevin well enough by now to realize that was a joke and laughed accordingly. "I almost broke my father's nose *before* the ceremony. Does that count?"

Kevin rolled his eyes. "What did he do now?"

Scarlett waited to speak again until she had a drink—whiskey, neat. She downed half of it in one slug, then said, "My mom was murdered when I was eleven years old. It's not something I talk about for a lot of reasons, not the least of which is that it still fucking hurts every time I think about it. She was killed by a guy named Marshall Raider, a nutcase with a thing for blondes. He stalked her for weeks without my father or his thugs noticing and snatched her when she was walking home from work." A faint smile tugged at her lips. "Mom liked to do that instead of sitting in Manhattan traffic for an hour each way. And that was *way* more information than you probably wanted—"

A hand touched hers, a light press of fingers that made her look at Kevin. Instead of the sympathy or pity she expected to see, he watched her with a… a *soft* expression. "I'm so sorry about your mom," he murmured, setting his hand on the bar top, palm-up in invitation. "I can't imagine how horrible that was. And I can't say that I'll understand how you feel, but I'm willing to listen. If you want."

Scarlett looked at him for several seconds before lifting her hand and placing it on top of his. "I'd like that." She paused. "After this." And then she kissed him.

When they broke apart, Kevin stared for a moment before he grinned. "I guess this is a real date after all."

~***~

The asset clambered from tree to tree with a silenced Remington Modular Sniper Rifle, and each time she looked through her sights a man in a suit outside the Mount Washington Hotel fell like a domino in the fading sunlight. Despite the fact that she was producing the result desired by her handler, the asset thought there was something missing. The gun was good, it was fine… but wasn't it supposed to be bigger? Less something she could prop on her shoulder and fire at will, and more something that needed to be stood on a flat surface?

She shook her head to clear it and dropped out of a sturdy oak, crawling on her belly into some bushes with the rifle slung over her back. The asset watched for signs of movement or reinforcements, but she had killed all of the private security personnel stationed around the main doors and the courtyard entrance to the ballroom by being patient and waiting for each one to be alone. Using the growing shadows to her advantage, the asset snatched a keycard from the jacket pocket of one of the dead men before using it to gain access to a side entrance which led to a corridor.

She knew from her careful study of the building's schematics that the second door on the left was a maintenance closet that contained the electrical breaker box for the entire hotel. Just flipping the main switch would blackout the ballroom and be enough to cause panic and chaos…

But as always, her handler had grander designs.

~***~

Frankie never felt more like himself than when he was looking through the viewfinder on a camera. It was a hobby he'd kept private until Caitlin had announced her engagement to the family at Sunday dinner and Maureen had suggested they get some photos taken. All the Sullivans had immediately turned to Kevin, fully expecting the soulful librarian to have a friend who liked to take pictures. Instead, much as Frankie had outed Jake to their entire school, Kevin had simply pointed at Frankie and said, "He has a camera with four different lenses."

And so Frankie found himself not only taking his sister's engagement photos, but her wedding ones too. Not a bad gig all things considered, and he'd already given out six business cards to various members of the extended family for everything from First Communion to prom. Did he need a sideline when he was already a BPD officer? Probably not, but his old man was right when he said it was always good to keep his options open.

He'd snapped candid shots of almost everybody by this point of the reception, after the cake was cut and people were on their second or third (or fourth or fifth, if you were a Murphy in from County Tipperary) alcoholic beverage. The band—which consisted of Lacey Stahl, her father Samuel, Kevin, and one of the waiters who happened to play bass—were currently playing a cover of Paramore's "Still Into You" and the dance floor was churning with people, mostly teenagers.

Frankie spotted a familiar head of red hair and drifted in Jake's direction, watching from behind a pillar like a freaky stalker as he talked to Detective Kamienski and Christopher's campaign manager, Nikki. The way Jake gestured with his hands as he spoke hadn't changed despite the injuries inflicted by the Mass Art Murderer, and without conscious thought Frankie raised the camera and snapped off a few pictures.

He'd intended to get photos of the three of them, but when he glanced at the camera screen he realized the pictures were portraits of Jake right as he'd laughed, which Frankie could always anticipate from the way his mouth flattened out. What the hell did *that* mean? Before Frankie could figure it out (the butterflies in his stomach gave him a *very* scary idea), the ragtag group on stage finished their song and Lacey tapped her microphone to get everyone's attention. It mostly worked—two-thirds of the room turned in her direction, while the rest were too shitfaced to do much besides swear at the feedback.

"Hey everybody," she said, taking a sip off of a water bottle, "there's someone who was supposed to be here tonight and couldn't make it... or at least that's what you thought until now." She pointed toward the ballroom doors. "All the way from Greece, let's give a warm and not-slurred welcome to Josh Wolfe!"

Frankie almost dropped his camera when the eldest Wolfe sibling walked in, smiling bashfully in the face of cheers. Since he'd been working with Doctors Without Borders for almost four months it was no surprise that he was as tan as a saddle, which looked great with his gray suit and black shirt. When he clapped Wolfe on the shoulder and leaned in to hug him their resemblance was striking, save for the kinder tilt to Wolfe's brow and his broader build. He went to Caitlin and Ryan next, hugging her and shaking his hand, and then bent down to kiss his mother on the cheek.

Movement in his viewfinder caught Frankie's attention—Jake all but ran in the direction of the bathrooms like his ass was on fire. Frowning, Frankie put down his camera on the gift table (his family was many things, but thieves were not one) and started to walk after him, wondering what the problem was. Why hadn't he gone over to greet his brother along with everybody else? Was it because Josh had left for his volunteer mission on the same night that Jake was tortured by the Mass Art Murderer?

Before he could make the connection regarding that particular coincidence, a gunshot cracked through the ballroom. Frankie dove for Jake's ankles without conscious thought, tackling him out of harm's way. They hit the floor hard and Frankie scrambled to cover Jake's shaking body with his own, wishing he'd worn his gun to the wedding despite a strict no-guns rule with an exception for Peter and his men; at the last family reunion some Sullivan cousins got drunk and one of them ended up in the ER with a gunshot wound to the foot.

There was a cry of pain from somewhere in the crowd amid the panicked screaming and diving for cover... and then the power went out, plunging the ballroom and the rest of the hotel into darkness.

~***~

Chapter Twenty

Ears ringing from a combination of the gunshot and the screech of dropped instruments, Wolfe pushed himself up from where he'd knocked Sebastian and a Murphy relative to the floor and started scanning the room as red emergency lights flared to life near the exits. Through the glass doors leading out to the courtyard he saw the bodies of Peter's guards sprawled on the ground; they would've been impossible to spot with the glare from the lights, but now that they were enveloped by near-darkness it was easy. What wasn't easy was discerning who had been shot, since there it was absolute calamity as three hundred people were either in the midst of taking cover or trying to get outside.

Wolfe stuck his index finger and his thumb in his mouth and whistled. "HEY!" he yelled in his sergeant's voice, and everyone froze. "The exterior doors locked automatically when the power failed—and you don't want to leave the building anyway, not until we know what the threat is. Now, who's hurt?"

"I… I think that's me," Patrick said, raising a shaky hand from near the punch bowls. He was bleeding sluggishly from a wound to his thigh, and Maureen was already wrapping her shawl around it. "Shot came from near the main doors."

Josh went over to check on Patrick along with Caitlin and some of her friends from work, so Wolfe was sure he'd be fine. He grabbed Diana by the elbow, and he knew she must've looked at building schematics before she ever agreed to stay in the hotel. "What's the most fortified room in this place?"

"Probably the security room behind the front desk," Diana replied. If there was one thing Wolfe admired about her, it was that she was excellent in a crisis. "Everybody, pay attention! We need a few people to carry Patrick, and you all need to follow Detectives Kamienski and Hale—they'll take you somewhere safe."

"I'll go too," volunteered a tall black-haired man that Wolfe belatedly recognized as Scarlett's ex, Keane. "Come on, everyone, let's keep things calm and civilized."

"We'll call the local police," Kamienski said to Wolfe, "but I wouldn't expect them for at least twenty minutes, not in the dark with the roads we had to use to get here."

The three men started herding guests and employees alike toward the doors at the end of the ballroom opposite from where the shot had been fired, and soon only a handful of people were left in the dilapidated space. Streamers hung halfheartedly from the ceiling, and pieces of balloons were scattered on the ground, popped by trampling feet. Overturned tables were everywhere, along with food on the walls and ceiling.

Wolfe stood in the shadows furthest from the wall of windows and surveyed who he was working with: his father, Constantin, Scarlett, Sebastian, Diana, Flynn, Lottie, Peter, Frankie, and… Jake? "Whoa, whoa, what are you doing here?" he asked, both hands landing on Jake's shoulders. "Why didn't you go with the others?"

Jake looked pale and shaky, and Wolfe couldn't tell if it was from the shooting or something else. "I… I just couldn't, Jimmy, okay? Let me help, if I can."

"Somebody needs to check the breaker box," Scarlett said, pulling off her high heels and ripping her bridesmaid's dress so she could run. "Maybe you and Frankie could do that?"

"Sure, no problem," Frankie agreed, an expression on his face that Wolfe couldn't quite decipher. He put a hand on Jake's shoulder when Wolfe's slipped off and steered him toward the doors. "C'mon, Jakey, let's see if we can get the lights back on."

Peter's in-ear communicator crackled and Wolfe was half-aware of him speaking into it, but didn't pay attention until Peter tapped him on the shoulder. "Wolfe, Aiden Parker's here," he said, and held out the comm like a weird olive branch. "He took a comm off one of my guys, and he wants to talk to you."

"Fuck me," Wolfe muttered before he put the comm in his ear, doing his best to ignore the sticky feeling of someone else's earwax touching his own. "Aiden? It's me, it's Jim. Listen to me, you don't want to do this—turn around and walk away."

"I can't," Aiden replied, a thin quality to his voice that Wolfe didn't like. "This is my fault, it's all my fault."

"The only person to blame is Anton, man." Wolfe felt sweat on the back of his neck and under his arms and yanked off his jacket, rolling up the sleeves on his dress shirt. "And I promise you, I'm going to find a way to bring him to justice. But stepping in front of Laine right now? That's suicide and you know it."

No response. Aiden had dropped the comm.

Wolfe dragged a hand over his mouth and ripped the comm from his ear, handing it back to Peter. "Goddammit, the last thing we needed was another freewheeler. He's going to get himself killed."

"Peter," David started, patting Wolfe on the back, "where did your guys store their extra gear? You must've brought SMGs—" subcompact machine guns "—at the very least, right?"

"We did," Peter said as Frankie and Jake slipped back into the ballroom, rejoining the huddle when they got close. "There should be bags of weapons stockpiled in all the closets off the main hallways."

"I'd say that sounds like overkill, but right now I'm grateful for it," Lottie commented.

"Power won't be coming back on anytime soon," Frankie said, holding up a large knife by the handle. "She drove this into the middle of the breaker box and fried everything."

Everyone was quiet for as they absorbed that.

"As much as I don't want to be the guy in the horror movie who suggests we split up to cover more ground," Flynn said, "I think that's exactly what we need to do."

"Are you sure that is a good idea?" Sebastian asked, raising a critical eyebrow. He was twirling a butterfly knife between his fingers, the blade spinning in a gleaming arc but never touching his skin. "It's usually how everyone except the B-list celebrity dies."

"You're both right." Wolfe wasn't wild about the fact that Sebastian was there—and from the look on Constantin's face neither was he—but he was capable of defending himself. "We'll split up into pairs—I'm presuming there's extra comms in these caches?" When Peter nodded, he continued, "Then when everybody finds comms, get online and we'll coordinate from there. If anybody's not online in ten minutes, we presume they're engaging a hostile. Be careful."

~***~

"You know, when you asked me to be your date to this wedding, I thought we'd at least get to dance," Diana said as she and David crept down a carpeted hallway. She had a stun baton held down along her leg, a long lock of black hair hanging over her shoulder where it had slipped free of her chignon. "But no, somehow these formal events always end in bloodshed."

"Maybe we bring the violence with us?" David suggested, regretting not ignoring Caitlin's decree against guns. Something occurred to him and he put his free hand out to stop Diana. "Wait… you *wanted* to dance with me?"

Diana glanced at him before quickly looking away to peer around the corner. "Yes, I did. I have wanted to… *dance* with you for a long time, actually. You just never noticed."

David was ninety percent sure he wasn't misinterpreting what his partner was telling him and felt himself blush to the roots of his hair. "D… I want you to know, it hasn't always been like this. When you were younger I never would've—"

She smacked him in the gut. "David, don't be stupid—I know that. You're not some creepy old man, and I am not a little girl anymore." They reached the closet and she tried the knob, both of them breathing a sigh of relief when it turned. Slipping into the closet she tugged David with her and turned on the light inside, shutting the door behind them before looking up at him with those big hazel eyes. "I am not good at feelings, you know this."

David's mouth was dry and his palms were sweaty. "Dijana…" he said softly, reaching out to push that errant lock of hair behind her ear. "Maybe once this is over, we can—"

An explosion rocked the building, making them stumble and almost fall on the oversized black duffle bag on the floor.

"That must be Laine's idea of a distraction," Diana said, unzipping the bag and pulling out two M4 carbines and a couple of in-ear communicators. As soon as she had her comm in, she tapped it and asked, "Peter, do you copy?"

"I'm here," Scarlett's father replied. "I'm with Frankie and Jake, we were headed to block the main entrance when we heard the explosion."

"Keep going," David told him, slipping an extra magazine of ammo into his pocket just in case. "We'll go check out the blast site."

~***~

In a closet off the hallway that ran behind the hotel kitchen, Scarlett knelt down and unzipped a duffle bag exactly like the one David and Diana had found. She heard Wolfe's sharp intake of breath when he saw the weapons the bag contained—M4 carbines, the same kind of gun he used when he was a Ranger. She grabbed one and held it up to him, trying to be casual about it even though she knew this was a delicate situation.

Wolfe took the gun from her after a moment's hesitation, one scarred hand folding around the grip, the other one settling in the groove between the magazine and the handguard around the barrel. "Jesus Christ," he whispered. "Scarlett, I…"

She stood with her own gun held at port-arms and looked into his eyes. "Haven't held one of these bad boys since the Sandbox, huh?"

He shook his head and licked his lips. "I started carrying a handgun—never even crossed my mind to get one of these." Wolfe's voice dropped to something low and pained: "I spent so much time trying not to stick it in my mouth and pull the trigger back then."

Scarlett knew that already, but hearing it said aloud still made her shut her eyes briefly, an ache behind her breastbone. "Well, I'm damn fucking glad you didn't," she said, her own voice staying miraculously steady. "And the sooner we figure out where Laine is, the sooner you can put that thing down. But she's got high-powered weaponry, so it's only fair that we do too."

Wolfe cleared his throat. "Whatever rifle she has isn't as big as the last one—can't be if it's silenced—but it was enough to take out all of Peter's men *and* knock Patrick halfway across the ballroom. She'll be up high, probably waiting to see if Christopher reappears… the question is where?"

Scarlett stuck a comm in her ear and did the same for Wolfe, pinching his cheek at the same time. "I don't know, but we need to find her first. That boob isn't getting shot on my watch."

~***~

"What did Scarlett and Wolfe say when you told them about Sang's plan?" Constantin asked as he and Sebastian walked cautiously down a hallway near the interior balcony on the second floor, which overlooked the lobby. Neither of them had turned on their comms yet. "I know that is why you wanted to meet with them at their office."

"They were surprisingly amenable," Sebastian said, adjusting his hold on the M4. He'd done some target shooting with a gun like this in the past, but being prepared to use it on a person was a different animal. "Anton has caused Jim plenty of grief, and Scarlett is loyal to him—plus in case you haven't noticed, she understands what is like to have a father who's an asshole."

Constantin nodded. "That makes sense, I suppose. Are they going to help us?"

"Yes." Sebastian glanced at his bodyguard as they rounded a corner. "They said they could get Frogger to—*rahat*!" The slip into vulgar Romanian was caused by a collision with two people that he recognized as Flynn Walker and Lottie Tran—and thankfully he and Constantin were recognized in return, so nobody got shot. "Damn, you scared us. I take it you have not found her?"

"Nope," Flynn said, the lines around his eyes tightening grimly. "Heard that explosion, though. Can't decide if it was a distraction or her blastin' her way outta here."

"She doesn't have demolitions experience, right?" Lottie asked. She shifted her stance and Sebastian saw the faintest shadow of movement behind her. "Because if she does, then—"

The butt of a modular rifle struck Lottie in the back of the head before Sebastian could warn her and she hit the floor, unconscious. Flynn was turning when the gun cracked against Lottie's skull, but he was at a bad angle to use the M4 in his hands. Laine dropped her gun in favor of grabbing the barrel of his and used it to yank him forward so she could head-butt him hard enough to stun and followed that up with a chop of her hand to his throat.

309

Constantin shouted for Sebastian to get behind him, but that was all he managed to do since Flynn's body blocked his shot in the instant it would've been effective. Laine wrenched Flynn's M4 out of his hands and swung it around like a bat, clipping Constantin across the face and sending him careening into Sebastian, who couldn't fire without risking hitting someone else. He went down in a heap underneath Constantin's considerable bulk, the wind knocked out of his lungs.

Laine turned the M4 around and shoved the stock against her shoulder, raising it so it was level with Constantin's head, but someone rounding the corner caught her attention and she froze. Sebastian twisted around as much as he could and saw Aiden Parker standing at the end of the corridor, his hands raised in supplication and sweat shining on his forehead under the flare of the emergency lights.

"Lainey," he said, his voice cracking with what Sebastian suspected was fear given his last encounter with his sister. "Please, stop. You don't have to do this."

Laine's head tilted to one side, and while her aim at Constantin did not waver she was looking at Aiden with an unsettling, almost reptilian stare. "I don't know you. Go away."

"But you *do*—" Aiden started, and then he made a frustrated sound. "I'm your *brother*, you idiot! God, why do you always have to be so *stupid*—?"

BOOMBOOMBOOM from the M4 in Laine's hands, so loud Sebastian thought it burst his eardrums for a moment. He watched in horror as Aiden's body was riddled with bullets—two in the chest and one in the head, right between his wide-open eyes. Movement at the end of the hall beyond Aiden's corpse as it fell signaled the arrival of Wolfe and Scarlett, their big guns raised and aimed at Laine who turned and fled at the sight of them.

Wolfe started to run after her but paused for a half-second at Sebastian's side, fingertips grazing his forehead. "You okay?"

Sebastian nodded, gasping in a relieved breath as Scarlett moved Constantin off of him. "I'm fine. Go."

Wolfe touched Scarlett's shoulder. "Help them."

Then he was gone.

~***~

Sometimes when Jim Wolfe was awake, he was terrified he was dreaming.

This was one of those times.

Running down a cramped corridor in near-darkness surrounded by doors that could conceal any kind of threat felt exactly the same in New Hampshire as it did in Iraq and Afghanistan. For a second he forgot he was wearing the remnants of a tuxedo and instead felt the weight of a helmet on his head and gear on his body, the rifle in his hands merely an extension of a tool designed to kill.

He turned another corner and ran into Laine, who had her feet planted for the impact and her stolen M4 raised horizontally to fend off Wolfe's incoming body weight. He put the brakes on at the last second but while he stumbled to try and keep his balance Laine was throwing her gun aside and wrenching Wolfe's away to do the same. He feinted back in time to avoid her fist as it swung at his face, but just barely, and her follow-up kick caught him square in the chest and sent him reeling.

"*You*," Laine snarled, throwing another kick that Wolfe managed to sidestep. "Why do you keep showing up in my head? Why are you so fucking important?"

"Because you saved my life," Wolfe replied. The next time she swung a fist his way he blocked it and grabbed her wrist, spinning her and bending her arm behind her back. "You need to remember, Laine—if you don't Anton wins, and the woman I knew would never want that."

"You don't know anything about me," was her response, and then she flipped him forward over her shoulder to break the hold. "And you're going to die that way."

Wolfe rolled to avoid the boot she tried to stomp down on his head and sprang to his feet, adrenaline flowing now, every part of his body tuned to the fight like an antenna. While it was true that Wolfe was larger and stronger than Laine, her smaller size made her quicker and being female put her center of gravity much lower than his own. The latter was something Wolfe could exploit, but he'd only get one opportunity to do it, and if he fucked up he had no doubt she would make good on her promise. He stepped backward and turned abruptly, so the roundhouse kick that Laine aimed at his head fell short—but not short enough that Wolfe couldn't grab her leg with both hands. He pivoted and threw her to the ground, wincing when her head hit the concrete floor.

She didn't move right away, and for a second Wolfe was afraid he'd killed her. He also thought she might be playing dead, so he didn't approach her prone form, choosing to call out to her instead: "Laine?"

Her body twitched and she pushed herself up with her arms, slow and unsteady, head bowed toward the carpet.

"Wolfe?" she asked, and that flat quality in her voice was gone, replaced by the kind of trembling horror that made the hair on the back of Wolfe's neck stand up. "Where am I? What…" She trailed off, one hand going to her forehead before moving higher, fingers fisting in her hair. "Oh God… oh my *God*, I *k-killed* him." Her next words came out as a barely-audible whisper: "I killed my brother."

"Laine, it's not your fault, it wasn't you—" Wolfe started.

Her hand was reaching, stretching out pale-white against the green of the carpet as she grasped for one of the M4s. Wolfe felt a spike of fear race up his spine and took a half-step toward her but because he was so far away, and it seemed like he lurched in slow motion while she moved at full speed. He knew what was going to happen and couldn't do a damn thing to stop it, his mouth opening to beg her to change her mind—

A single BOOM from the M4 that Laine stuck under her chin, and Wolfe was sprayed with blood and brains and bone as he watched her body fall backward, the gun following suit a second later. He fell to his knees beside her and was helpless to do anything but stare as the wail of police sirens filled the air.

Chapter Twenty-One

When the sun rose the following morning, the wedding party plus a few others crowded into Patrick's room in Memorial Hospital in North Conway, about thirty miles from the Mount Washington Hotel. Haphazardly packed suitcases leaned against the walls or served as beds for small children, and several people were asleep on the floor. Orderlies and nurses stepped over them to get in and out of Patrick's room, miraculously not waking anyone in their non-skid shoes.

After what happened at the reception some of the guests—including Jake, Lacey and Samuel, and a few others—chose to rent cars instead of waiting for the chartered buses that would come to get them later in the day. Those who chose to stay as moral support but didn't fit in the room were relegated to a waiting area down the hall, and from what Wolfe had heard the chairs were uncomfortable but they were close to the coffee machine.

He sat in the hall right next to the door with his phone in his hands when Scarlett approached him with a couple of generic paper cups in her hands. "Josh grabbed a car and head back to Boston early too," he reported, taking the ridiculously hot cup of watery coffee from his partner. "Philanthropy never rests."

"Is he going back to Greece?" she asked, sitting next to him on the floor. Licking her thumb, she wiped away a speck of blood

Wolfe had missed when he cleaned himself up. "Hear it's nice this time of year."

He shook his head. "Nope, says he's done with Doctors Without Borders, but he has an interview with the American Red Cross later today."

"Good for him." They lapsed into silence for a moment. "How are you?"

"Honestly? Shitty as hell." Wolfe cradled the cup in both of his hands and shifted enough to rest his head on her shoulder. "Watching Laine… kill herself, it was like the cherry on top of a PTSD sundae. And I don't like sundaes."

"Oh, come on," Sebastian said, coming out of the room across the hall, where Constantin was being treated for a grade three concussion. "Everybody likes ice cream." He sat down on Wolfe's other side and peeled one of his hands off the cup to kiss the back of it. "Scarlett, back me up here."

Wolfe saw Scarlett's lips curl into a smile out of the corner of his eye. "Our intern is right, Jimmy. Even Timothy McVeigh liked mint chocolate chip."

"That was his last meal," Wolfe countered, but he felt himself smiling too. "I don't know if that helps or hurts your position. How's Constantin, Bash?"

"Whining, as you can imagine," Sebastian replied with a roll of his eyes. "He has gotten your mother to agree to play nurse for him… I think he plans on staying over at her house once they release him from here."

Wolfe shuddered theatrically. "I'm not touching that with a ten-foot pole. Like… if Ma's happy, I'm happy, but I don't need to know what's happening there."

"I don't think anybody wants to know about a parent's sex life," Christopher commented as he and Melissa came back from their own coffee run, Kamienski and Silent Mark trailing behind them. The Republican gubernatorial candidate had fired Peter as soon as the cops showed up at the hotel, and the men from Vaughn Securities had gone back to New York with their tails between their legs. "Well, except maybe in every Greek myth ever."

"You have a point," Scarlett said, "and it's not on the top of your head." She raised an eyebrow when Christopher took in a breath to speak, adding, "To answer the question you're about to ask, no, Jimmy and I won't work for you again. No more jobs for family, even if they're the black sheep."

Melissa clapped a hand over Christopher's mouth before he could say anything potentially insensitive. "Thank you two for what you did. Bill me for the rest of your time and we'll call it even?"

Wolfe glanced at Scarlett for confirmation, then nodded. "Sounds like a plan."

At that moment Nikki Shaw came around the corner at the end of the hall, car keys clutched in one hand and the other one holding the strap of an overstuffed messenger bag. Her eyes were wild and her shoulders were tense until she saw Christopher, at which point her whole body seemed to deflate. She closed the distance between them and yanked him into a hug by the front of his wrinkled dress shirt, pulling Melissa into the embrace a second later.

"I got here as soon as I could, I'm so glad you're okay," Nikki said when she stepped back, flicking a tear off her mascara-coated lashes. "How's your dad?"

"He's going to be fine." Christopher looked truly touched by her concern. "Thank you for coming. Any idea what we're going to tell the press?"

Nikki opened her mouth to respond, but her eyes caught on movement over Christopher's shoulder and stayed there. Wolfe craned his neck to see what she was looking at and hid a smile when he spotted Frogger with a cafeteria-issued bagel in one hand and her phone in the other, tapping out a text with her thumb. Her curly hair bounced with every step she took in her battered red Chuck Taylors, and she looked up when Nikki made a choked-off sound in the back of her throat, clearly struck speechless.

Melissa caught Wolfe's eye and winked. "Oh, I don't think you two have met! Nikki, this is Frogger Sampson." She was much more chipper than she'd been a moment ago. "Frogger, this is Nikki Shaw, Christopher's campaign manager."

Nikki seemed to snap back to reality. "Um. Hi. You're, uh... nice to meet you?"

Frogger blinked rapidly behind her glasses, and if Wolfe wasn't mistaken he thought he saw a blush darken her cheeks. "Hey. You, too." She put her phone away and squared her shoulders. "I seem to have forgotten to get coffee to go with this bagel, and if you just drove up you're probably hungry. Do you want to come with me to the cafeteria?"

Nikki nodded and shoved her keys in the messenger bag before thrusting the bag into Christopher's arms. "Yes, I do. Very much."

The rest of them managed to stifle their good-natured laughter until the two women were out of earshot, but just barely.

~***~

That evening, as the sun sunk below the tall pines that surrounded the town of Petersham, Sebastian rode down Route 2 in the backseat of Constantin's Mercedes—but due to his concussion and his overall disagreement with this plan, Constantin wasn't the one driving it. Instead Scarlett was behind the wheel, her blond hair tucked up underneath a black driving cap and her M1911 on her lap. They'd deliberately waited for the late hour in the hopes that the night shift might be less familiar with Anton's habits.

Wolfe occupied the passenger's side, and he adjusted the cufflinks on the black suit that Sebastian had stolen for him from one of his father's bodyguards. He twisted around in his seat to look at Sebastian, his freshly-shaven face pale in the illumination from the dashboard. "You sure this is gonna work?"

"Not in the slightest," Sebastian replied. His fingers itched for a cigarette. "All I know is that short of a missile launcher, this is the only way we can get into Blakely Manor to retrieve the Rapture formula for Danh Sang."

"Are these guards gonna buy the story?" Scarlett wondered as they pulled up to the chain-link gate. "That you're doing a surprise quality control check? Is that even a thing with drug cookers?"

"Let's hope so," Wolfe muttered, checking the angle of his tie in the visor mirror.

Sebastian buzzed his window down and leaned out of the car to speak into the intercom next to the driveway, glancing upward to make sure the rotating camera on the fence caught a good shot of his face. "My name is Sebastian Codreanu. I am here on behalf of my father to inspect your facility." A pause for dramatic flair. "I suggest you let me in."

The intercom buzzed an acknowledgement and the gate swung open, so Scarlett drove through. Even with the ample headlights on the Mercedes it was difficult to see their surroundings until the trees parted to reveal Blakely Manor, its stone arches and barred windows stately and intimidating in equal measure. Scarlett pulled around the fountain in the middle of the circular driveway to drop off Sebastian and Wolfe, then parked with the nose of the car facing outward in case they had to make a quick getaway.

Wolfe walked a step ahead of Sebastian as Constantin always did, reaching for one of the heavy oak doors but pausing to glance back at Sebastian. "You ready?"

Sebastian took in a measured breath and forced his expression into his best impression of his father's stern condescension. "Let's just get this over with."

Wolfe opened the door, and together they walked into the lion's den.

~***~

Unbeknownst to Wolfe and Sebastian, they were not the first ones to infiltrate the bowels of Blakely Manor. That honor went to Diana Johnson—or rather to Dajana Jagr, with her recently bleached hair cut into a ragged bob and coke-bottle glasses masking the hazel of her eyes. Getting admitted to Blakely had been easy once Tara combined some false police reports with an equally fake letter from Dajana's concerned (and wealthy) parents. They only wanted what was best for their troubled daughter and were more than willing to pay for it.

Diana had taken the three medications they'd foisted upon her after admission, holding them in her gullet until she could sneak off to a bathroom and stick her fingers down her throat. Not the most elegant solution, but it was better than being drugged to the gills and unable to defend herself if need be. She hoped violence wouldn't be necessary, since the only person in Blakely Manor who could recognize her from her work with Anton was Elena Ivanova. She was easy to avoid—after all, she spent most of her time in the basement torturing people.

That was why it was a bone-chilling shock when Diana came out of the bathroom and found herself face-to-face with none other than Xander Murray.

The Mass Art Murderer's former campus snitch stared at her for a moment, clearly just as surprised as she was and no doubt drugged for real. Any hope that he wouldn't know who she was went out the window when a slimy smirk curled his thin lips. "I remember you," he said, the words a bit slurred but understandable. "You were in the parking lot the day Jake and I got into it at Caruso's—you work for Codreanu, don't you?" Then before Diana could strike him, he drew in a huge breath and screamed at the top of his lungs: "HELP!"

Diana turned and found herself faced with two huge orderlies clad in white, a coffee stain on one of their shirts indicating they'd come from the break room down the hall. Footsteps indicated there were more of them on the way, and when Xander's hand snatched the glasses off her face she kneed him in the balls. She saw the syringe as it swung toward her bicep, snarled and tore at it but the orderly had already pushed the plunger down.

The fall to the floor felt like it happened in slow motion, her body going numb as her vision began to fade.

Before she lost consciousness, Diana recognized one of the faces floating above her as that of Doctor Ivanova. "Bring her downstairs. We have some work to do."

At around two o'clock in the morning, Scarlett pulled Constantin's Mercedes into the parking lot at Pope John Paul II Park in Dorchester, the lights from North Quincy visible across the dark gleam of the Neponset River. There were no other cars around at the late hour save for one, a dark blue Lexus sedan belonging to Thanh Ngo. When Wolfe and Sebastian emerged from the Mercedes Ngo signaled to his boss with his hand and Danh Sang got out of the back of the Lexus.

Sang raised an eyebrow when he saw Wolfe. "Where is Constantin? I miss his scowl."

"He was indisposed and not a fan of working with you," Sebastian replied. He stuck a hand into the pocket of his leather jacket and held it out to Sang. "The Rapture formula is on here."

"It could not have been easy to retrieve," Sang said, his dark eyes flashing with excitement when he saw the drive. He plucked it from Sebastian's open palm and examined it like a jeweler would a diamond. "I must admit, I was skeptical when I received your text message."

"Let's just say that when you dislocate your shoulder as a distraction in a place like Blakely, you don't get the best care." Wolfe rolled the aforementioned shoulder to try and get circulation back into it. "Are we good here?"

Sang held up one finger for patience, and handed the drive to Ngo. He plugged it into a small laptop computer sitting on the hood of the Lexus, and a second later he gave Sang a thumbs-up. "We are indeed. It was a pleasure doing business with you."

They started to get back into the car, and Sebastian took a step forward. "Wait—what about my father?"

Sang paused. "He will be dealt with accordingly, but the less you know about when and where, the better. It might be a good idea for you to take a vacation."

Wolfe watched Sebastian carefully as Sang and Ngo drove away and they got back into the Mercedes. "You okay?"

Sebastian stared at him for a moment before he shook his head. "How can I be? I just signed my own father's death warrant." He looked out the window, hands curled into loose fists in his lap. "I wish it had not come to this."

They were all quiet for a moment as Scarlett drove back to Morrissey Boulevard, buzzing up the Expressway past National Grid and The Rainbow Swash. "This is probably a terrible time to mention this," she said, the natural rasp to her voice as familiar to Wolfe as radio static, "but Constantin told me something the other day, after he saved Lacey and Jake." Her fingers tightened around the steering wheel. "Said he has a daughter that he's never met somewhere in Romania. And since Sang just told us in no uncertain terms to get the fuck outta town…"

Wolfe's brain processed that little revelation and he sighed. "I'll have to find my passport and book some plane tickets. Can you fly with a grade three concussion?"

Scarlett glanced at him with one eyebrow cocked. "Do I look like a fuckin' doctor?"

"I haven't been back there," Sebastian said quietly, catching their attention. "I speak the language and eat the food, but we left when I was a child, and the memories I *do* have are... horrific." Then in a whisper that conveyed equal parts surprise and hurt: "Why? Why would he tell you and not me?"

"That's a question for him," Scarlett replied, not unkindly. She was gentler with Sebastian than she was with most people, which Wolfe appreciated. "And I think that the only way he's gonna be able to answer it is if we go find his kid, so let's do that instead of getting roped into your old man's murder."

~***~

Epilogue

It was the beginning of October before Danh Sang got word that Sebastian Codreanu and his little friends had left Boston for Bucharest. Once that happened, he used a burner phone to send two text messages to the Mass Art Murderer. According to Anton—who gave up the information under duress, to put it mildly—the famed killer was understandably concerned about privacy and would only respond if the messages were sent to a similar burner phone in a particular way.

The first message was four lines from Shakespeare's Sonnet 71: *"No longer mourn for me when I am dead/Than you shall hear the surly sullen bell/Give warning to the world that I am fled/From this vile world with vilest worms to dwell."*

The second message was a time and place for a face-to-face meeting: **Public Garden, 10am. Middle bench on north side of pond.**

At five minutes to ten Sang approached the bench in question, hands in the pocket of the raincoat he wore over his suit. It was cloudy and gray, a light drizzle falling on the joggers and clusters of tourists walking the paved pathways and pausing to take photos with the Robin Williams Bench or the Make Way for Ducklings sculpture. At first the bench was empty, and Sang felt a flare of anger—had that damn Rom lied to him?—but right as he reached for his phone, a man in a long trench coat sat down on the bench.

He carried a *Boston Globe* rolled up under one arm, and he looked familiar even from behind—almost like Jim Wolfe, but not quite. Something different about his gait and the way he carried himself, less like the weight of the world was on his shoulders and more like he enjoyed piling bricks on the bodies of others. He snapped open the newspaper heedless of the moisture, like he didn't plan on staying in his spot for long.

Sang rounded the side of the bench. If it weren't for decades of being a hardened criminal he would've balked when he realized that the Mass Art Murderer was none other than Joshua Wolfe, older brother to James and Jacob and the state's former chief medical examiner. Even so, he had to clear his throat before he could speak. "Doctor Wolfe, what a... surprise."

Josh glanced at him, his face eerily blank for a half-second. Then a smirk curled up one side of his mouth. "Danh Sang. Figured you'd be the one to take Codreanu out eventually. None of the others had the balls."

"I will take that as a compliment." Sang sat at a polite distance on the other end of the bench and took the sports section of the paper when Josh offered it. He held the newspaper in front of him but couldn't make out the words, fight-or-flight making his vision warp. "Once he had the proper motivation, Anton was quite... *informative* regarding his arrangement with you. I understand that he did not intend to utilize your services again, but I think we could come to an agreement that would benefit us both."

Josh didn't look at him again and Sang was grateful for it; when the man wasn't pretending to be normal, he was downright terrifying. "I'm listening."

"With Anton indisposed and the Rapture formula in my control, the Red Dynasty is poised to take its rightful position at the head of Boston's criminal underground," Sang explained, checking his peripheral to make sure Thanh Ngo was still nearby. Just because he thought the Mass Art Murderer might be useful to his cause didn't mean he wanted for a second to be truly alone with him. "His son doesn't have the work ethic to run Stela, let alone the rest of Anton's interests, but he isn't stupid. I am planning a complete takeover—however, if it is not executed with surgical precision it will surely fail."

"Cut the shit, Sang." Josh's voice was flat and cold like a sheet of ice. "What are you asking for?"

Sang suppressed a wince. "A distraction for the police and the politicians. Perhaps the return of the Mass Art Murderer?"

The smirk from before turned into a grin, full of shiny white teeth and devoid of any human emotion. "It just so happens I have some unfinished business, so providing we can iron out the details... you've got yourself a deal."

Josh stuck out a hand and Sang shook it.

This city will not know what hit her, Sang thought, too lost in his own ambitions to see he had made a deal with a much bigger devil than himself. *And neither will Sebastian Codreanu.*

THE END

Acknowledgements

They say the sophomore season of a TV show is always harder than the first one. I have no idea who "they" are or if that's true, but I *do* know that writing and self-publishing my second book was infinitely easier than my first. These acknowledgements sections never get any easier to write, mostly because there are so many people in my life that I'm grateful for and want to thank.

Mom and Dad are always going to be first, because you've continued to believe in my crazy dream even when it's not going so great. I've learned so much from both of you and I love you to pieces.

Nurse Caitlin will always have a huge role in the Wolfe & Vaughn universe, and like I said the last time, it wouldn't be what it is without her. She's pretty cool and I'm so glad we're friends.

While I was writing this book I met some super-cool people, including my best friend. Kaja, you're a kind, supportive, all-around awesome human being and I am so happy you decided to message me that day. My life is better with you in it, babe.

To Katie, Aimee, Lavender, MK, Thistle, Delta, Tuuli, Pluto, Erin, Erin, Frankie, Sarah, Lexi, Nev, Paige, Twelve, Loch, and the rest of my Tumblr fam: THANK YOU. Whether you know it or not, you helped keep me sane while I was doing this—and yes, you fall into the category of "super-cool people".

I probably forgot somebody I wanted to mention, so presume that if we've ever interacted at all I appreciate the hell out of you.

If you like the cover of this book, it was created by Mindbomb Design on 99designs!

Last but certainly not least, I want to give a huge shout-out to my Kickstarter backers! Without them this project would not have been possible. In no particular order, thank you to: Katie F., Faith G., Geoff R., Katelyn, Lyndsey Aldous, Miley Doerr, Jaxon Fischer, Ryan Wildgoose, Georgia Sokolov, Tango Charlie, Tuuli Ruponen, Giovanni Rivera, Enzo Rivera, Brizeida Rivera, Kaja, Dżaneta, Robert Thomas, Joseph Yankech, David C., Rai Knightshade, and Aimee Schwintz.

About the Author

Samantha Simard possesses a deep love of books and she's been writing stories since she learned to read. She's a fresh voice in the mystery fiction world, and wants her characters—many of whom are LGBT+ and/or minorities—to reflect the broad, ever-changing world in which we live. Her other interests include reading, archery, video games, and searching for a way to consume coffee intravenously. She holds a Bachelor's degree in English and Creative Writing from Southern New Hampshire University and is continuing her education with a Master's of Fine Arts, also from SNHU. You can visit her website or follow her on social media to tell her she needs to write more.

Website: samanthasimard.com

Facebook: @thesammykinz

Twitter: @Sammykinz

Instagram: @the_sammykinz

Tumblr: thesammykinz.tumblr.com

Made in United States
North Haven, CT
22 April 2022

18448366R10202